Ghosts and Angels: A Memoir

How, During an Epoch of Terror, Goodness Vanquished Evil and Restored Faith

Also by Stanley Goldstein

Fiction
Lies In Progress

Park West: A Novel of Love and Murder and Redemption

Nonfiction
*Troubled Children/Troubled Parents:
The Way Out
2nd Edition*

*Shopping For A Shrink:
Finding the Right Psychotherapist For You or
Your Child*

STANLEY GOLDSTEIN

Ghosts and Angels: A Memoir

How, During an Epoch of Terror, Goodness Vanquished Evil and Restored Faith

WYSTON BOOKS, INC.

WYSTON BOOKS, INC.
P.O. Box 1280
Warwick, NY 10990-1280

Tel.: (845) 986-6888
E-mail: wystonbooks@yahoo.com
Please visit our website: www.wystonbooks.com

Goldstein, Stanley
Ghosts and Angels: A Memoir/
How During An Epoch of Terror, Goodness Vanquished
Evil and Restored Faith
A Novel/Stanley Goldstein
    1. Terrorism—Fiction
    2. Religion—Fiction
    3. Clergy Life & Duties—Fiction
    4. Military Life & Duties—Fiction
    5. Military Weapons—Fiction
    6. Scientist Life & Duties—Fiction

Library of Congress Control Number: 2010943084
ISBN 978-0-9832326-0-5 (print)
ISBN 978-0-9832326-1-2 (E-book)

Cover photograph by Tom Haseltine/
Photographers Choice Collection
Licensed from Getty Images

I will save you from the hands of the wicked
And rescue you from the clutches of the violent.

JEREMIAH 13:,21

Therefore shall Heaven be shaken,
And earth leap out of its place,
At the fury of the LORD of Hosts
On the day of His burning wrath.

ISAIAH 13:13

That, like voices from afar off,
Call us to pause and listen...
—Longfellow, *The Legend of Murderer's Creek*

Contents

Editor's Note

...at each epoch the world was lost, and at each epoch it was saved.
— Jacques Maritain
...on the subject of ghosts. I do not in the least pretend that such things cannot be.
— Charles Dickens

Paulie phoned me eleven months ago. When we last spoke nineteen years before, he had looked and sounded much like his present day namesake on *The Sopranos* though being shrewder and more talkative. He wanted to hire me.

"I'm not looking for a job."

"It's not the typical freelance gig," he told me, in his wheedling fashion which I still remembered. "Think of it as being this year's mitzvah*." Hearing these words, I suddenly remembered my Italian grandmother's advice to be wary of non-Jews when they use Jewish expressions.

"Like the favor you did after that last meal at my house?"

---

*Literally translated, a *mitzvah* is a *commandment* though the term is often loosely used to mean any act of human kindness which is intended to help one come closer to holiness and God. According to the teachings of Judaism all moral laws derive from divine commandments of which there are six hundred and thirteen given in the Torah (the first five books of the Bible).

"You have nothing to complain about," he said, sounding hurt. Which was doubtful for no one had as thick a skin as Paulie. "You got an agent and book contract in three weeks. With Puzo's publisher too! How many new writers get that break?"

Though he knew that wasn't what I was referring to, Paulie was right. I still owed him and he had called to collect.

"How is Denise?" I asked. My ex-wife was no longer a painful subject for me.

"She's having our fifth child. Seventeen years to the month after our first," Paulie proudly informed me. Removing Denise from my life was something else I owed him for: they running off together had ended our stormy marriage. Yet I still cared about her and was grateful to Paulie for making her happy. But I was puzzled why he called me now and pressed him about this.

"The manuscript of an autobiography badly needs editing. It's a rush job and my boss begs you to do it."

"I'm a writer. There are plenty of editors around."

"These pages need someone who thinks like the author. You both have doctorates. He's a mathematical physicist and Denise said you have a background in science."

"College calculus and physics. My last books were thrillers with religious themes."

"That's how we'll be marketing this book. And we'll say *you're* the author."

Now I was really suspicious for no writer gives up credit for their work unless they absolutely must. I sprawled and prepared myself for a long story. "Tell me about it."

"Read it first. *Then* give me your answer," he pleaded. "There's no way to contact the author and I don't know how much of his story is true. But the manuscript sat for months on government desks waiting for clearance. Where it would still be except for the pressure from a senator who's also a minister. This is a touchy point."

His congenial lie—that we *must* get together soon—followed, and our conversation ended. I agreed to read the book because, like I said, I owed him.

It arrived at my door the next day, four hundred pages held together by two large binder clips. It was typed and paginated but far from ready for publication, being undivided into chapters and written in that style typical of scientists who use multi-syllabic words where a small one would do. So after calling Paulie and agreeing on my fee, I created its chapters, shortened the sentences and simplified the language*, and took out all of the mathematics and most of the technical terms.

"Change the title. It's too long and will never sell," Paulie had instructed me, and I did. But I anguished even as *Ghosts and Angels* went into production, feeling that the author's original description was more accurate: *How, During an Epoch of Terror, Goodness Vanquished Evil and Restored Faith.*

---

*Though all of this book has been cleared for publication by the required government agencies, I have left the original security classification of documents intact.

Of an earlier time, Anna Freud wrote about the power of the individual to battle tyranny, stating that "for every gang of evil-doers...there is always at least one 'just' man or woman ready to...sacrifice his or her own good for fellow-beings."*

This book tells how, sixty years later when freedom again became threatened, it was saved by individuals: a wounded soldier, an orphaned girl, a dying minister, and perhaps another.

Despite Paulie's offer I left these pages unsigned, being unable to decide whether I wanted my name to be associated with this book. For I'm convinced it isn't possible that what the author described could have happened. Unless—*unless*—ghosts and angels *do* exist.

*Gardiner, Muriel (1983) *Code Name "Mary"*. New Haven: Yale University Press, p. xiii

Introduction

*"You've worked on crime victims before. Why was she
so different?"*
*"Because of the expression on her face...and that there
was no blood left in her."*
United States Senate Select Committee on Intelligence
Hearing – Appendix B

*"...foreign nationals who engage in domestic terrorism...are
violating international law and not protected by provisions of
the Geneva Convention which govern the conduct of war. Thus
they may, following their apprehension and without judicial
oversight, be immediately deported from the United States for
whatever further actions are deemed necessary."*
United States Department of Justice Memorandum
Opinion – Appendix C

Fate leads the willing and drags the unwilling.
—Seneca

At first there was just blackness. Then came a
memory: my bullet wound from long before when I was
losing blood, shock set in, and my thinking grew foggy. But
now I felt increasing self-control as my consciousness
slowly returned. I heard the murmur of quiet machines.
Then the sound of a door opening and closing with the
smooth precision clicks which one associates with well
constructed automobiles and prisons.

I unsealed my eyes cautiously, being afraid that
opening them to the brightness would increase the dull
throb in my temple.

When my eyes were fully opened I found myself
lying on a metal bed in a barely furnished room with

whitewashed walls. A soldier sat in a chair at the foot of my bed. An officer was seated in a corner of the room. Turning my head to the right, I saw a white enameled night table holding a clock. When I tried moving toward it I discovered that my left leg was shackled to the bed.

Another soldier then entered the room. He was dressed in the same odd military clothes which the other two wore. Like theirs it had a Mandarin collar which could be worn up or down. Its color wasn't the traditional American army uniform of green for woodland combat or gray for urban warfare or sand brown for desert fighting. This style was new and I remembered reading about it in an alumni newsletter which had been mailed to me from the Royal Military Academy at Sandhurst.

The uniform's color was derived from the United States Marines' MARPAT camouflage scheme. It had a digital pattern which suggested colors and shapes without actually being them, as if one were viewing an incompletely downloaded photograph. Instead of traditional buttons this uniform had zippers. Insignia and patches were fastened with Velcro, not sewn, and placed on the front rather than the side. Moreover, boots were now suede brown and not the usual polished black.

This soldier's name tag read, not surprisingly, Smith, and he allegedly held the rank of colonel in the United States Army. My ability to grasp these facts made me realize that my thinking abilities had recovered enough to permit me to risk speaking and to be interrogated.

The man seemed short though from my prone position I couldn't be certain. What I felt surer of was that despite his uniform and insignia he was no ordinary soldier, that this was no conventional hospital, and that my interview was being recorded and likely broadcast elsewhere.

The man seated himself gingerly on the hard wooden chair by my bed as if his back hurt, leaned his expensive Coach briefcase—certainly not military issue—against the chair leg, and hung his beret from the edge of the night table. He had balding gray hair and a warm smile which left his shrewd gaze untouched.

After folding his hands over his stomach he crossed his legs as if preparing himself for a long talk. He spoke in a soft, even voice. His powerful build contrasted with his gentle, almost feminine manner, one which he may have cultivated to deceive the unwary. Intelligence plus deception is a highly successful combination, I reminded myself, echoing a line from the *Eton College Chronicle*. This is a dangerous man.

"Welcome back," he said.

"Where am I?"

"In a hospital room. You were shot. The bullet just grazed your forehead but we kept you sedated to help you heal."

"How long have I been unconscious?"

"For four days."

"That's not the usual treatment is it?"

"No, but we're not a typical hospital," he said with a small smile.

Suddenly I remembered—"Holly," I screamed, and tried to raise myself.

The guard at the foot of the bed immediately moved towards me and I focused on the large pistol in his shoulder holster. But the colonel waved him off and, after placing his hand against my shoulder, forced me down with a strength which I didn't expect from someone nearing sixty.

"She's down the hall and doing fine," he said. "Being so young, we woke her three days ago. Since then she's been playing poker with a nurse for dimes. I staked her with ten dollars in exchange for half her winnings and she was up seventy three dollars as of an hour ago. We already let her see that you were OK—she wouldn't eat otherwise."

The man lied persuasively but I knew Holly was dead. There was no way she could have survived *that* afternoon. No way. But because he held all of the cards I played along with him.

"When can I see her?"

"Maybe soon, maybe never," he said smoothly, as if he had prepared this response in advance. With experienced interrogators you can never tell for sure. Then I used my only ace.

"I realize that I'm just a British Green Card holder but the U.S.A. is still a nation of laws. What if I insisted on seeing a lawyer?"

"There's none on this base to take your case. You're in Azerbaijan on a facility under that nation's jurisdiction. But we do control a non-denominational cemetery here," he added pointedly. "Besides, even in America no lawyer valuing his career would represent you: the crazed scientist who murdered ten people including clergy and children. Though there's an even better reason why no one but us can help you."

"And what might that be?" I asked, gritting my teeth and trying to keep a snotty tone from my voice.

"Because," he said slowly and using words which drained all hope from me, "both you and Holly are officially dead. Her funeral is this Sunday. There's a closed casket ceremony to hide the evidence of your sadism and a moving tribute which I wrote myself. Students from her grade will be there. The Connecticut governor too."

To confirm this he removed a Greenwich newspaper from his briefcase and laid it on the bed. "It's three days old."

ENGLISH SCIENTIST KILLED AFTER MURDERING TEN. TORTURED BODY OF KIDNAPPED GIRL FOUND, the blunt headline read.

"It wasn't like that," I said, with a sense of resignation.

The colonel opened his Mandarin collar with an awkward gesture as if being unfamiliar with it. He glanced towards the corner of the ceiling where I noticed the glint of what was probably a video camera lens.

"Yes, we know. But only some of it," he murmured in a surprisingly understanding tone. "And now you can tell us the rest." But then his voice hardened. "Which better be everything if you hope to get Holly back to America."

Why did I break then? Because, upon hearing her name, I hungered to spin words into colors and make Holly live even if only in speech. And to be permitted to return to America and mourn at her grave, the final refuge for the child I risked loving and failed to protect.

So I did tell him everything—even what I wanted to forget. Plus some matters he may not have been allowed to know. Like the questionable reliability of the W-76 atomic warhead and my work with Pulsed Energy Projectiles. Not unless his security clearance went as high as mine once did. Had I really been a "crazed scientist?" Sometimes, I admitted to myself.

"Can I have some water?" I asked, wanting time to organize my thoughts. The colonel nodded and a gray uniformed nurse quickly entered the room. She placed a tray with two bottles of Poland Spring Water on the side table. After holding the straw to my lips for a long sip, she returned the bottle to the tray and left the room.

"It all started with my first sight of Holly," I said. "She was drenched with blood." Then, surprisingly, tears flowed down my cheeks though I had never cried before. Because I so rarely shared my feelings, I thought. The colonel placed his hand on my arm and, soon, I began my story—which was unlike any he could have heard before.

A tale of love, tortured bodies, and an unsolved riddle concealing the power of the universe. About a girl in danger; a dying minister's prophecy, and his unusual explanations of pain and Sin and Grace. Then, finally, how when America battled extraordinary evil, the Heavens intervened. Yes, a ghost or possibly an angel joined the fray. Which, being a scientist, I knew must have sounded crazy. Except that it really happened.

Chapter 1

The leaves will whisper...and if you listen she will call.
Edwin Arlington Robinson, *Luke Havergal*
...rescue came in the nick of time out there/from this little mite by me.
Ibsen, *Terje Vigen*

I felt as if I existed only so long as I was loved by Julia who grasped the sadness of my life more clearly than anyone I knew. I could not understand her but nothing else seemed to matter. Only later did I remember the saying of Walter Badgett, that people are most credulous when happiest; and the older proverb I should have paid special attention to: be careful for what you wish since there is always a price to pay. Yet probably I always needed Julia—or a woman like her—to raise my emotions to that level by which other people live.

Though feeling controlled by her will there is only one test of what I wanted: what I let happen. For despite the frequent searing pain our relationship left me with something priceless: a glimpse of joyfulness, a faint sense of optimism and home.

And this figure looked so like Julia. Both even had the same rose tattoo on the left arm: a purchase after her divorce. But I knew it couldn't be Julia for she was dead I reminded myself. Maybe not, I still hoped, as the figure slithered towards me.

Although she was forty four when we met, six years older than me, Julia had always looked younger: a "genetic gift" from her otherwise inadequate mother she explained. This enabled her to dress youthfully as she was now. Denim jacket. Embroidered suede skirt. Long necklace. Even her makeup—peach and pink—reeked of youth, I noted, for this was one of my rare dreams in color.

The figure undressed seductively as she approached, a knowing smile on her face. Her short jacket was closed with only one button. She opened this while she walked and cupped her breasts in her hands. But suddenly—as I lay naked awaiting her on the bed—-she froze, reacting to a low whimper originating from outside of the room.

Then the figure—Julia?—continued towards me. Her lace bra dropped to the ground and, as I stared at her small pointed breasts, she smiled and massaged their nipples. By the time she reached my bed her panties had joined the rest of her clothes and jewelry on the floor. I noted the odd sight of her completely shaved pubis: though I preferred this, Julia had always left a small tuft of hair.

The figure hovered over me and kissed my face. But then she again froze, responding to the same sound I had heard earlier. Like from a wounded animal protesting the pain which it could not understand. Quickly, although it couldn't be soon enough for me, the sound disappeared and Julia was in my arms. "You're gorgeous," I murmured as I had so often in the past. Running my fingers down her arm, across her belly, inside her. She moaned and stroked my face until the strange cry again interfered. Now it was closer, louder, more insistent.

Slowly—struggling not to—I opened my eyes and found myself sprawled on the auto seat with the car door open and the usual foul post—alcohol binge taste in my mouth. Julia—or whoever the figure had been—was gone. Except for her increasingly faint image which I could still dredge up and a feeling of moistness on my face.

That was the first moment I felt the terror which, without warning, had already entered my life. Though in that instant it was from my realization that reality could never equal fantasy and I hadn't fully valued Julia until I lost her and would never have her again. Not in this life.

Dreams are wondrous things, I reminded myself as I rubbed my cheek. Which *did* feel wet. Then, in the illumination of the overhead car light, I saw that my fingers were colored blood red. Moving the seat's lever, I jerked to an erect position and searched my face in the makeup mirror but could find no cut.

Now I heard the same sound which had roused me from my dream and moved towards where it seemed to be coming from: a few feet outside of the car. There, in the dim light off its interior, stood a girl of about ten. She was dressed in a sweatshirt with "MIT" logo and pajama bottoms with grinning characters from the Peanuts comic strip. Some were difficult to make out for they, like her hands, were stained everywhere with blood to a degree which couldn't have been from small accidental cuts.

"Pleeze," she begged in an exhausted desperate voice. Then she collapsed into my arms.

Chapter 2

The academic mind is filled with alternatives.
—author
The fact of twilight does not mean that you cannot tell day from night.
—Samuel Johnson

For moments I just stared at the dead weight of girl in my arms. Alcohol does that to you. It makes one uncertain what they are seeing and should do even if I was sure that the blood and the girl were real unlike the events in my dream. And, though I feel ashamed to admit this, I did consider walking away and staying uninvolved.

Because it had been my past heroic acts in the British army and with Julia which placed my life in free fall. Following which I concluded that there is too much pain and surprisingly little reward in being a hero. Certainly not with a child who, given my luck, I might even be accused of having injured.

Yet while I considered abandoning her I was already planning. My leg, which had been crippled during a past good deed, was starting to bother me. I would have to investigate further while sitting on the ground or in my car. But how *did* one talk to a child? There were none in my life and my having learned to cope with Julia's tantrums didn't qualify me to speak with this girl. Whose name, it then occurred to me, I didn't yet know. Finding out would be a good first step in opening communication between us, as they say in the best bureaucratic jargon. Also, a familiar question might help to pull her out of the panic she was obviously experiencing. So I cleared my throat and spoke with the calm, slow cadence which one uses with melodramatic girlfriends, traumatized soldiers, and terrified children.

"Hello. My name is Alan. What is yours?"

The girl didn't immediately respond. When she finally did it wasn't as if she saw me although I was directly in front of her.

"Holly." Her voice had the haunting atonal characteristic of one who is dying and had accepted their fate.

"Holly is a pretty name. Holly, I hurt my leg when I was a soldier. That's why I use the cane in the back seat. Can we sit in the car while we talk? Come."

I took her hand and she followed. Step by step we slowly approached the passenger's car door. I opened it and, because she then stood rigidly, I told her to lower her head so she didn't hurt it. After she seated herself I closed the door and walked to the driver's side.

When seated, I quickly began speaking. I was afraid that if I stopped talking her frozen state would deepen or she would become hysterical. "You look really tired. I guess we're both tired. It's past our bedtimes and we should be asleep." I was about to add the words "in our beds" to my last sentence before thinking that her living nightmare had likely begun there.

Being a former soldier, I was accustomed to unpredictability and confusion. And the sight of blood was certainly familiar to me. But having to cope with an impenetrable child in a situation about which I lacked *any* information was not.

I felt that to keep her calm I should not yet ask what happened. But I wondered what else to say, having used up my capacity to communicate with children. Then I remembered a past experience.

Six years earlier, while doing research at the Institute, I was cajoled into teaching a summer class in introductory nuclear physics to a group of gifted high school youth. This was a pet project of my boss so his courteous request had left me no choice. Being an inexperienced instructor, I quickly used up my day's supply of lecture notes within the first few minutes of the class. Then, being forced to improvise, I told the students a story about the young Albert Einstein, in those days when he still worked in the patent office in Berne, Switzerland.

After receiving a colorfully scripted letter, Einstein threw it into the trash. He didn't realize that it contained an invitation to attend a ceremony at Geneva University where he was to be presented with his first honorary doctorate. Feeling that my time-consuming story should have some educational purpose, I advised the students to never immediately conclude the obvious without investigating. Using as an example that even such a popular term as "energy production" is incorrect since no force can produce energy. Rather, there are different forces in nature (gravity, the so-called weak force; electromagnetism, the so-called strong force) and their interaction can *change* one type of energy into another but the total amount of energy always remains the same.

So, years later when facing the terrified Holly, I also told her a story even as I thought how oddly I was behaving.

When confronting danger a person naturally seeks others. Yet I didn't take her to the nearest home for a phone and help. Why? Because (I concluded with my best scientific reasoning) I must unconsciously have determined that those who threatened her were close by and presented greater danger than the tiny sheriff's department on this Maine resort island could handle.

"Donald Duck was my favorite comic book when I was your age," I told Holly, "In one adventure his nephews, Huey, Dewey, and Louie, wanted to bake him a birthday cake but needed honey. When they climbed a tree to get it they got stung by bees who didn't want anyone taking their honey. Those stings really hurt! Do you hurt anywhere?" These sentences were my non-threatening way to learn the extent of her injuries.

As Holly shook her head, I heard the crackling of brush and small animals scurrying past. Sounds I last heard years before during a nighttime battle in the jungle when I felt surrounded by moving things which seemed the stealthy enemy approaching. I was wet, cold, confused, and afraid because I couldn't sense where or how many they were. Now I felt that identical primitive dread and with it came the same certain knowledge: like vultures homing in on their prey, this bloodstained child was being hunted.

Chapter 3

It is in the nature of the hypothesis...that it assimilates everything to itself as proper nourishment and from the first moment of begetting ...it generally grows stronger by everything you see, hear, read, or understand.
Lawrence Sterne, *Tristram Shandy*

I am thinking too slowly, I told myself, and cursed the vodka still lingering in my blood stream. Spirits may be a gift from the gods but my frequent overuse was a torment. So, wasting precious moments that we didn't then have, I condemned my weakness. Until the adrenaline created by my fear kicked in, counteracted the effects of the alcohol, and my more productive though tentative conclusions followed.

First, my life was also at risk. Having had contact with Holly, I could not be permitted to live. Who knew what I might have learned from her? And I had no doubt that she *was* in mortal danger. Parents or the police would call aloud while looking for a lost child. Not search silently to be announced by the sound of startled animals.

Second, while I was believed to know too much I really knew nothing and considering Holly's emotional state, wouldn't be able to learn anything from her for awhile.

Third, and most important, we had to escape her pursuers.

Some facts seemed certain. That, being a child, she was living with her parents when they were attacked. If still alive, they probably needed medical attention. Also, she must live close by. No young child could walk on such rough ground for a great distance as Holly had done. I could learn more only at her home. And going there wouldn't be as dangerous as it seems for only foolish criminals lingered near their deed.

The military had taught me that any action was better than none and the importance of moving fast. I did both even as I hoped that I wasn't making the common tactical error of behaving most deliberately when I was least certain.

"Holly," I whispered, interrupting my Donald Duck story, "we have to get away from these scary men. Can you be real quiet?"

She nodded and her thumb entered and remained fixed in her mouth. Likely it was my sense of her psychological regression which caused me to tell this ten year old a story so babyish that any six year old would have wrinkled their nose at it.

To avoid further delay I buckled her shoulder harness. For comfort, I gave her the only soft object I had: a folded blanket from the rear seat. Then, hearing a loud curse, I quickly turned the key in the car's ignition and pressed the starter button.

Chapter 4

...like a stairway to the sea,/ Where down the blind are driven.
—Edwin Arlington Robinson, *Eros Turannos.*

My car is nearly one of a kind. A fully restored 1953 Kaiser "Hardtop" Dragon with its original 14-carat gold hood ornament re-plated; exterior emblems, script, and glove box nameplate re-chromed; and new thick carpeting and modern safety features. It was the most luxurious model built by the long defunct company of Henry J. Kaiser, the World War Two genius who turned the ship construction industry on its collective ear and later tried doing the same to the auto industry.

My car was first owned by a Seattle collector. When he died it was sold by his son, a musician who had no interest in cars. Then again the car's body had begun to rust after being stored under a tarp for two years in the rainy North West and he could have had no idea how impressive it would look once it was restored. Which the car's next owner did, driving it daily until his death. After which it lay in a garage, unloved and uncared for. Like me until Julia entered my life.

It was she who convinced me to buy the car feeling that, among the other things I needed besides her, was a livelier image. Her typical stunt was to order cognac over grapefruit for breakfast because, as she put it, such behavior caused one to be remembered. Now, because of her innocent suggestion, were our pursuers to glimpse just the outline of my striking car they could easily discover my identity.

The car was parked on the side of the road in a small turnaround space. Despite the earlier soaking rain (which sometimes played havoc with the wiring), it started easily. I kept the headlights turned off for the first quarter mile.

I felt safer once we were moving though our safety was far from assured. The island's one man winter police department was incapacitated by shingles. "There's never any crime," he told the townspeople, before taking to his bed.

North Folk Island, Maine, has about four hundred permanent residents though its population swells twenty fold during the summer. It is forty-five miles north of Bar Harbor, Maine, another historic resort area but one with wealthier vacationers.

I came here in early September after being placed on paid medical leave from the Institute. The island was recommended as a quiet setting where I could recuperate, it being far from the daily pressures of scientific research which my "breakdown" was officially attributed to. Though the technical problems on my job were the smallest cause of my stress. The major issue lay unspoken. Partly because affairs were common among the young staff but mostly since mine involved Julia, the widow of the Institute's founder and chief financier.

To psychologically remove a scientist from their work is harder than simply relocating them. Though nowadays the popular image of the solitary researcher is mostly fantasy.

But during my first days on the island I did try to relax, being aided by the reality that there wasn't much to do, The only Internet access was at dial-up speed, so slow that accessing the Internet was painful. Our telephone service was via microwave circuit and erratic and, of course, there wasn't cable TV. I tried to occupy myself with magazines and the local newspaper until, as I felt my brain begin to rot, I returned to my persistent quest: trying to win a million dollar prize, the goal which drove mathematicians crazy for decades.

Prime numbers are numbers which can be evenly divided only by themselves or one, such as five and seven and one hundred ninety nine. Bernhard Riemann was a nineteenth century mathematician who described how prime numbers were scattered along the number line, this theory becoming known as the Riemann Hypothesis. Though widely accepted, his idea remains unproven.

Riemann's work is important. It underlies today's code breaking, research on the energies in atomic nuclei, even how long you have to wait in line to cash a check at a bank. Which is how things go in science where curiosity can improve civilization—or lead to Hiroshima.

The logarithm of a number equals how many times one must multiply a constant number, e (approximately 2.718), by itself to get that number. What Riemann discovered is that the number of primes about a number is equal to one divided by the logarithm of that number. Thus the logarithm of one million is about thirteen and about every thirteenth number is prime. And the logarithm of one billion is about twenty one and every twenty first number is prime. What Riemann wanted to figure out was how prime numbers were related to logarithms. He managed to guess at the general formula but the million dollar prize, offered by the Clay Mathematics Institute in Cambridge, Massachusetts for its proof, remains unclaimed.

I got hooked on this problem in graduate school and, like so many others, failed to solve it. Though I recognized that since my major expertise was physics and not mathematics my attempt to gain the prize contained more than a little grandiosity.

So on early mornings, late evenings and weekends—outside my usual job hours—I too obsessed about this puzzle in a manner which many psychiatrists might be concerned about. Perhaps like the London doctor who diagnosed as "schizophrenic" the habits of the great American physicist, J. Robert Oppenheimer, during his student days in England. Mind you, this was well before he managed America's Manhattan Project which built the first atomic bomb.

After working on this problem for a few more days, I finally accepted my failure and began spending my time drinking in what passed for the island's only bar: a curtained–off section of its diner which served beer and wine.

"The island now has *four* doctors," the waitress recently said.

"I thought Plazey was the only other here." He was the town's elderly resident physician.

"Dellum family just arrived. Both husband and wife have Ph.D.'s like you."

So Holly might be *their* child, I thought, remembering the "MIT" logo on her sweatshirt, an emblem of likely little significance to the island residents I had met.

Chapter 5
A soldier must renew their conscience each evening.
—author

There is only so far to drive on a one hundred fifteen square mile island and leaving it immediately wasn't possible. Until late spring the ferry ran only on Fridays. So unless a person owned a boat or could beg a ride, at other times they were as cut off from the mainland of the United States as if they lived in Iceland. A place, I was told, that the weather had been compared to.

For medical emergencies a helicopter could fly in from North Maine General Hospital in Bangor. But to satisfy other needs—a computer part, Chocolate Pop Tarts or broccoli florets—if it wasn't on the island a person would have to suffer a few more days.

The island's roads were dirt and gravel, a bond issue to pave them being voted down by a margin of six to one in the last election. It was opposed by a coalition of environmentalists and homeowners who feared that paving the roads would lead to greater development and higher taxes. With such formidable opposition the measure never had a chance. Which side the angels were on didn't concern me. What did were the large potholes which the voters' decision was forcing me to try to avoid, and often unsuccessfully.

Missing potholes during the day was hard enough. Even then one had to concentrate on the road and not a CD. With such distraction, by the time your brain announced "pothole" you already drove over it. Now, music wasn't causing my inattention: the presence of my terrified companion proved enough. After hitting the second pothole at high speed I slowed down. On this drive becoming immobilized by a broken axle presented far greater danger than simple delay.

I alternated between using the car's bright and normal headlight settings but neither cut through the heavy fog. The weather and darkness isolated me in my thoughts, which again turned to Holly.

What could have happened to her family? The self-serving boast of the resident police officer was true. There was no crime on this island. The small weekly newspaper reported minor criminal activity, though in excruciating detail. From it I had learned the niceties of mailbox vandalism and shoplifting. A year round resident did tell me of the burglary of expensive jewelry. But this happened fifteen years earlier and involved insurance fraud. The gems were found in a mainland pawnshop where they were sold by their owner.

Assault and the pursuit of a child *here* seemed incredible. Maybe I was overreacting, I thought. Projecting my personal anxieties onto Holly. Perhaps she had been sleepwalking with the blood coming from cuts made while she trampled through the woods, her fright being caused by she awakening and finding herself alone in an unfamiliar place.

This explanation was logical except for the extent of blood stain. Yet if true, it would permit me, without guilt, to take Holly to the nearest house and transfer her responsibility to the parents. Who existed in nearly every home on this family-centered island. Soon after my arrival I learned that, despite my advanced education, my single status rendered me unwelcome. For it was widely assumed that I must be awaiting the arrival of other unmarrieds for our periodic drug laden orgy.

I quickly rejected these thoughts, knowing that probable conclusions could be wrong as was evidenced by my life. No one predicted I would join the British army after my university graduation for I had never expressed any martial interest and the decision made no sense from a financial perspective.

So it would be safest, for both Holly and me, to continue to act on my earlier conclusions. That her parents were attacked and, through luck or assailant error, she managed to escape. Now being the only witness to their crimes, she could not be permitted to live. Nor could I for it would be believed that she had likely told me about this event.

By this time in my thinking we reached the fork in the road separating the town from the route back to the outlying cottages. Driving left would bring us to the tiny village of Clarksburgh which would certainly be deserted at this time of night. Turning right led to the outlying cottages, including mine and Holly's. Without further deliberation I turned right. Towards the horror from which she fled must have begun. Where the explanation of how she became blood stained must lay.

My logic seemed impeccable and I felt as confident as one could be given the situation. But I wouldn't have been so pleased with myself had I known that my career as a scientist—which I deeply loved and to which I committed my life—had just ended.

Chapter 6

You're probably thinking, colonel, that despite my vow to never again be a hero I still craved it. But it wasn't that. I just wanted to survive and was sure that by being with Holly I had become as much a target as she was. They —whoever *they* were—wanted us both dead. Since they hadn't found her they must have realized that she gained help. So they needed to learn who I was and I had to find out who they were.

I took my foot off the gas. The car slowed by the side of the road. Holly stared straight ahead, thumb in her mouth, my ancient khaki army blanket clutched to her chest.

"Holly," I asked, "when you looked out your kitchen window did you see the water or a hill?" I knew, from the real estate agent, that just three cottages were rented for the off-season. Only one had a kitchen facing the water.

"Water," she replied in a dull tone.

Now I knew her house. It was the one I first wanted but the owners would only rent to a family. It was a two story/three bedroom/two bath affair with a ceramic tile kitchen and a stairway leading down to the dock. But, alas, no boat. The owners were a retired couple who used theirs to travel Florida's inter-coastal waterway during the winter. It was too big a house for just me but I was raised in a crowded orphanage and thereafter sought roomy accommodations whenever possible.

Beyond the next turn in the road lay Holly's house. Bringing her inside to view its bloodied inhabitants wasn't a good idea. Leaving her alone in the car was a worse one. There seemed no alternative—until I remembered Mickey's Manor.

Another attraction of this rental was the tree house which came with it, two hundred feet away on the opposite side of the road. It was built long before by the owner for his six year old son. Over the years it had acquired a table and chair, small bed, even electricity and running water. Being thirty feet above ground and reached by a barely visible staircase, it would be easily missed at night if one did not know where to look. It was named Mickey's Manor after Mickey Mouse, the child's favorite cartoon character.

I placed my arm about Holly, "I'm going into your house to see if your mommy and daddy need help." Her body begin shaking. "Not with you," I quickly added. "You can wait for me in the tree house. Mickey's Manor. Have you ever been there?"

Her wordless reply seemed to indicate "no."

"It's very nice," I said, in my now familiar singsong manner. "I'll take you there. You can nap in the bed until I return in a very few minutes. A big stuffed bunny is probably sleeping and you can nap with her. She's very friendly and won't mind. Let's go there now." I wanted her moving before terror paralyzed her further.

I left my seat, went to her side of the car, unbuckled her seat belt and helped her out. Stooping low and keeping the bulk of the car between us and the house, I held her hand as we approached the tree house. Though the rain had stopped, the skies remained black and I used a flashlight sparingly to light our path.

When we reached the tree I pointed the beam at the bottom of the ladder. "Here's the first step. It's only a little harder climbing a ladder in the dark. I'll be right in back of you. Put one foot in front of the other. Soon you'll be near the top and I'll raise the lid."

Holly climbed tentatively and I followed, During our ascent, an unforgettable memory passed through my mind.

Once, while walking across an African field, I looked down and saw tiny prongs showing through the earth just inches from my foot. The barely visible sign of an anti-personnel mine called a "bouncing betty." I instantly yelled "mines" to warn my men to watch where they walked.

These devices were hidden, deadly, and worked in two stages. If one stepped on the prongs or touched the trip wire with five pounds of pressure, the first explosion was set off. The mine then shot up like a small rocket until, when ten to twenty feet above ground, it exploded again. This later blast scattered hundreds of ball bearings like a shotgun, maiming or killing anyone within thirty-five yards. Moreover, the second explosion is so close to the first that there is hardly time to move. And falling down—doing what is natural—just exposes more of your body to the blast. We managed to make it across the field unharmed and spent that night, one equally as black as this, by a stream just beyond.

The moments climbing the steps with Holly seemed as weighty as during that experience. Though, as we pushed aside the wet leaves and rose into the tree's bosom, our personal world gradually seemed less forbidding. Holly's steps became surer too.

Tree houses are now fashionable and may even include such luxuries as a full kitchen and whirlpool bath. But this was a simply carpeted two rooms and bathroom, totaling about two hundred fifty square feet. The interior was painted in light shades of orange and blue to conceal the watermarking stains on the wood where the rain penetrated before it was fully constructed. It had a covered deck along one of its sides with a ladder opening onto this.

To protect the structure from vandalism, the windows were double-glazed, of industrial strength; and the trapdoor was locked with an ingenious eight number coded lock which had been proudly explained to me by the rental agent. The combination changed daily through a battery operated mechanism. Though simple, the code was one which would not be easily guessed by a vandal: the two digit day of the week and month, with Monday being "01" followed by the four digit year. At the top of the ladder I found that the lock hadn't been changed. I felt for the buttons, entered the combination and, with my gentle push, the trapdoor rose smoothly. Holly and I climbed onto the deck.

In the house, I shone my flashlight about the rooms, pointing out and naming each piece of furniture. At the bed, she mechanically lay down beside the large stuffed figure though not touching it.

"You can nap while I go to your house," I said softly. "There's electricity but don't turn on the lights while I'm gone. No one will bother you. I'll be back in a few minutes," Then, for moments, I stood immobile as she had been.

I was afraid. A destroyer of fear before battle is the desire to care for your men. The more combat responsibility you have, the easier it is to remain calm. But I had no soldiers on this island, only Holly. I began to feel helpless and out of control, no longer having a soldier's basic psychological armor: the conviction that death happens to others but not to them. My anxiety increased until I spoke to myself as I always had before combat: I was indestructible, would be no one's target, and would survive!

All of which I almost believed as I re-entered my terror filled night and discovered a sight of unimaginable horror.

Chapter 7

Dilemmas are never simple.
—author

I listened closely: hearing slight noises had saved my life twice in the past. But there was only the wind. I waited fifteen seconds and then moved, staying below the horizon so I wouldn't be seen from the house. Approaching it slowly with the familiar zigzag pattern of soldiers. I was making progress. Ten yards remained. Five yards.

Though the building was entirely lit it remained silent. I opened the unlatched screen and kitchen doors as noiselessly as I could. At first glance the kitchen looked normal. Brightly colored dishes and cutlery were drying in a black plastic drainer on the sink.

Then I smelled what turned out to be Holly's mother: the obnoxiously sweet odor of her putrefying flesh. Something which, once experienced, is never forgotten. It aroused further memories from my military service.

I stooped to investigate several large pebbles on the floor before realizing what they were: cut-off, blackening human toes. Like colored stones along a pale walkway, they drew me into the dining room. There, my eyes jolted towards the body of a woman, if one could still call her that. Her feet were fastened to the legs of a wooden chair. Her hands were bound by gray duct tape so they resembled a cross. The nails had been torn from their fingers.

Her face was scarred with cigarette burns and conveyed such anguish that I instinctively looked away.

Having been at war, bloody wounds and nakedness no longer surprised me. But those sights were in far-off perennially feuding lands, not an American home. It was obvious that the help which I had promised Holly to provide her mother wouldn't be useful.

When I killed as a soldier it was because it was my job and for self-preservation. Those I slew would have delighted in killing me. But I never used torture for this adds a slippery edge down which even experienced interrogators can drop. Becoming an end unto itself rather than a means towards gaining the truth. Besides, if you have the time and can engage your prisoner, eventually they run out of stories to tell. And after giving up these rehearsed tales you will get the truth.

Not that torture doesn't work. It does, though eliciting both accurate and poor information. But, perhaps from squeamishness, I always permitted myself the luxury of believing that the natural disorientation and fear which were experienced after capture, and later courtesy and apparent concern, were more effective in gaining helpful intelligence than cruder methods. Here I viewed the results of one who disagreed. Or maybe he just enjoyed his work.

There were so many wounds that I couldn't guess which was the lethal one. Perhaps Holly's mother had died from the heart shock caused by intolerable pain. Her nipples and the area around her vulva were burned, probably with the still plugged-in electric iron on the ironing board beside which, incongruously, lay a half-full laundry basket. The blood which no longer drained from her body stained her slashed arms and thighs from which the skin had been peeled away.

I gripped the carving knife which I earlier picked up in the kitchen and held it combat style for self-defense. I tried to avoid stepping on the blood stained carpet as I entered the living room. This room seemed normal. It was strewn with books and scientific journals, children's crayons and toys. Even an old style Daisy air rifle and I wondered if Holly had a brother.

I searched the house quickly. Holly couldn't tolerate being alone for more than a few minutes.

Approaching the stairs, I looked forward to breathing deeply again. But the second floor also stank from the odor of bodily decay.

In the bedroom farthest down the hall lay two fully clothed bodies. The boy, about five and likely Holly's brother, was dressed in pale blue pajamas enlivened with Disney figures. He had been shot once in the temple. Apart from the wound and blood which seeped from his head onto the blanket, he appeared to be sleeping.

A man in his forties, wearing a plaid shirt and tan jeans, lay nearby—probably Holly's father. He was shot in the back, likely while trying to protect his son.

I felt baffled. When I left Holly I hoped that her parents were merely injured. So I expected, after helping them, to happily reunite everyone. The extent of blood stains on clothing, which were extensive on Holly's, doesn't necessarily mean that the injury was lethal so long as treatment is prompt. But her entire family had been slaughtered and I didn't understand why.

Was her mother tortured for information or from sadism? Then why not her husband and son too, or were their murders unplanned. These events made no sense to me even as I knew that from some perspective they must. Perhaps that of thrill seeking teenagers or older Manson devotees.

No, colonel, I wasn't being one of those armchair detectives whose thoughts ramble amidst strewn bodies. For while thinking I tensely searched one room after another until finding what I was looking for. In an old-fashioned hat box on the floor of a bedroom closet lay a Colt .380 caliber semi-automatic pocket pistol and nearly full box of fifty cartridges. Though almost an antique for its greatest sales had been seventy years before, the gun looked new. Judging by its smell, it was recently oiled. I loaded it and left the kitchen knife—reluctantly. Because, you see, it was my suddenly developed fear of guns which had led to my discharge from the British army thirteen years before.

The rest of my search was unproductive. I found none of the drug paraphernalia or money counting machines which are associated with similar crimes in newspaper reports. Nothing to account for the doom which swept this family. And, judging by their journals and books, the parents had even been physicists like me!

Who could have wanted them dead, I repeatedly asked myself, until the banging of the screen door interrupted my thinking: I was about the learn the answer. Welcome visitors not usually arriving after midnight, I felt sure that it was the slayers of Holly's family. As bad as things had been that evening I knew they were soon to become worse. Much worse.

Chapter 8

Chance favors the prepared mind.
—Pasteur

The pistol I held reassured me but I knew that a having shoot-out would be the least desirable outcome. Because of my phobia about guns it would probably be unsuccessful too: I wasn't the well-functioning soldier I once was. Moreover, I couldn't risk being injured with Holly depending on me. And I feared, despite my instruction to the contrary, that at any moment she might leave her treetop refuge and fall onto the ground. Or return home into the arms of the monsters who murdered her family.

Why *did* they return to the crime scene? I wondered. Perhaps they believed that Holly might have returned home and she knew the location of what they sought. But what goal could justify such torture and three deaths?

The sounds from downstairs were of breakage and footsteps on creaking boards. I hungered to see who they were but feared, because of the light in the hallway, that peeking downstairs would betray my presence. Their noisy search seemed unfocused with their anger arousing random destruction. Soon, frustration must drive them upstairs.

As they approached the second floor, I heard the murmur of words. Seeking greater distance from them, I slipped into the nearest room. But once there I became trapped into what was likely Holly's bedroom judging by its furnishings. A half-sized make-up table strewn with toy cosmetics. A pink diary and Cinderella bedspread atop an adult sized bed, beside which was a play tent.

The room was small, cluttered by its few pieces of furniture. The bed lay against the window with a dressing table and two canvas deck chairs filling the opposite side of the room. A multi-colored throw rug added a splash of color.

Where can one hide in such a bare room, I asked myself. Then another question arose. Since the room has no closet, where does Holly store her things? Apart from the small drawers in the make-up table I saw no storage space except, maybe...

Concealed by the bedspread lay a full-length storage drawer suspended beneath the bed. While I couldn't fit inside I could, by leaving it open and scrunching myself, hang between the rails. Though too painful a position to be held for long, it seemed the only possible hiding space. And an open drawer would appear to hold no secrets.

As the footsteps became louder I quickly pulled the drawer and crawled into the empty space, letting the bedspread fall after me. Seconds later a figure entered the room. He walked aimlessly, seeking inspiration for his search.

People have distinctive smells. That of men and women are different particularly with soldiers who haven't bathed for days. And because fear has its own odor, I wondered if what I smelled was him or me.

An idea seemed to strike the figure who then began walking deliberately. I heard objects crash to the floor as he approached the bed. Once there he made crisscross slashes with a knife through the mattress before calling loudly to his companion. His words surprised me for it was years since I had last heard the timbre of that language.

I tend to notice the oddities of language. Take Farsi, the language of Iran or Persia as it was once called. Psychologists say that the human brain is programmed to learn every language at birth so for a baby no language is more difficult than any other. But learning a foreign language as an adult is different. At that point in development some *are* harder. An instructor at the British Army's language school, who was fluent in five tongues, insisted that the only way to learn Mandarin was to have had a Chinese grandmother. Farsi is like that.

First, it has thirty-two and not twenty-six letters as in English. And to make it harder to learn, Farsi doesn't have vowels but instead has written sound symbols on or under the letters to make them readable. Moreover, the language is read from right to left. These few basics, which were mentioned by that teacher, are what I remembered years later. Plus just one word from all his failed educational attempts with me.

A word which I hadn't heard in many years was now uttered in a frightened tone by one of these killers—"motehaer.rek." It means *trembling.*

Which my arms began doing.

Chapter 9

My arms felt paralyzed. As if they had always held this aching position and knew no other. I couldn't support myself much longer. Still, the man lingered in the room.

Unable to see what was happening, I listened and smelled. A chair scraped along the floor. Then the scratching of a match and odor of burning tobacco. The smell before Holly's mother was burned. And me, were my arms to give way as they soon must.

The sweat dripped from my armpits and I feared that he must be smelling this or, as animals reportedly can, be sensing my fear. After what seemed an hour but couldn't have been more than another minute, the man left the room. I kept my rigid position until I heard footsteps on the stairway followed by the door slamming. Then my arms gave way and I collapsed onto the floor, laying there until I could again control my limbs.

I searched further after the killers left the house but again found nothing to explain the murders. Help might be just a call away as telephone companies advertise, but this house's phone line had been cut.

I returned to the tree house in a more direct fashion than I arrived since the immediate danger seemed gone. Holly was sleeping. She now clutched the large stuffed bunny. Dawn would be in a few hours. For the present our tree house was as safe a sanctuary as any though who knew what might happen in the morning. So, though exhausted, I tried to plan. As much as the idea repulsed me I would have to return to the house to get food and clean clothes for

Holly. Suddenly, fatigue and grogginess overcame me and I fell into a deep sleep.

Now my dream wasn't of Julia but of her late husband, Bryll, as we all called him. This lifelong nickname derived from the Brylcreme hair dressing he used ("a little dab will do you," its ancient marketing jingle went).

In this dream, Bryll was in his seventies, which was when we first met. He was relaxing in one of the over-sized art-deco armchairs facing the huge fireplace which dominated the library in the Institute's main building. I was there along with his first wife, a tall, too thin woman who projected an aura of illness and fragility. Henry, the lab's resident clown and head mathematician, was there too. We nursed our coffees: apart from the yearly formal dinner this was a non-drinking establishment. Bryll then said, in the sad tone he playfully affected when describing one of my errors in logical thinking, "You're missing the obvious." Whereupon I suddenly awoke and remembered a story he once told me about a French Curve.

This is a plastic scientific instrument, often used by children to draw smooth curves. While in college, Bryll was asked by a classmate whether this tool's curves had some special formula. It did, being constructed so that at the lowest point on each curve no matter how you turned it, the tangent was horizontal. The derivative (tangent) of the lowest point of any curve is zero or horizontal. So this classmate already knew what he didn't realize he knew.

"You're missing the obvious," Bryll told me in the dream, and I hungered to search Holly's house again.

I rose from the chair, having slept longer than I intended. It was five twenty. The sky was black and the weather forecast was stormy.

Though I tried to wake Holly gently, speaking her name and rubbing her hand softly, she jolted upwards. I quickly explained. "I'm your new friend, Alan. I'm going to your house for food and clothes and will be back in a few minutes. I woke you because I didn't want you to wake up and find yourself alone. You can sleep more with your bunny friend and get up when I return." Apparently unseeing, Holly hesitantly closed her eyes and fell back asleep. No nightmare she experienced could be worse than hearing the screams of her mother being tortured, I thought, as I covered her with the blanket before leaving.

Chapter 10

While walking to the house I puzzled over my dream. Though not naturally introspective, I do take dreams seriously for great scientific discoveries and artistic works have originated from them. So its warning, that I missed the obvious seemed too important for me to ignore. My next search would be more careful.

Because people have a thing about avoiding bodily odors, deodorants are a growth industry. But death does smell, as this house now did. Not a nice odor, like of babies, but of earthly corruption and the end of possibilities. Having expected this, I held stuffed tissues to my nostrils and steeled myself against the putrid odor.

Once inside, I slowly wandered the house, gathering supplies while waiting for an inspired thought to arise. In a kitchen cabinet I found black pepper crackers, Skippy Crunchy Peanut Butter, and Smucker's cherry preserves. Which seemed odd, for it was my favorite flavor. Then, long-lasting Parmalat packaged milk, plastic cups, plates, and utensils. All went into the plastic shopping bags I found in the cupboard under the sink.

I quickly passed the body of Holly's mother. It's familiarity made it less shocking than earlier that night. In the living room I could distinguish only a few of the family's possessions. Which didn't surprise me since the house was rented furnished from its owners who had filled it during their long marriage with large heavy furniture meant to last a lifetime. What had Holly's family brought with them? What did I miss seeing earlier?

The answer rumbled from my dream. You were blinded by ordinary things, unable to see the clue which was hidden in plain sight.

Now the family's belongings did stand out for these were very different from the style of the house's owners. Academic pursuits and IKEA thrift against a backdrop of early Americana. On a table, out of its black case as if waiting to be used, lay an AlphaSmart word processing keyboard. These are mostly purchased by schools who want children to learn typing skills on other than costly, fragile laptops. I turned on the machine. Only one of its files was written to. It held the tale of a lively baby moose and was likely written by one of Holly's parents for their children, or perhaps by Holly herself.

The only other family items seemed drab volumes in structural physics and electrical engineering, and colorful children's books explaining astronomy and chemistry.

Then I saw it. All but hidden under the sofa flashed an instantly recognizable blue edge which had been obscured by the nearly identical color of the rug. Julia had redone the Institute's journal with a red/white/blue color scheme which the patriotic Bryll instantly approved for the cover of our Journal of Military Nucleonics. The word means atomic nuclei and was chosen to emphasize the cutting edge weapons he hoped to devise.

This special issue concerned the American attempts to build laser based weaponry. Atop its Table of Contents page written in an expansive script were the following words: *It will shake the heavens.*

Chapter 11

I gathered Holly's clothes from her room. Socks, underwear, jeans, T-shirts, and a hooded winter coat. Then, trying to avoid seeing her parents' and brother's bodies, I retrieved the bags of food from the kitchen and left the house with a sense of relief.

Where should we flee after breakfast? To remain in the tree house longer wasn't wise. The murderers might return to repeat their search..This problem occupied my mind as I sat on the edge of the bed watching Holly. Suddenly she opened her eyes and looked at me..

"They're dead aren't they?"

"Yes."

She didn't cry or speak more and I didn't know what to say. How could one comfort a child after the catastrophe of her entire family's destruction? You don't, Julia seemed to whisper to me, first involve her with familiar matters.

"Holly," I said, "the bathroom is in back. You can wash and change into the clothes I brought for you. I'll make breakfast."

I handed her the sack filled with her clothes. Then I left to make peanut butter and jelly cracker sandwiches and to open the packaged milk. There were Nabisco Blueberry Pop Tarts for desert.

I felt comforted by the familiar sound of running water. Would we later lunch at the island's diner? Not unless I intended it to be our last for the attackers would shortly have our photos. Holly's, obtained from the house;

mine, after a search of the state Department of Motor Vehicles' database for the owner of my classic Kaiser auto.

With the few facts gained, the Internet would provide more. Though, once I contacted the mainland police, our safety would be assured. *Unless* since I shared the same profession as Holly's parents, the murderers erroneously believed that I too possessed the information they sought—if it was information they were seeking. Maybe Holly knew what they were looking for and could tell me.

While I was setting the table, in as formal a manner as possible under the circumstances, Holly appeared. Dressed in her likely daily costume of jeans, T-shirt, and sneakers. Without a word and behaving as if this were an ordinary morning, she sat at the table. I shared my thoughts with her slowly.

"Bad men are looking for us. We can't stay here and because they'll soon know who I am we can't stay at my house either. There are no police on the island and we have to hide. The ferry won't leave until next week. Where can we stay till then." I inflected my last sentence as a statement, feeling that to phrase it as a question would place additional stress on her. And if I lacked a solution, I couldn't imagine her coming up with one.

"Do you know what the men wanted?"

"No."

"What happened last night?" After a long silence, Holly did speak.

"I woke up...in my Princess tent. A man with a gun ran past my room. Mommy was screaming. I hid till they left. I should have helped her." Her face began breaking up so I changed the subject quickly.

"You're still a little girl and they were grown men with guns. I'm glad you found me. I hope you like cherry jelly? It's the only flavor we have."

Holly viewed the food on the table as if not recognizing it. Then she haltingly picked up one of the crackers which I earlier spread and bit off a corner.

"The milk isn't cold." I filled a cup for her. I wanted to continue my questioning but was afraid this would cause her to shut down again.

"What will we do?" she asked.

I continued making cracker sandwiches. Finally I spoke. "We'll get off this island. Find the police and be OK. Do you have an uncle or aunt you can stay with then?"

"There's no one," she said, with a finality so firm as to make her statement seem indisputable. I didn't question this for certainly others, including myself, lacked known relatives.

My immediate worry was where we could safely hide until I contacted the mainland police. My next was their response upon learning that I was an exceptionally skillful killer. One of the best that the SAS ever trained.

Chapter 12

Death occurs naturally, accidentally, or deliberately. I was much too often involved with all three. Those learning of these events in my life would joke that I was a risky acquaintance. "You're a dangerous person to be around," a general observed, after he viewed the corpse of a prisoner I had been guarding. "He attacked me with a smuggled knife. What would you have done, sir?" I asked. "The same," he admitted, though now with a friendly smile. "But one shouldn't make a habit of killing people."

I didn't, but people continued dying around me. So I wasn't looking forward to a new investigation. "Were you a scientific competitor of the Dellums?" they would ask. "Did professional rivalry exist?" Then their final question to which they already knew the answer: "Have you ever killed anyone?" "Yes," must be my responses to all these questions. Being honest was necessary since, as a British citizen and working in the U.S.A. at that government's sufferance with a Green Card, I could be quickly deported for little or no valid reason.

Which I very definitely didn't want. I greatly enjoyed my cushy job and the social informality of America as contrasted with the stratified social climate of England where the comforting myth of rags to riches never took hold. Moreover I loved Manhattan and spent many weekends there since arriving seven years earlier at the Institute's main campus in Tuxedo, New York, a wealthy gated enclave forty miles north of New York City.

Bryll had long vacationed at his home in Tuxedo though few would have described his twenty room mansion with outbuildings and tennis courts as being "just a summer cottage."

It was Bryll who rescued me from the Senate and FBI investigations into what was, essentially, just a business dispute. The university where I was teaching included the use of my patented invention in their application for a government grant. They wanted to set up a laboratory and seek commercial and military uses *of my* discovery, claiming that their plan represented an exception to the copyright law since they would be using my invention for research. My lawyer insisted that creating a facility to seek commercial contracts was far from one of the exceptions intended in the copyright law and that they had no right to do what they were doing. So, following this favorable legal opinion, I entered their lab in the middle of the night and removed my invention. Whereupon they fired me, accused me of theft and, since my laser had potential military applications, pushed for a government investigation. Until Bryll heard of the matter.

Wanting to hire me and to have the exclusive use of my invention for *his* Institute's work, he aroused his friends in industry who, whatever their differences, recognized the danger to their profits in diluting patent protection.

Now recognizing the depth of controversy they created and the threat it presented to the university (for much of the research which *they* conducted involved the permitted *free* use of inventions patented by corporations), they caved in. The university recognized my patent *and* apologized for the trouble they caused me. They also offered me back my teaching job—and with tenure too.

So thanks to Bryll I quickly went from being a potential felon facing twenty years in a federal prison to Scientist Of The Week in *Time* magazine. After which I would do anything for him. Particularly once I visited the Institute and became familiar with a luxurious lifestyle which I previously only viewed in movies. It was there that I first experienced having a chauffeur and butler. It takes only five minutes of this personal service to expect such treatment thereafter.

There were economies after Bryll's death when the Foundation he set up took over. But even with these (as, being charged two dollars for the formerly free meals), I was already too spoiled to work elsewhere. No, I very definitely didn't want to leave America.

Indicating that I was thinking too long, Holly "accidentally" spilled her milk, I cleaned the mess and poured more. She seemed to be coming out of her dazed state though she still spoke as if she knew words but didn't quite remember how to use them.

"Is my brother dead?"

"Yes. Your mother and father too. They're all dead," I felt, despite her youth, it was important that she accept the facts.

"Will there be a funeral?" she asked, a minute later.

"Soon."

"I want to go."

"We'll both go."

"He was so young." Individual tears rolled down her cheeks, followed by rivers of them.

"Let's sit on the sofa," I said.

There, I held my arm about her and spoke as I had in years past, to the relatives of the dead soldiers I visited. I said that her mother and father and brother would exist forever in her memory. And that the depth of her sadness revealed how deep their love had been.

I used simple words, wanting to be sure that Holly understood. They seemed to help but maybe what really comforted her was my tone and our closeness. I was always suspicious of words.

While we sat, the sun briefly rose before disappearing behind thickening clouds.

"Marian needs me," Holly said.

"Who's Marian?"

"My doll."

"I'll get her from the house before we leave," I assured her. And at that moment it occurred to me where we could hide: in an empty house. With most of the island's population gone for the winter many houses were now vacant. Our pursuers couldn't search all of them. But I needed one with a garage, to hide my too noticeable car.

"You're thinking again," Holly said unexpectedly. Having kept my thoughts to myself for so much of my life her observation seemed intrusive yet also something which I hungered for since Julia's death.

"I'm making plans. We have to clean up, like when you go camping." And so others wouldn't pick up our trail, I thought.

I remade the bed and placed our trash, her soiled clothing, and the damp towels in plastic bags. She watched me work but didn't help.

We climbed down from the tree house and returned to my car. "Sit here. I'll bring your doll friend," I said. "If anyone comes, run quietly and hide in the woods. Come out only when *I* call you."

I walked slowly, not wanting to re-enter the house. No matter how often death is viewed it never becomes ordinary. Even among undertakers who cope with their daily stress by creating soothing concepts, like describing death as being "God's final blessing." Not being religious, I could not do so and had always reared from its ugly sight: deformed body parts; corrupting, insect ridden flesh. No longer people but "remains."

Yet Holly's doll was important to her and I felt that I had no choice.

As I approached the door I remembered that I hadn't asked Holly where her doll was. Now I might have to search all of the rooms. Would this take me twenty minutes? Forty minutes? An hour?

I opened the screen and kitchen doors softly, hesitating to disturb the dead even as I realized how irrational this concern was. Entering the kitchen, I instinctively looked towards the floor—for the blackening, cut-off toes of Holly's mother.

Suddenly I felt hot and unwell and instantly told myself that I was having a heart attack. Then that these feelings and thoughts just indicated I was having another of those panic attacks which had plagued me since leaving the military years before. These produce symptoms which unnecessarily bring many people to Emergency Rooms. All erroneously believing that they are suffering from a heart attack rather than anxiety, which can mimic virtually any physical disorder. "Tell yourself you're in good health but simply feeling anxious," the military psychiatrist had advised me. "*Believe* that your symptoms are psychological, not physical, and the terror will vanish."

So I did. I told myself that I was *not* having a heart attack but was just very afraid. I repeated this mantra aloud as I wandered the rooms in my search for Holly's beloved doll. Once again, the doctor's advice worked. My fear that I was deathly ill disappeared.

But despite this, even as my chest felt less heavy and my pounding heart rate decreased, my terror remained. For it hadn't derived from a fantasy about my health but to what I just saw in this house. Or, rather, that I didn't see.

Those horrifying body parts on the floor, the deteriorating corpses of Holly's mother and father and baby brother: the sights which so upset me the evening before. All were gone—having disappeared as if they never existed.

Chapter 13

...there is always an easy solution to every problem—neat,
plausible and wrong.
H. L. Mencken

Finally, I found Holly's doll. It was two feet long with pale skin, flowing blond hair, and green eyes that blinked and made it seem alive when I picked it up. Besides me, the eyes were the only thing that moved in this house.

The doll was dressed in a long, white, old-fashioned sleeping shift and cap, which I was careful not to let slip off. On the dressing table were the doll's hairbrush and a diary entitled *Holly and Marian—Our Adventures*. I slipped these into my pocket, feeling they might comfort Holly. Marian, her doll, was the only family she had left. I cradled it in my arms as if it were an infant and left the house, still dazed by my experience of minutes before.

When I tried to understand it, disturbing thoughts arose. Maybe my panic attacks had developed into true madness and this was the real reason I was discharged from the British Army. Not because of my limp and fear of guns, though these do limit a soldier's activities. My having gone crazy would also explain the demand of the Institute's new director that I take a "medical leave for stress" from my job.

Perhaps the bodies I saw last night were delusional, a daytime equivalent of the recurring nightmares I experienced since my military service. Psychoanalytic theory insists that traumatic events must be repeated until the unconscious fear is laid to rest.

But what I saw had seemed so real. And Holly certainly existed, as did her terror. Unless it was me who killed her parents and kidnapped her, I then forcing myself to forget the truth in order to reduce my overwhelming sense of guilt. So Holly's real fear might be: *of me.*

How I managed to drive down the road with such bizarre ideas I'll never know. But as my anxiety left me so did they. The bodies *had* existed and *I* didn't hide them. Our danger *was* real. And despite my army medical discharge and mandated job leave, I wasn't crazy. Just experiencing the normal stress of a person who is going through a most trying time. As was Holly. Moreover, there *must be* a logic to what happened. For some good reason the crime scene had been cleaned up. Why, and who did it, I didn't yet know. After accepting these logical conclusions, I relaxed a little.

Holly was calmer too now that she regained her doll. I increased the car's speed. Not knowing where our pursuers were, I wanted us off the road and into a vacant house as quickly as possible.

I passed one house. It had bicycles beside an open garage door: the sure sign of a family still in residence. Farther down the road lay a second house. But this one lacked a garage to conceal my notable car. Finally, when I had begun to despair at finding something suitable, I glimpsed a possibility.

This house lay behind high shrubs which grew almost to its front door. I stopped the car and asked Holly to accompany me. A parent and child convey far less suspicion than does a lone male stranger. Hand-in-hand, as she gripped Marian to her chest with her free arm, we walked towards the house. It was a two story affair with a garage to the left of the front door and a covered porch to its right. Standing just outside, I saw no lights and heard no sounds, No one answered my knock.

"Let's walk around back and see if anyone is home," I said to Holly, after returning to the car for a screwdriver.

A London policeman once advised me how to make my rented house be least attractive to a passing burglar. "Place deadbolt locks on all the doors, not just the front one. That's most important. Many people treat back doors as if they're different and use simple knob locks there. But these doors are invisible to neighbors and are the most vulnerable. After you protect the doors, drill a hole through the top of the lower window's frame and partially into the upper window's frame. Then insert a nail or eye bolt into the hole."

The condition of this house would have alarmed him. Its heavy shrubbery made it easy for burglars to conceal themselves. The back windows were fastened by latches; and the door at the rear of the house had glass panels and a knob lock.

My heavy knock on this door produced the silence which my banging on the front door received. After waiting a minute, I shattered the pane closest to the door's lock with the handle of the screwdriver. After knocking out the jagged edges, I slipped my hand through the opening and unlocked the door.

"That was a crime," Holly observed.

"Yes, but we need help and not everything bad is always bad. If the people were home they would help us. Before we go I'll leave money on the table to repair the window and pay for the food we use." Despite her dubious look, my explanation seemed to satisfy her.

The door's entrance led into a kitchen. Then, much like soldiers, we explored the house before settling in.

Next to the kitchen was a laundry room. This was bordered by the veranda beside which was a nearly empty single car garage. The tricycles there indicated young children. The family had likely returned to the mainland before school began in September.

On the other side of the laundry room was a functioning bathroom with the water in the pipes being set to run at a trickle. The bottled gas heater was full and the temperature had been set at fifty to avoid the pipes freezing. I relaxed: it would do no good to elude our pursuers but freeze to death.

Past the bathroom was a bedroom about twelve by fourteen feet. A larger living room, small dining room, and covered patio made up the main floor of the house.

The second floor held three bedrooms and another bathroom. "I'm going outside to put the car in the garage," I told Holly, feeling it was important to keep her informed of my location. "Do you want to stay here or come with me."

"With you," she said, and I thought of how quickly we had become a pair. But I wondered when she would experience that normal rage felt by people whose relatives were murdered and how it would be expressed.

Chapter 14

You can't say civilization don't advance...
in every war they kill you in a new way.
—Will Rogers

The biting wind and darkening sky foretold snow and our longer stay on the island. When we returned to the house I replaced the broken window pane with waxed paper and duct tape which I found in a kitchen drawer. The phone was disconnected. After making us cocoa, I sat Holly down for another chat.

"Did your parents ever take you to their office?"

Holly didn't answer immediately. As if she had to deliberately reach back into her mind, to the normality before the murder of her family, to be able to respond.

"Yes."

"What did you see there?"

"I wore goggles." Her parents' work in physics must have involved lasers, I thought, the goggles being used to protect eyes from its harmful effects.

I thought for a moment. "How big was the machine they used?"

"They had two. One was big, the other small."

"Would the small one fit on this table?" I asked, indicating the kitchen table at which we sat.

"Yes."

"What did your parents do with the machine?"

"They shot light at a piece of steel."

Holly seemed annoyed by my persistent questions but she continued answering.

"What did you see after it was smashed?"

"Little pieces."

"Did your parents say anything?"

"My mother said now that they knew how to control anti-matter they should work on the matter of their daughter. My father yelled a number and jumped up."

I caught my breath. "Do you remember what it was?"

"A thousand. No, twenty five thousand."

They did it, I thought, and felt like leaping into the air myself. Her parents had discovered how to increase the energy in a small laser to make it capable of producing two hundred and fifty times the strength of current ones. Which could already punch a hole in a sheet of metal from several miles away.

Laser is an acronym for "light amplification by stimulated emission of radiation." Using this technology, atomic particles can be changed into light having enough radiation to destroy an object. How much damage depends on the amount of power generated and the precision of its focus on the target. A small laser gun, capable of fitting on a table, might be installed in aircraft or ships. Then, nearly instantaneously and without visible warning, they could vaporize troops or a missile from hundreds of miles away.

Lasers can be produced using chemicals or electricity. Chemical lasers are more powerful but require huge quantities of material, making a small weapon impractical. Holly's parents had succeeded in producing a small electric laser with many times the power of the current largest chemical laser. They might even have solved the problem of targeting: how to create a beam of high enough quality—one sufficiently narrow, intense, and well focused—that it wouldn't diverge on its way to the target.

And her mother's offhanded comment, that they had learned to control anti-matter, indicated an even far greater discovery.

What Holly witnessed on possibly a community wide "Take Your Daughter To Work Day" was the dawn of a revolutionary weapons system. Perhaps like all valuable inventions it had invented itself for it offered speed-of-light precision engagement and destruction of battlefield targets like artillery, rockets, and mortars. A nation with this weapon would be invulnerable against inter-continental missile attack; and were they the only possessor of an anti-matter weapon they could conquer the world. This explained the deadly interest of Iranian or other foreign agents in Holly's parents. Holly's information crystallized the huge personal danger I had to avoid overtaking us.

While these weighty thoughts consumed me, Holly sprawled on her chair, looking increasingly listless. To distract her from her mood, I suggested, "Let's see what food there is."

I opened one cabinet and asked her to explore another. A glance evidenced that we could survive for months without leaving the house. The top pantry held tins of tuna and sardines, vegetables, spaghetti, and condensed milk. Even crackers and jelly. Holly found more cans of vegetables, macaroni, and spaghetti sauce.

In addition to knives, spoons, and forks, we found the usual castaways of kitchen cabinets and what we most needed: a can opener.

For the first time since the previous night I began to feel safe. Until my paranoid/watchful instinct kicked in. I paid attention for this had saved my life in the past. You'll need a disguise to get off the island it told me—there will be watchers at the dock.

So, though the ferry wouldn't arrive for a week, I considered the camouflage we needed. It would have to be not only external, like a false mustache, but internal—psychological. We would have to adopt and maintain the mood and temperament of other people.

An intelligence instructor once told me of several American officers who were parachuted into Nazi Germany a month before D-Day. Both had lived in Germany before the war and spoke the language fluently. Traveling by train, wearing authentic clothing and holding excellently forged documents, they were stopped by Gestapo agents who were interviewing all travelers. The Americans readily offered their papers. Despite speaking colloquial German they were quickly arrested, interrogated under horrendous torture and, barely alive, finally released from a concentration camp at the end of the war. What tricked them up? They didn't show the normal anxiety which civilians always had when confronted by the police. So Holly and I would have to *become different people* in order to remain safe.

Which also meant that I'd have to keep her calm and her mind off what she endured just one day earlier. Hopefully, we could find games to play.

"What did you like to do when you weren't in school," I asked Holly."On Saturday, after breakfast," I added, trying to be helpful.

"I wrote in my diary."

"Did you write every day?"

"Not when I had to help...my brother." Her words trailed off.

"What else did you do?"

"I drew."

"That's really good. I never could draw," I responded honestly. "Let's look around, Maybe we can find crayons and paper."

Without affect and walking stiffly, Holly followed my lead during our search. We skipped the downstairs, largest bedroom since it obviously had been used by adults. Against one wall of an upstairs bedroom lay a low bookcase holding pens, pads, crayons, Peanuts and fairy tale coloring books, chess and checker pieces and a play board. Also several popular games including Chutes and Ladders. I remembered playing this as a child though in my British version its name had been changed to Snakes and Ladders.

"Lots for us to do," I observed, in the exaggeratedly optimistic tone which parents use to brighten a child's spirits. Then I thought how well Holly was adjusting to the extraordinary change in her life. Deadly men invade her home and murder her family. She flees and, seeking safety, bonds to a stranger. Who will protect you, I vowed silently.

Chapter 15

Having no television or even adequate radio reception to distract us, Holly and I amused each other by playing Chutes and Ladders, Connect Four, and Monopoly. I didn't suggest that we play the Operation game, fearing that the comical picture on its box—a man being operated on—might arouse painful memories. When we weren't playing we planned and cooked meals and went to bed at the times when families usually do. During this period, while awaiting the arrival of the ferry, I tried to forget the recent past, focusing on the future and our achieving safety. .

I didn't know where Holly would live once we reached the mainland. Perhaps some previously unknown relative could be found. But that problem was for later. Soon I would teach her how to conceal her identity but that too could wait.

The repetitive activities soothed us and one afternoon we played Chutes and Ladders seven times. The pervasive fear and increasing cold were unable to penetrate the warmth we created about us.

One night when Holly was asleep, I lay in my bed fiddling with the radio dial. Stations came on briefly but quickly disappeared into the static. Suddenly, with a clarity which surprised me, I heard information which kept me awake for the rest of the night. Between the reports of an actor's marriage ending in divorce and the collapse of a Michigan bridge, the announcer exclaimed that a "missing scientist" was being sought by the police. That scientist was me.

Chapter 16

Most people think that the world revolves about them. Still, there is a sense of disbelief when you hear your name on a broadcast. So it took a few moments for the news to sink in.

"The disappearance from North Fork Island, Maine, of vacationers, Melinda and Jackson Dellum, their five year old son and ten year old daughter, was reported to the police in an anonymous call. The couple are teachers at the Massachusetts Institute of Technology. Because of the military applications of their research, the investigation is being considered a security matter. The fingerprints of another missing scientist, Alan Higginsen, a British subject, were found at their home. He was identified by authorities as being a person of interest and is sought for questioning. He is six feet three inches tall with an athletic build and walks with a limp. His behavior was described as 'odd' by co-workers, before his recent medical leave from his job. Listeners seeing this man should not approach him but instead inform the police or nearest FBI office."

The accusation didn't surprise me. The unusual events of the past days had made me shock proof though this news did test my limits. My next thoughts concerned the biggest mystery.

Who removed the bodies of Holly's family and cleaned up the slaughter scene? And, though her parents were certainly dead, who reported this lie about their disappearance to the police? My mind whirled at possibilities.

The most fantastic was that the murderers themselves did so in order to gain the assistance of the police in finding Holly. Who, they believed, had the information they wanted. But this explanation made no sense. Were Holly to be found, the truth about her family must come out: Holly was ten years old and not a barely verbal infant. Because every hypothesis I generated seemed illogical, I stopped making them and turned my thinking to our immediate concerns.

The first was to avoid both the police and the murderers of her family. Were I captured by either my fate wasn't enviable: lengthy interrogation with possible imprisonment or certain torture and death depending on who caught me first. Moreover, if the police refused to believe my apparently fantastic story about foreign agents they would do little to protect Holly. So she and I were joined at the hip until I could gain evidence to support my story.

My second problem was where to find this evidence and about this I didn't have a clue (to make a bad pun). Moreover, that Holly's parents were doing critical research might seem less relevant than my fingerprints being at the crime scene. And even if Holly spoke convincingly, would the police believe her considering her traumatized state. They might believe I brainwashed her. Past experiences had taught me to distrust investigators working under pressure. Unless I discovered something quickly, our odds of surviving looked slim.

The only good development was that our initial problem was less pressing. If contacting the mainland police represented danger and not safety, then there was no hurry to leave the island. We could remain in this house until late spring, before its owner returned for the tourist season next summer. Provided that our supplies and sanity held out and they didn't decide to visit earlier. But since remaining anonymous was easier on the mainland than on a small island, reaching it was still desirable.

One sure way out of our mess was to find what the killers were seeking. This would convince the police. This information, it was logical to assume, involved the Dellum's military work.

Then another thought arose: Holly *might* know where *it* was. Before falling asleep, I decided to question her further in the morning.

But I woke long before dawn, aroused by a sound which I couldn't immediately identify. Fearing the worst, I reached for the pistol on the floor by my bed. My fingers had just touched the gun when I realized that the noise was being made by Holly, who was walking slowly towards me. I moved the pistol out of her sight.

"I can't sleep," she said.

"Did you have a scary dream?"

"No." I suddenly remembered a television factoid which explained that when children awake at night they likely had a nightmare which they might or might not remember or want to discuss. It also advised how to help the child cope with their fear.

"Are you hungry?"

"I'm afraid to sleep alone," she hesitantly revealed.

"OK. I'll lie on your bed with you until you fall asleep." .

Holly seemed comforted by my suggestion. She gripped my hand until we reached her bed. Then she got under the blanket and looked expectantly. I lay beside her.

"All dreams are good even if some are scary, They are our friends, telling us what is going on inside us and how we see our lives. But this message is hidden, like in a mystery movie we have to figure out."

Holly listened knowingly as if she had been told this before. Unfortunately, for I had run out of things to say. So I said what I planned to tell her in the morning.

"We're going to have to pretend. The men who hurt your family are looking for a man and girl who don't know each other. We'll be safe only if people think that I'm your father. It'll be our 'pretend' game. Can you do it?"

Holly looked uncertain.

I continued. "To become convincing, we'll have to act all of the time. So starting now, you'll call me 'daddy.' But we're only acting. Soon we'll be just good friends again. Can you remember?"

Holly suddenly turned and stared past me into the open doorway. I followed her gaze. There was no one there.

"Mommy said I should do what you say. That I can trust you."

"Your mommy..." I began arguing but stopped myself. If it comforted her to believe that her mother still existed as a ghost or an angel what right did I have to take this fantasy from her. I kissed her on the forehead, said we would talk more in the morning,, and returned to my bed. Holly didn't object. Her face was relaxed and she now looked like a normal child for the first time since we met.

But I didn't sleep well, having another of those dreams where horrors abound, all goes wrong, and no efforts manage to get them right. In its beginning I heard booted steps and began to run. Holly was beside me and I whispered for her to move faster. Finally, I picked her up and carried her into a castle with many rooms and glass doors. I glanced through several and saw children lying in agony and begging for help, their bodies scarred from torture. I ran down the corridor until bullets cut me down. In the next scene we were both tied down and I could hear Holly's screams as the skin was being peeled from her small naked body.

Chapter 17

Next morning Holly still looked happy. During breakfast she spontaneously addressed me as "daddy." Later she became animated and taught me a card game, "I Doubt It," and beat me with a gleeful expression. In this game one player lies about the cards they hold while their opponent tries to determine if they are lying. Great practice for our future, I thought.

It was in the midst of our fourth play of this game that Holly stared directly in front of her. Then she nodded and a smile lit her face. I shivered slightly as I realized what was happening: Holly was again speaking to the fantasy of her dead mother. These incidents occurred frequently over the next few days. It was after one of them, when Holly seemed particularly relaxed, that I gave her my final instructions.

"Hold my hand when we walk. If someone stares at us, squeeze it tightly and call me 'daddy.' Or ask me a question like, 'how soon will we be home?' And never leave my side!" Then we cleaned the house and packed our few belongings. I placed two—one hundred dollar bills on the kitchen table to cover the cost of repairing the window I broke and for the supplies we used. It was Friday and I wanted us off the island that day.

But our efforts were fruitless. An hour later I noticed snow flakes. By early afternoon, several feet had fallen and the storm intensified. We unpacked and planned our supper. The ferry wouldn't arrive that day, not until the following Friday.

Chapter 18

I celebrated my graduation from the Royal Military Academy at Sandhurst by spending more hours drinking alone in a local pub. As I became increasingly drunk on Laphroaig single malt Scotch whiskey, an instructor of tactics joined me. I had sensed a similarity between us since we first met but because of our difference in rank, real conversation wasn't possible until I received my commission. Which he saluted by inviting me to address him by his first name.

"Call me Charles," he said, as he seated himself opposite me in the booth.

"Charles." I grasped his hand, seeming more drunk than I was, a pose which I often adopted to avoid even casual intimacy. But, also being a reserved Britisher, he didn't comment on my behavior. Not at first.

"What are your plans?"

"Camping in Scotland for the next three weeks. Then two courses at Cambridge: 'Political Terrorism,' and 'The Politics of Acceptable Military Risks.'." "A fellowship," I added, my pride at gaining this award being leavened by a simultaneous shrug. As if to indicate "it ain't that much." Boasting, no matter how well deserved, is considered boorish in England.

He briefly let me bask in self-congratulation. Then he leaned forward and, gripping my shoulder lightly, smiled to reduce the sting of his words.

"You're about the most unsocialized but talented recruit we ever had. Which is why you got your commission considering the record number of instructors you pissed off. And because people with big offices believe in you.

"But the military doesn't like special people. So in the future, *try* to remember that you're not the only person who was homeless. I spent a year in foster care and still remember how it feels." Perhaps this explained the bond I sensed with him.

"You won't achieve all that you're capable of unless you stop pushing people away. A high IQ gives you a leg up but creates enemies no matter how careful you are. You don't have to hide your talents. Just get a job with the smartest person you meet and hang on. You'll learn from them and they won't feel the need to drown you in bureaucratic bullshit.

"Pretend to be friendly," he added. "Adopt the mannerisms of the most social person you know. Deliberately, until it becomes natural."

I sipped my drink.

"You sound like a psychologist," I said.

"A good officer must be one."

My lifelong suspicion arose.

"Why are you telling me this?"

Now he gave his broadest smile.. "Because someday you might be able to offer me a job. And keep off the booze," he ordered in a mock tone before leaving, "that self-medication is worse than what doctors push."

I sensed his advice was good but didn't enjoy hearing it. Few people welcome unpleasant information about themselves even if it is accurate. But I followed his suggestions. Thereafter, I tried to act friendly and keep my rage submerged. Though I only risked sharing my real feelings when I met Julia, many years later.

"It's your move," Holly exclaimed petulantly, interrupting my train of thought. We were now on our third game of chess. I taught her the rules that morning and by our second game she had them down cold.

"Sorry." I moved my piece unthinkingly and she captured my queen.

It was partly the snowstorm which saved us. No effective search could be mounted while it lasted. But I also credit the ghost or angel of Holly's mother, or whoever Holly spoke with during those three days, for these contacts kept her calm.

Not that I didn't help by playing innumerable games with Holly and responding to her needs, like any real parent would. So though I had earlier feared being marooned by the snow, our experiences during it reduced Holly's pain. .

Our moods were brighter by the afternoon when the sun briefly appeared. Now I began to feel real contentment and not just the substitute enabled by alcohol. Which I hadn't touched since meeting Holly. Even after I found an unopened bottle of Scotch in a kitchen cabinet.

But this mini-euphoria doesn't excuse my carelessness which could have ended our lives. For I had missed the noise of the kitchen door opening and that it was masked by voices from the radio doesn't excuse my laxity. Nor does the radio's reception having been briefly static-free, and my need to learn about events concerning us during our three day snowbound isolation from society,

I felt shock upon hearing the footsteps creak in our direction. Holly froze too. I grasped the small pistol in my jacket pocket and unlocked the safety.

Chapter 19

I motioned for Holly to be silent and quickly hid her in the space between the sofa and the bay window. Then I stood behind the door and waited. Because of the radio's chatter I couldn't tell how many were coming through the kitchen. The image of Holly's dead mother arose in my mind.

My defensive position wasn't to be envied: alone with an underpowered pistol and a child who might scream and reveal our location at any moment.

A shadow passed in the space between the partially open door and the wall which concealed me. Then it spoke in an annoyed female voice: "Paulette, Chuck—where *are* you?"

I replaced the pistol into my jacket and slipped from behind the door.

"I'm a neighbor," I said, the first thing which came to mind. Being unshaven for days, it was crucial for me to make a reassuring statement given my disreputable appearance. Thankfully, my image would bear little resemblance to any newspaper photo of me she might have seen.

Holly chose that moment to stand up, giving rise to one of my less plausible brainstorms.

"We were playing Hide and Seek." I blurted out, before realizing that this game would be far too babyish for one of Holly's age. But I wanted to give further evidence of our innocence to this stranger.

The woman seemed surprised but not frightened. She was about four inches shorter than my six feet three inches and stylishly dressed in a black jacket and jeans. Her clothes were chosen to emphasize shape, not for outdoor activities. Her skin was pale, unlike the ruddy complexion of island residents. I feared what Holly might say and quickly spoke first.

"We're renting at the other end of the island and had a car problem. I didn't think the owners would mind our staying till the weather cleared."

"Daddy, I'm hungry..." Holly interjected helpfully, as my capacity for invention flagged.

"I'm sure they won't," the woman said evenly, as I wondered if she accepted my story. But I began to relax: the arrival of a friend or relative was far preferable to the murderers I expected.

"How did you get here in this storm?" I asked.

"Dumb luck. I wanted to get away and drove here on impulse, not thinking of whether the ferry was running. But it was taking someone with acute pancreatitis to the hospital. The medical helicopter couldn't get through. A four wheeler taxi took me from the pier." She added in a rueful tone, "so I won't be alone," as if she would have welcomed solitude.

"We'll be leaving as soon as the storm lifts," I said. "Can I make you coffee?"

"Sure."

As she spoke I became aware of what disturbed me about her. Despite the warmth of the room, she hadn't yet taken off her jacket. As if she were waiting for the right moment to flee.

"I'm hungry, daddy," Holly repeated, sensing the tension in the room and following my exact instructions of a previous evening.

"OK, honey." Then, as if having just remembered to do so, I introduced ourselves. "I'm Alan and this is Holly, my ten year old troublemaker." The woman offered her hand to both of us and introduced herself as Pat Wrenson. Still, her coat remained zipped tight. I returned her smile and led Holly to the kitchen before she made another remark. She sat quietly at the table while I boiled water for coffee and opened cans of tuna and lima beans for her lunch.

"How long did you plan to stay?" I asked Pat.

"I'm not sure. I'm out of work at the moment."

"What do you do?" I used that typical American question to foster a friendly atmosphere.

"I'm a lawyer."

"What type of law do you practice?"

She paused before responding. "White collar crime: securities fraud, tax evasion. What about you?"

"I teach physics at the University of Maine," I said, keeping my lie very close to the truth. The best liars tell few, to reduce the chance of exposure. Also because except to their students, college instructors are generally considered harmless. But the woman looked uncomfortable as she glanced at the improvised covering in the window pane which I broke. Her luggage stood between her and the door and the expression in her eyes caused me to suspect this was also her thought.

Suddenly, as if having made a firm decision, she opened and lay her jacket on a chair and sat by Holly. "Bet you're tired of canned stuff," she said, in a friendly tone.

Holly ignored her, her acting capacity having likely reached its temporary limit.

The tea kettle's whistle and my bustle to make coffee interrupted the silence.

"I hope instant is OK."

"It's fine."

Pat stared at Holly for she wasn't really eating but just re-arranging the tiny lima beans on her plate. She made them into the pattern of a snake with an elongated head.

I sat in the chair opposite Holly. "Maybe we better have lunch too," I suggested.

That's how my relationship with Pat began. During an interlude between storms when our casual contact radiated into something far deeper and, for me, unimaginable. Over the following days, while playing games and sharing chores, we developed that trust which enforced isolation produces, though I couldn't yet tell her of mine and Holly's peril.

Each morning more snow hit the windows. Once I awoke to Holly sleeping beside me. And, as she became more of a real daughter to me, Pat became my friend. By the time the storm finally drew down, on the fourth day after her arrival, we had begun sharing events from our pasts..

I was playing Battleship with Holly, that long popular board game in which players try to sink their opponent's ships by determining their positions. As we called out our guesses, Holly removed the red and white plastic pieces from the cubicles on her board and began lining them compulsively on the table. We stared, much like when she had acted similarly with her food.

"Nervous habit," I explained.

"I bite my nails on holidays," Pat said understandingly.

"Vacations affect people differently. I did worse when I wasn't working," I added, before catching myself. Then didn't seem the moment to reveal the extent of my past drinking.

"It was how my job ended which made me nervous," she said.

"You quit your job?"

"Sort of," she said. Lowering her voice so Holly, who was now coloring in a coloring book on the other side of the room, could not hear what she was about to say.

"I stabbed my boss."

"That was a mistake," I said evenly and suddenly remembered the comical sticker on her suitcase: "PMS—Punish Men Severely." After the events of the past week nothing would surprise me.

"You haven't heard the whole story."

I couldn't wait.

Chapter 20

Pat began her explanation. "Lawyers aren't nice people. They dress and smile good but all the while they are just scheming to take your money. There are overflowed workshops on how to arouse the most fear in clients for the bigger the worry the larger the fee.

"They work outrageous hours and get to know their co-workers better than their spouses. Cops understand this. Maybe scientists too.

"Women lawyers get additional—unspoken—orders. Dress well enough to command authority but not so carefully as to attract attention or seem frilly. Look like a woman, not a smaller man. One boss got me a tiny tie which I threw out. I never could figure out why it's OK for a man to wear khaki's but not for a woman to wear capri pants on casual Fridays.

"I followed the rules but still got hit on and didn't know what to do. A guy told me he passed the word that if a woman didn't stop touching him he'd slug her. She stopped but for a woman to threaten would cause her to be appear *unfeminine*. How to appear both feminine and assertive is a big problem for women in business.

"So when sexual abuse happens, women tolerate it and hope that it'll stop. They often blame themselves for their dress or behavior which they mistakenly think caused this trouble.

"I did the usual. Smiled at crude remarks, backed off touches, refused invitations to work over dinner. I couldn't avoid traveling with colleagues but since lawyers don't share rooms I figured that I'd be safe but I was wrong.

"One night I awoke to find someone on top of me. He was ripping my panties and trying to force my legs apart. When I tried to claw his eyes I got a punch on the side of the head which dazed me." Pat paused to control her rush of emotion.

"What saved me was a simple industrial error. To economize, our firm had bought what seemed like a bankrupt stationery company's entire stock of inadequately perforated legal pads. This forced us to keep a small blade knife available to cut off sheets cleanly. I was working before going to sleep and the knife was on the night table. I managed to get one arm free, found the knife, slid its blade open, and stabbed the back of the rapist's thigh. He screamed, I pushed him off me, got up, and smashed a table lamp on his head.

"He was knocked out and while running for the door I thought of putting the scissors In my luggage to good use like Elaina Bobbitt did. I flicked the light switch on, opened the door, and looked back at the rapist for a moment. Then I calmed down, closed the door, and returned to the bed.

"The stab in the rapist's thigh was an obvious flesh wound and had bled only slightly. With luggage straps I tied his hands in back of him and his feet together. Then I took pictures of him from all angles. His wig and nakedness made for impressive photos. By now my fear was gone and I seemed to be operating according to an unconsciously formulated plan which became increasingly clear to me.

."I was a lawyer. Lawyers negotiate situations coolly. I would talk terms with the rapist—who was also a managing partner of my firm!

"I knew that my job was over. No way could I stab him and hope to remain—even if he had tried to rape me. The only question was how I would leave. I *could* have him arrested but pity any woman who goes through the typical questioning during that kind of trial: "Have your ever practiced 'rough sex'? Not even to achieve an orgasm?" "Did you ever hit anyone? Never? Not even as a child?" Being paid off was a much better deal.

"He agreed to my terms as the hotel doctor arrived. Before which I untied him and left the explanation of his injuries to the doctor's lurid imagination. No one wanted police involvement, not us or the hotel. I left the firm with an excellent letter of recommendation and a seven hundred fifty thousand dollar check. More than enough to support me until I find another career. Lawyering ain't in my future!"

Chapter 21

Holly was coloring silently while Pat told me her story. Though unable to make out what Par said, Holly seemed calmed by the flow of words. We had tended to speak briefly when it was just the two of us. Maybe she felt better, I hoped, and would now eat and not play with her food. A sick child requiring a doctor was a complication we didn't need.

"You don't look like a physics teacher," Pat said, interrupting my thinking.

"I don't teach much. Mostly do research."

"You don't look like a physicist either."

"What do I look like?" I was curious.

"Shaved or not?"

"I should have shaved. I try to every morning but being a parent is another job in itself."

"A wife's too."

"She died recently. So what do I look like?" I repeated, wanting to change the subject.

"A pirate who lost his earring."

This was little different from how Julia once described me, as "a Park Avenue thug," that being Manhattan's most affluent street.

"I grew up an orphan. My early struggles sometimes show."

A few minutes later Pat left for her room.

"I talked to mommy last night," Holly told me, in a low tone.

"What did she say?" I now felt comfortable relating to her fantasy.

"That you'll protect me from the men."

"You can count on it. Why do they want you?" I asked hesitantly, fearing this intrusive question would damage our developing rapport.

Holly looked about the room.

"I don't know," she said, and I sensed that it would be unwise to press her. Her ability to speak of past events depended on her healing. I hoped this would occur quickly for I had another upsetting dream the previous night. Holly and I were fleeing through a dangerous area of a city but no help was to be found.

Chapter 22

While Maine experienced its greatest storm in eighty three years, the three of us became a real family.

Each morning Pat got up early to prepare breakfast. And, though not knowing much about cooking, she did try. Sometimes Holly helped her and they became so close that Holly no longer came to my bed when she awoke at night. Instead, she invaded Pat's bedroom, with whom she increasingly shared her dreams. But not the fantasy of her mother's ghost or angel, about which she still spoke only with me.

Our family became even more traditional when I began sharing Pat's bed. Whether from simple lust or mutual anxiety this seemed natural. As it also did to Holly who only once referred to this change, telling me what the ghost had said: "It's not good to be so alone." A shiver went through me after she spoke for Julia had used identical words.

"Loneliness is like having a mild headache," Pat said one night, after we bundled Holly into bed along with Marian, her doll.

"How's that?" I asked.

"A mild one, not a migraine, causes you to feel that something isn't quite right but doesn't disable you. You try to ignore it and when it's gone you hardly remember it. That's the difference between how I feel now and before we met. As if my past was completely gone."

I moved her beside me, down from the edge of the sofa where she was sitting, and pressed her head onto my chest. I wanted to say something equally loving but talking was never my strong point. Even as I began to feel that particular loneliness which those who cannot confide in anyone feel. Like the spy who hungers to share something real, even tangentially. I swept this thought from my mind and changed the subject. But kissed the top of her head so that she wouldn't mind.

"What were you like growing up?" I asked.

"A rebel. I got thrown out of *two* high schools."

I kissed her head again. "What for?"

"At the first, a typical suburban school, just for a prank. The next—religious—school was more than a little strange. For starters, you had to address the principal as 'ma,' If you didn't she ignored you. I already had one mother and naturally refused.

"But there was a bigger issue. Ten percent of the students in this Christian school were Catholic and there was prejudice against them. One day I was walking with a Catholic friend down the hall. Some boys taunted her with their ultimate insult, insisting that 'the Catholics killed Christ.'" The girl was timid so I answered back for her."

I was intrigued. "What did you say?"

"I said they spit on Catholics only because they dared not spit on their Savior who introduced the idea of morality to the world. These weren't my words but what a French theologian described as being the underlying reason for antisemitism."

"You were quite a girl? What happened?"

"My parents were told that I didn't have the right spiritual attitude and must leave the school. They were proud of me but getting tired of the all the trouble I got into. Incidentally, nothing happened to the boys. I transferred to another Christian school. They took us to London for our graduation trip."

Chapter 23

The storm ended and I needed to make decisions. Where would we go? How would I tell Pat our real identities and what if she then refused to help us? What if the terrorists found us before we left this house?

The answer to the first question was easiest. Being off the island anywhere was safer. Once holed up on the mainland Holly would, hopefully over time, provide me with enough factual evidence to clear me and get protection for us both. Admittedly this was a thin straw on which to rely but it was all I had. If the murderers found us our safety would depend on the speed of my reflexes and our luck, which was always an important factor. The difference between life and death for a soldier is often luck.

Pat posed the greatest difficulty. How do you tell your lover that you and your apparent child are other than who she believes them to be? Like most people with a difficult decision I procrastinated, waiting for the perfect moment whenever that might come.

Which never did arrive for it was Pat who raised this issue. While we lay in bed as she alternately fondled and mildly clenched my testicles—to give me the clearest message.

"Whose child did you say Holly was?" Pat squeezed gently.

"It wasn't *quite* the truth," I admitted, remembering how close to the groin she had stabbed her boss. "What gave me away?" I wanted to establish a friendlier tone.

"Little things. Holly making 'daddy talk' *after* getting your visual approval. And that she never touches you."

"You were probably a very good lawyer," I mused.

"So who really are you?" she asked, giving a less gentle tug to my appendage.

"Just now I'm really her father. Her parents and brother are dead. If their killers find us—and they're seriously looking—we'll be goners too."

Pat stared. "You're scaring me."

"Join the club. I've been terrified for weeks."

Pat"s hand loosened its grip and my breathing became less strained.

Despite my story being astonishing, Pat didn't seem surprised. Probably because lawyers have heard everything. She also didn't respond immediately and I sensed her thinking being in high gear. Did I look like a murderer? How does a murderer behave? What did she know about killers anyway? Her legal practice had consisted of thieves. Did Holly seem afraid of me? Finally she asked what I would have.

"Why didn't you call the police?"

"To say what? That a strange child came to my car while I lay drunk. After which I heard sounds and thought people were chasing her. That we continued running after I found her parents' bodies and then broke into a house to hide? Also, there's my background. I'm British and in the U.S.A. on a work visa. I was thrown out of the SAS for medical reasons and placed on leave from my current job for 'stress.' I've been investigated and cleared after several deaths. For me to now trust the police, considering the high profile of this crime and the concern about aliens, is a risk I won't take. I love living in America. And you too," I added.

I didn't tell Pat about the bodies having disappeared. That was too fantastic for even a lawyer to believe. Though I think it wasn't my apparent truthfulness but my vow of love which convinced her.

"That's a pretty strange story," Pat observed.

"Only a little more than how you lost your job."

"Maybe you're the murderer."

"Do I look like one?"

"Frankly, yes."

"Then quiz me on physics. Probably no physicist was ever convicted of murder."

"Maybe. What's more telling is that I don't think you'd have let Holly live if you were her family's killer."

"If you already decided I was innocent, why the third degree?"

"I'm not good at love. Can you blame me for wanting information?"

Her words changed the atmosphere. Holly chose that moment to enter our room and, as we three cuddled, I felt for the first time that things might turn out OK but not yet how. Or maybe my feeling simply evidenced that on which both Julia and the ghost agreed: it's not good to be alone.

The morning sun rose. Pat lay by my side with Holly tight against me. When I stretched, Pat nuzzled my neck and Holly opened her eyes. Then she sat up and addressed us in a matter of fact tone.

"I spoke to mommy last night."

"What did she say?" Pat asked. I had told her earlier of Holly's fantasy.

"That we must travel someplace safe."

"Did she say where?" I asked, and then mentally kicked myself. Was I so desperate for a plan that I would seek one from a delusional child?

"To the house where the parents who are God's messengers live."

Ask for advice from a traumatized child and what should you expect, I thought, and tried to think of something positive to respond. But a frightened look appeared on Pat's face. She actually turned white, and spoke before I could.

"Both my parents are ministers," she sputtered.

Some people believe in ghosts and angels. Arthur Conan Doyle, physician and creator of Sherlock Holmes, did, and he spent many years consulting mediums. I never believed in spirits except for those you drink. Nor did I consider fairies, elves and the like to be worth a moment's consideration.

And religion, apart from an occasion for holiday parties, meant as little for me as for many ex-soldiers who saw too many horrors to believe in a supposedly benevolent God. To which sights I added that of Holly's mutilated family.

But I did believe in chance for this had led to some of the greatest scientific discoveries. Consider the unschooled London blacksmith's son, Michael Faraday. He became the major scientist of his age by inventing electromagnetic induction which made the industrial revolution possible. Was it likely that such a discovery would arise from his uneducated mind? Not to me. So I accepted that there could be experiences which were improbable and made no logical sense but, nevertheless, were useful. Like the presence of this ghost or angel.

Holly's mother, father, and brother were dead. I saw their bodies and there is no way any of them could walk or talk again. So Holly, to endure her unfathomable loss, had created an imaginary friend. Just like many children do. That this character could create valuable insights from within Holly's unconscious mind made sense to me, though how she knew that Pat's parents were ministers was a mystery. Perhaps Pat mentioned it to her and forgot. Or Holly's statement, like the prophecies of fortune tellers, was vague enough to lend itself to innumerable interpretations, one of which was bound to be accurate.

So we adopted Holly's suggestion of visiting Pat's parents. Not because Pat or I really believed that Holly's fantasy figure existed. We simply had no other plan.

And this ghost or angel *had* helped us. Before she arrived there was, emotionally, my depression, Holly's detachment, and Pat's understandable rage caused by her boss's rape attempt. But the presence of Holly's odd, unexpected figure aroused our reserve of strength and optimism. So I hoped she would remain with us though, of course, Pat and I knew that she really didn't exist.

Chapter 24

We left for the ferry an hour before its departure. Pat managed, despite Holly's considerable resistance, to cut her long blond hair into a short but eminently attractive bob. Dyeing it would have made her less recognizable but we lacked the chemicals. Reading glasses and beard would have to serve as my disguise. Pat didn't need one unless she was already associated with us by the murderers. If so then they already knew our location and we were in even greater danger.

Moments after we left the house Holly became cranky and wailed for her favorite (grape) juice. She said that she was too tired to travel and had a stomach ache. But these woes disappeared when Pat offered to piggy-back her to the car and then did, revealing a strength which surprised me. "She needs to be babied," Pat whispered in my ear.

I drove slowly while scanning the empty road. Holly sat in the back seat hugging Marian, her doll buddy. When I parked my beloved 1953 Kaiser in the town's lot a half mile from the dock, I sensed that I would never see it again and mourned its loss. Like other loners who come to love lifeless objects.

Fear unlatched my imagination. The walk to the dock seemed endless with terrorists' eyes seeming to peer from every tinted windshield. Maybe Holly sensed my tension for she began gripping my hand tightly.

A hundred yards from the corrugated shack which housed the ferry's ticket booth, men loitered on fence posts . They periodically raised their eyes from newspapers to scan passersby. At the foot of the dock stood uniformed police officers, equally intent.

. My breath caught and I became self-conscious of my limp as we approached the men. One of them passed judgment over me but returned to his reading. Then he glanced at me again, apparently being unable to make up his mind. His stare deepened when he focused on Holly. Folding his newspaper, he moved towards us—until he saw Pat and immediately froze.

I tried to reach for the pistol in my jacket but Holly held my hand firmly, which was probably for the best. My phobia about guns made even touching one chancy, and with police officers so close, brandishing a gun could be fatal.

My nose grew stuffy and mouth grew dry as my terror increased. This is the first stage of a heart attack, I began thinking. Until I regained self—control by telling myself that these symptoms reflected anxiety and another of my panic attacks, not a physical disorder, I forced myself to breath deeply and regularly, and managed to walk slowly past these men. Which occurred without incident.

We approached the last barrier to leaving the island: two police officers in uniform and apparently one in plainclothes.

Twenty feet from them my injured leg gave way and I stumbled, not having the support of the cane which I often used. I picked myself up quickly but had already drawn their attention. To reduce suspicion, I asked Holly loudly, "How does your stomach feel?" She said nothing and I silently cursed her for forgetting my instructions. Finally, as we came abreast of the police, she tossed off an unbeatable statement. One which immediately allayed their suspicion and aroused my belief that she possessed acting ability.

"Daddy, I have to vomit." One of the policemen hurried us through the ticket booth and onto the boat. Pat scurried with Holly to find the bathroom.

My heartbeat slowed as I navigated the few passengers on board. Pat and Holly didn't re-appear until the boat was underway. While waiting for them I again began worrying for something seemed very wrong.

Even granting Holly's dramatic gift, things went too smoothly. We were the only family boarding with a young girl yet no one had tried to stop us or even to question us. Not even the loiterers who peered with such suspicion. So was I wrong about them or had they identified us but were unable to do anything with the police close by: they wanted us alive for intensive questioning, not being dead potential witnesses to their crimes. And that they didn't follow us aboard meant nothing. Other of their agents could be among the passengers or waiting for us on the mainland.

The behavior of the police was equally puzzling. One seemed ready to grab me until the plainclothes officer placed a hand on his arm. To which I could think of only one—admittedly ridiculous—explanation. That despite their well-publicized and strenuous efforts to the contrary, and for some unknown reason, the authorities *did not want to arrest me or cared a damn about protecting Holly!*

As these disturbing conclusions sunk in, Holly approached me and I grabbed her hand.

"You're a real actress. Saying you had to vomit was a wonderful idea," I gushed.

Holly made a face. "I did vomit."

You're just learning to be a father, I consoled myself. "How do you feel now?"

"OK."

We returned deck side and found seats along the mid-section of the boat, the most stable location. I raised several topics but neither Holly or Pat was interested, causing me to wonder how long our closeness would continue. Then Pat slipped her hand into mine, Holly leaned against me, and we became a family again.

"Don't act surprised when you see my father," Pat said. "Treat him matter-of-fact."

"Why wouldn't I? Just because he's a minister whose daughter I'm sleeping with doesn't mean I can't be tactful in other ways."I whispered this so Holly couldn't hear. I always felt strongly that children should be kept from adult matters as long as possible. The presence of bare breasted photographs in English tabloids, which could be easily viewed by children, had always revolted me.

"He won't care about that," Pat said. "Since my sister's marriage fell apart he's given up advising his children. Dealing with his multiple sclerosis put things in perspective. It was diagnosed when he was thirty-six. Though considered the disease of the young go-getter, it can hit anyone."

"I thought you died quickly from it."

"Most people confuse it with Lou Gehrig's disease. But with MS you can live for decades and be normal most of the time. Until you get an attack which might affect your vision or ability to move. What's scary is that you can't predict when it'll happen. He uses a wheelchair. Not all the time but his condition is getting worse. I didn't want you to be surprised."

My limp, about which I long anguished, now seemed unimportant.

After reaching the mainland we planned to travel to her parents' home in Greenwich, Connecticut. And later? I didn't know except to hope that our miraculous survival would continue.

Our lives were drifting like that of most people, though appearing self-directed when viewed within the framework of a neatly constructed resume or later obituary. Yet perhaps the mind has a wisdom of its own, I thought, it being composed of unconscious impulses and naive sensibilities which channel behavior toward productive goals. This was another of my hopes as we reached the mainland and left the ferry.

Despite my optimism, I doubted that we had succeeded in escaping the danger. A secret worth three killings was certainly worth more effort—and murders.

Chapter 25

We had talked little during the ferry ride, being content to watch the brilliant sunset which contrasted so strongly with our earlier snowbound state. Once ashore, the issue of transportation became central. Air travel, with its security procedures, was impossible for this family which was officially sought by the police. There was no local bus or train and using my credit cards to rent a car presented a problem. They must already be on a "watch" list and would create an easily followed trail. Stealing a car seemed our only option, this adding another item to my already puzzling resume of military officer and physicist.

Pat suggested she use her credit card and draw money from her ATM account.

"That ties you in with us. Now you become a target too," I whispered.

"I'm already in with you."

Holly heard the affectionate tone and leaned against her.

A sign in the ferry station advertised a low-cost car rental business: Rent-This-Wreck. It was located in the back of a business complex which included a diner, a used car dealership, and a garage. Chick and Len owned all of it, as their huge sign informed travelers. While Pat negotiated the car rental, Holly and I ordered lunch in a back booth of the Heavenly Rest Diner, a name which aroused my concern.

Holly's head drifted towards the table.

"She's tired," observed the waitress, a woman in her fifties.

"Being cooped in by snow makes one logy."

"And drives kids crazy," she added, apparently welcoming conversation to relieve the tedium of her job. "A teacher from New York moved his family here for the cheaper housing, thinking that even with our lower salaries he'd be better off economically. When winter came, his daughters couldn't find anything to do and started hanging out with gang members. After two years the family returned south."

"It takes getting used to," I agreed, warmed by the comfort of her ready acceptance. Until I caught myself and wondered where our pursuers awaited us. "Only the paranoid survive," a Silicon Valley genius insisted in his popular business book. Could this red-haired waitress be an "innocent": a terrorist agent residing legally in America? Was our food doctored and did a van outside await our limp bodies? Or had we really escaped—for now.

Chapter 26

Last Testament of Hasan Al-Nebil, Commander of the Faithful

(This document was discovered by FBI agents in a terrorist safe house in suburban New Haven. The translation was declassified just before my manuscript was completed. I thank Major R. for informing me of its existence and for the following information: that the first line was plagiarized from Dostoevsky; of Al-Nebil being grandiose in assuming for himself the caliphic title of Commander of the Faithful; and that Hasan means *handsome* or *good*. The explanatory footnotes which follow are mine.)

Nothing is easier than to denounce the evildoer. Nothing is more difficult than to understand him. I write these words that, after my death, those who love me will understand.

Though abhorrent, the execution of innocents is sometimes needed to cause others to mend the error of their ways.

All of Islam is one. Our struggle is against Western countries who, with their pornography and dissolute customs, seek to separate the faithful and destroy us. They who build their fortunes on the misery of our people will be punished. It is these hands which force my deeds. When our goal is achieved I will be proud.

The caliphate* will spread across the world. None can escape this future.

Allahu akbar!**

(SIGNATURE)

Caliph comes from the Arabic word *Khalifa*, which means successor to the prophet Muhammad. After his death a dispute occurred over his legitimate successor. This resulted in schism and the development of the Shiite and Sunni branches of the faith. While the Shiite line of Islam stopped selecting caliphs, in the dominant Sunni tradition this office embodies the ultimate religious and political authority. The ideal of a caliph as being the earthly head of a community of believers derives from the traditional heart of Islam and contrasts with the Western ideal of secular heads of nation-states. One caliph, Abdul Hamid II, studied the American principle of the separation of church and state and regarded it as being consistent with Islamic principles. His intervention in the Spanish-American war of 1898, forbidding Muslims of the Philippine Islands to enter into hostilities against the Americans, saved the lives of "at least twenty thousand troops in the field" according to President McKinley.

**God is great

Chapter 27

Holly seemed listless and depressed. Pat tried talking to her but this didn't help. Holly ignored her and clung to me. So I did what I found had helped in the past when I became puzzled by her behavior. Watched, listened, and occasionally said a word or two to indicate that I was still there. I also saw that she got enough food and rest. Soon, while sipping grape juice, Holly spoke more of the ghost who now directed our journey. And, absurd though this might seem, I managed to convince myself that by following the advice of this imaginary figure, things would turn out OK.

During these hours of mutually contented fantasy, with Holly sometimes dozing in the large back seat of our rented Chevrolet Impala sedan, I considered our situation logically.

The murderers must still be looking for us. Not because they feared our witnessing their crimes for they could quickly flee the country. But because they believed that Holly knew the location of the Holy Grail of weaponry: the secret of how anti-matter could be turned into a weapon. The technological breakthrough which her parents discovered.

Thus it was Holly and not me or Pat who was their real target. If caught, Holly would suffer the same unspeakable torture as her mother. Which is what Holly must sense and, understandably, so troubled her.

Despite her trauma I'll have to question her again, I told myself, as I fell asleep. Lulled by the car's rhythm as it passed from Maine through Vermont and on into Connecticut.

Greenwich is a small, wealthy town in southeast Connecticut. It is a major bedroom community for workers from New York City's Wall Street. My knowledge of Greenwich derived from a past stay with a girl-friend: an unemployed college graduate who wanted to strike out on her own and live apart from her rich family. With effort, she managed to find a tiny, cheap one-bedroom apartment above a dress shop on Greenwich Avenue, which is the main street.

The town has two beaches. One is fully developed with showers, lockers, and a refreshment stand. The other was kept undeveloped, like a nature preserve. Both were on islands which could only be reached by town ferry, admission being a quarter and a Greenwich resident identity card.

I liked the girl and loved the town for it reminded me of English villages with their small shops and sense of orderliness, Greenwich's police officers even wore white gloves while directing traffic. A doughnut shop which opened on Greenwich Avenue didn't survive for the rent was too high. But a bagel shop several streets away prospered. Which was a mystery since it endorsed such odd pseudo-ethnic spreads as chopped liver and grape jelly.

As we entered Greenwich I wondered how much of the town I would remember—and whether we would live to enjoy its beaches the following summer.

Soon our car left downtown and entered a less affluent residential area, the existence of which surprised visitors who were awed by the town's lavish estates. Pat's parents lived two miles further along a twisting road, past empty fields and an occasional abandoned appliance.

Though retired, they worked part-time as consulting or temporary ministers to small churches in Connecticut and neighboring New York State. Both were in their sixties and had survived cancer. When I complimented their youthful appearances, Pat's father remarked, in an amused tone, that "anyone still alive at our age looks good."

Their house was a large Victorian and resembled those lived in by English ministers in vintage black-and-white movies. Her parents even had such old-fashioned names as Cedric and Patience.

Holly slept during much of the ride and seemed better. My concern about her behavior and how to explain our sudden appearance proved unnecessary. Cedric and Patience accepted us as if we were relatives and asked no questions—which surprised me. "They're used to having people drop in," Pat explained. "Our teenager friends would live with us for months, after being thrown out by their parents. My mother wanted a big family but needed a hysterectomy after my sister was born. Those kids became her children too."

"How much younger is your sister?"

"Two years."

"A lawyer too?"

"She never went to college. You'll meet her. She returns to the old homestead every few weeks."

There was an undertone of resentment in Pat's words which I ignored. Every family has problems, I reminded myself. Coping with mine and Holly's were enough for now

"What did you tell your parents about us?"

"That we're friends. And would share a room," she added with a smile.

"It's OK with them?." I didn't want her parents feeling offended and gossiping about us.

Pat caught my meaning. "I don't know what they believe anymore. Their kids and health problems changed them."

Despite Pat's anger toward her parents, I liked them. Though not immediately for I begrudged anything religious, having been forced to attend long services at the orphanage where I grew up. Though that minister wasn't a bad person. Just underpaid and over-worked like most clergy are. Still, despite my attitude, he recognized the potential beneath my discourtesy and lamented my lack of ambition. But he did so privately and with great warmth so that gradually, with surprise, I came to sense that comfort was possible in human relationships.

Chapter 28

Our first month in Greenwich was a good one. The fear and instability which pervaded our lives receded and we entered a semblance of normal living.

Most importantly, we now felt secure. Pat's parents invited us—much as they did with her teenage friends years before—to stay with them for as long as we wanted. I like to think it was my charm which caused this but knew it was Holly's unconcealed sadness. They were told her mother was dead, believed that I was her father, wanted to help, and required no other information.

It was about then that Holly's hostility toward Pat began. I understood this for probably her mother's death was too recent for any substitute to be accepted. But Holly did meld with Cedric and Patience. They became the grandparents she lacked in her previous life as she became another of their daughters.

Patience taught Holly to cook and Cedric introduced her to the stories of Tolkien. As he read to her from *The Hobbits,* she told him of her mother's ghost and he listened reverently.

One afternoon while the women were shopping,, I lingered with Cedric over the one glass of wine which he allowed himself daily.

"You think it's crazy, don't you? Holly talking to a ghost," he said, toying with his half-empty glass.

"No. It's her normal reaction to the trauma of her mother's death."

"And what if I told you that I too saw 'the ghost.' Which technically should be termed an angel. Would you consider me mad too?"

I didn't know what to say. How can one reply to a crazy statement in a friendly tone?

"You don't have to answer," he said with a small smile. "These figures are on the edge of my profession and certainly not of yours. But I did see her," he insisted. "Or, rather, I sensed her. Which is how they usually appear: in smells, voices, and cold spots. Even electrical disturbances at times—now that *is* your field." He also said this with a smile.

Though grateful for his offer of shelter, I felt angry at being forced to consider the nonsense he spoke. And, unfortunately, speaking tactfully was never one of my strengths.

"Christian foolishness used to explain unknown phenomena." I snorted.

"Really...? Similar to Einstein's general relativity notion of a black hole?" he asked gently. "Which was first proposed by a geologist, John Mitchell, in 1784. Was there ever a more counter-intuitive explanation than that? But even the Japanese, most of whom aren't Christian, believe in ghosts. They call them *yurei*: females dressed in white kimonos, the typical burial costume in ancient Japan. These appear between midnight and sunrise and float about, frightening and tormenting those who wronged them in life but causing no harm. Unlike *goryo*, vengeful ghosts, who seek revenge for the evil done to them.

"The ancient scriptures also speak of good and bad ghosts. Disembodied souls that wander; and of demons, called *sheydim* in Hebrew. They were created just after humans and are neither of this world or the other but a little of both.

"Because spirits are not bound by the usual concepts of time and space and matter they can have knowledge beyond human experience. They may possess a person in need, *sod ha'ibbur*, it's called. The angel remains until the danger or struggle is overcome. Then it returns to the spirit world from which it was lent and the person feels a *loss of spirit*."

My anger suddenly disappeared as I recognized that Cedric was a scholar who was seeking to open my mind but not pressuring me to accept his beliefs. As the silence between us became comfortable, I sensed a cold spot directly in front of me—just before the room seemed to brighten. Then I felt relaxed and at peace. Or maybe, needing sleep, I had dozed off briefly and because of Cedric's words my imagination was operating in overdrive.

Perhaps because Cedric noticed my change of attitude, he began describing his life. And my interest surprised me, considering my long disdain of religion.

"I started out as a traditional minister, being educated at the Yale Divinity School. Patience's background was different. First she was an artist, a painter of considerable talent. She also modeled nude to help pay her college expenses. This makes her unique among American clergy and why I always insisted that its *her* genes which created our unconventional daughters.

"When I was diagnosed with multiple sclerosis the importance of church pomp diminished for me. This change was as far as I went until my interest in mysticism began. Though many believe otherwise, mysticism has little to do with any organized religion whether Judaism, Christianity, or our Eastern brethren. Mystics of all religions seek the same: contact with the unseen. This proves they have touched something objective with each religion being just a different pathway through which another type of reality may be achieved. But you look puzzled."

I was. "As a scientist I'm forced to disagree. That people have the same sensory experience doesn't necessarily make it objectively true."

"You're right. It's not the experience of mysticism that is significant for this can be gained using drugs. What's important is the destination the voyager achieves. This depends on his motives, constancy—and the grace of God.

"When I can't get out I write and lately its been about division. Not mathematics but the unnatural separation between the biological and spirit worlds. This disturbs people and causes them to associate the uncanny with death though there should be a unity between spirit and organism. Would you like to read my manuscript? I would welcome a scientist's judgment."

"Yes," I said, and our conversation turned back to Holly.

"She should be placed in school quickly. That's where normal kids her age are," Cedric suggested. I wondered how normal a child's life could be after her family was slaughtered and she hid from their killers.

"School would be good for her," I agreed, but then thought quickly. "Holly's records were destroyed during the trashing of her home. She can't be registered without them."

"The school district knows us. I'll vouch that she lives here and there won't be a problem. They'll test her for proper grade placement and ask you to get her files but soon forget about it."

Which is just what happened on next morning at the Hayes Elementary School. Holly, appropriately dressed in a pink top and blue jeans, responded to the principal's questions with the answers I had earlier prepped her. She said that her mother had died and she wanted to return to school. But a new one, where the children wouldn't know what happened and stare at her.

The principal was a tall, thin, gray-haired woman in her fifties. She listened with murmurs of sympathy and took us on a tour of the school. Holly was introduced to several of her future classmates when they passed us in the hall.

After her brief speech Holly said little to them or to us, ignoring the conversation about her. Several times an intent look would arise on her face as she stared at a point about a dozen feet in front of her. Like when she was at home and fantasizing her mother's ghost. Though I was afraid she would speak of this, she didn't. Instead, after a brief stare, she would become calmer and regain interest in her surroundings, once even comparing aspects of this school to her past one.

But Holly did become visibly upset: when a boy accidentally brushed against her arm as he ran past. She stiffened and her face froze with a look of panic. Then, after again peering as if towards someone, her face relaxed and she smiled. The principal was experienced enough not to comment on these episodes.

"Would you like to start school tomorrow or begin a whole new week on Monday?" she asked Holly.

"Can I start today?" Holly surprisingly responded, her tension gone.

"Of course. Whatever you feel most comfortable with. When I was your age I always wanted to get things like vaccinations over with right away. Though I hope you don't feel going to *this* school will be like getting shots."

The principal's words aroused our smiles and Holly readily accepted her hand as they went to her first class. Both looked more comfortable than I felt.

Even with Holly's new name, location, and hair style, she was far from safe. Where were the murderers? Were they watching the house and waiting? Since we left the island they seemed to have vanished but I doubted that they gave up their search. The police certainly hadn't. There were still daily updates detailing their lack of progress in finding Holly or her family and seeking information from the public.

So I felt nervous when I left the school. I told the principal that I would be driving Holly home and she should never be permitted to leave with anyone else. The principal quickly agreed, being annoyed by the implication of my statement: that school personnel would *ever* let strangers leave with *their* children!

While driving home with Cedric, I searched the streets for suspicious passersby. I saw none but my fear persisted. I again visualized Holly's mother's body. Her murdered father and brother too. I had read about Saddam's torturers, and what these methods could do to the human mind and flesh. To Holly's body too.

I continued studying the streets. They must be out there—somewhere.

Chapter 29

Intellectual passion drives out sensuality.
—Leonardo da Vinci

I became impotent. Not that I didn't continue to have sexual feelings for Pat. Particularly since she wasn't one of those women who run hot and cold, signaling their receptiveness by wearing panties to bed or not. Pat was always ready for sex, anywhere and however I wanted it.

I would still develop a sturdy erection as her legs spread. But then, to our mutual frustration, my penis limped, as if being ashamed of the role it was expected to play. Though I did manage to please her and you can guess how. After which she held me and said she loved me. This often led to another attempt and the same disappointment.

To avoid dwelling on this problem, when not driving Holly to and from school, I spent more time reading scientific journals on a computer in the Greenwich library

I once attended a U.S. Army conference in which the mock-up of a Future Combat System Vehicle (FCSV) was demonstrated. The FCSV would weigh less than twenty tons but be as fast and lethal as the latest M-1A2 Abrams tank. It would fire chemical or laser powered weapons emitting one millionth of a second discharges to destroy enemy tanks. It would have electromagnetic armor and repel not only pulsed but conventional weapons. This protective measure would be connected to the same generating system that powered its weapons.

An intercontinental or space based ballistic missile with such defensive armor would be virtually indestructible and present a threat to every nation, even one as powerful as the United States. And while researching laser weaponry, Holly's parents had discovered something far better.

Were Great Britain, Denmark, or even tiny Israel to possess their new invention, nations would be safe. But in the hands of fanatical purveyors of terrorism or bootleg marketers of advanced weaponry like Iran or North Korea, the entire world would tremble.

We at the Institute were greatly concerned about this possibility while we tried to discover the astonishing trick that Holly's parents had already accomplished: controlling the force of anti-matter, the theory behind which had been understood since the nineteen thirties.

Matter and anti-matter: the yin and yang of reality. Each subatomic particle possesses its antimatter element. When they collide they destroy each other in a cosmic burst of energy containing ten billion times that of a high explosive. One millionth of a gram of matter/anti-matter can generate as much energy as eighty three pounds of TNT. Thus a one pound weapon could be constructed which would be small enough to be held and, in the Institute's theoretical version, *not* emit radioactive fallout (though producing highly dangerous gamma radiation). Even antimatter aircraft engines, which would be capable of operating around the clock, might be possible.

Despite our round-the-clock study we considered these weapons possible only in the far distant future. Great problems needed to be solved before they could be manufactured. Foremost was the need to produce large quantities of antimatter. Doing this with our current particle accelerators would be tremendously expensive, costing six billion dollars for each one hundred billionth of a gram of anti-matter.

Moreover the needed positrons, the antimatter counterpart of the electron, are annoying creatures and must be stored in a quasi-stable form called positronium consisting of an electron and an anti-electron orbiting each other in a special electromagnetic field to keep them from colliding and exploding prematurely.

It was the unique characteristics of this field which we were unable to produce. But Holly's parents apparently did, making possible the Holy Grail of weaponry. For while laser guns are considered by the military to make victory probable, antimatter weapons would assure American superiority for generations..

Their achievement could not have been a simple matter. The Dirac equation which must be followed is complex. It is a crowning theory of modern physics and describes atomic particle spin in a way consistent with both quantum mechanics and Einstein's theory of special relativity.

So while waiting for Holly's school day to end, I puzzled over this equation's treatment of electrons. Its modification, the Majorana equation, which described neutrinos; and the Rarita-Schwinger equation, which concerns the behavior of spin-3/2 particles. Periodically I took breaks in the library's basement coffee shop to concern myself with local worries as were described in the *Greenwich Times:* Cost of New Y Pool Debated; Police Warn Of Check Scam; Drink At Your Peril, Students Told.

The more I struggled with my formulations the more frustrated I grew. I sensed that Holly's parents had found a unique way of solving the problem, much as the mathematician, Stanislaw Ulam, did with Edward Teller's flawed hydrogen bomb design fifty years earlier. My only consolation was that if even the brightest people at the

Institute were unable to discover this then, likely, neither could the scientists of rogue nations. *Unless,* a little voice told me, a physicist there possessed the same rare combination of intelligence and intuition as Holly's parents. This added another fear to my gnawing concern for Holly's safety.

I finished my brownie, went upstairs to the same computer terminal I left, and froze. A lovely lanky woman in her twenties was approaching it. She was unconventionally dressed in a long black dress with white satin collar. Cuffs covered her arms and the hem of her dress fell well below her knees. Her lipstick was deep red and she had shoulder length hair layered modern style. Despite this there was something old-fashioned about her. Was she be a foreign agent? Had I cleared the browser's search history? Why did she choose *that* computer? Who was she?.

Moments later five young children, four girls and a boy, approached and nuzzled her. All were dressed similarly but more colorfully and I relaxed. She was obviously a Hasidic Jew and *could not* be a terrorist. Members of that sect married young and had large families. But I knew that terrorists often adopted common mannerisms and customs. To conceal themselves and slip under people's personal radar, like those suicide bombers in Israel who wore the garb of Hasidic students. But this woman's clothes stood out in staid Greenwich so for an agent to wear them would make no sense.

I sat at another computer and resumed my study. Although nothing threatening had occurred since we left the island, I knew that it was just a matter of time.

Chapter 30

...no-work is worse. The mind preys on itself, the most unwholesome food.
—Charles Lamb

Despite my worry, things continued going well. Though Holly often appeared sad, which was to be expected, she enjoyed school and our relationship with Patience and Cedric remained good. Pat lustily shared my bed even with my erection problem; and the white-gloved police officer now waved to me in a friendly fashion when I crossed Greenwich Avenue. I still noticed no surveillance, subtle or otherwise.

In fact everything had become so uneventful that I nearly forgot the terror which propelled us to Greenwich. Until it reared and bit me one afternoon. Just after I arrived home from school with Holly, on a day when a Canadian cold front ended the unusual warm spell.

Cedric was snacking on his favorite Bahlsen Afrika Bittersweet Chocolate cookies in the kitchen. After his customary playful repartee with Holly, he gave me a letter. Written in elegant flowing script, it was addressed to my current pseudonym. I thanked Cedric and went into the living room to read it, knowing that It couldn't be good news. Who writes to a stranger with a phony name? The murderers had found us!

And I knew Holly's fate if I fell. Electric shock, burning cigarettes, the basic techniques taught in the "rape rooms" of torture chambers.

The letter, written on heavy cream colored stationery, began "To a Courageous and Honorable Comrade." I read its lines with growing disbelief.

Bismi 'llāh*.

Though Islam condemns infidels, I wish you no harm and even cherish the hope that you will join us in our universal fellowship, by following the teachings of the most holy prophet, Muhammad, peace be on him.

If men knew the outcome of wars there would be none. But you are too noble to be swayed by crass considerations. Scholars were revered even by Muhammad for it is stated in the Hadith**, "He who pursues the road to knowledge, God will direct to the road to Paradise...The scholar's ink is holier than the martyr's blood."

In truth, I lack your knowledge and intellect. And, though I am also a warrior, your military prowess. Perhaps you will become our modern Saladin, earning praise from the followers of the final messenger of God. Moses never reached his Promised Land and Christ was crucified but Muhammad died a spiritual and temporal giant. Al-hamdu li- 'llāh***.

*In the name of God
**Hadith are traditions relating to the sayings and doings of the Islamic prophet Muhammad and are classified into what Muhammad said (qawl), what Muhammad did (fi'l), and what Muhammad approved (taqrir). These are considered supplements to and clarifications of the Qur'an, Islam's holy book, and important in determining the Muslim way of life (Sunnah).
***Praise be to God

I digress. We need the positronium findings of Holly's parents. They refused our demand. One with your broader life experience would not behave so foolishly. Join us and ask whatever reward you wish. Or simply do our bidding and gain our friendship. Defy us and you and all who aid you will suffer torments, the like of which I leave to your imagination.

We need this information within three weeks. Indicate its availability by turning the light in your bedroom on and off for five seconds at 10:00pm any day. You will then be provided delivery instructions—and a cash payment to indicate our good will and concern for your future. Allāhu yukaththir khayraka*.

With the hope that I will soon be addressing you as "beloved brother."

HASAN

*May God increase your well being

Sherlock Holmes could undoubtedly identify this author by analyzing his phrasing, handwriting, and stationary. I sensed only his grandiosity. No one who viewed the butchery of Holly's family could feel anything but revulsion towards him. Now I knew that we were in far greater danger than I believed; I hadn't been as competent a bodyguard as I thought.

For despite my watchfulness, I noticed no one suspicious. Life in Greenwich had seemed as sedate as usual though several children did ignore the warning of the traffic policeman and dart across the street, a shocking sight here.

I had to do *something*. We could run. And go where? We might stay and fight though, considering my fear of guns, I wasn't optimistic about this outcome. Nor would the police help us while I remained their major suspect. Pat and her unwitting parents were our only allies.

Maybe I could gain from Holly the information she innocently possessed, But not even to save our lives would I reveal this to Hasan and risk the destruction of democratic nations with totalitarianism sweeping the globe. Should I show less courage than Holly's parents whose refusal led to their murder?

Until I could think of a plan we would have to roll with the punches. This was a dangerous situation for prize fighters and potentially lethal one for us. In any case, it was now time for me to play chess with Holly, who tended to become frantic when her expectations went unmet.

Chapter 31

That the murderers knew our location was clear. And, wanting information from us, they believed it could be most quickly gained through cooperation rather than harsh methods. So I considered it safe to walk around town with Holly. Engaging in a normal family activity might arouse her useful memories.

I knew that her parents must have kept a written record of their work close by. Scientists always mull over things, even when they are on vacation. Even if their original technical breakthrough came in a flash, the underlying formulas are complex and difficult to remember. Moreover, computers, which I didn't find in Holly's home, don't depict these easily. The essential Dirac equation, which describes the probability amplitude for a single electron and is a relativistic extension of the Schrödinger equation covering the time-evolution of a quantum mechanical system, reads: H\$\Box$(t)$\Box$=i ℏ d/dt \$\Box$ (t)$\Box$F.

Try to find these symbols in a computer's word processing program. See how long it takes you..

For the sake of argument, I asked myself, let us say that her parents did leave a written record, which would fit on several sheets of paper. Where might this be hidden so, were they to become incapacitated, it would be found? But not so easily that it might fall into unsavory hands.

Not within the pages of a book. This would be easily guessed as a hiding place or might be accidentally discarded. How about concealing it in a common household item like a biscuit tin? Perhaps, for there it could be quickly retrieved to make spontaneous changes. But a biscuit tin might be easily discarded and Holly's parents were clever enough to consider all possibilities.

It must be somewhere. Someplace missed during searches of the house by me, the terrorists, and possibly whoever disposed of the bodies. Perhaps Holly knew where it was and could help—*If she would answer direct questions.* She spoke little about her family since their murder. It was as if her earlier memories had vanished and her present life consisted only of me, Cedric, and Patience. She still ignored Pat but I wasn't concerned about this. Everyone develops dislikes for some people, and often for no valid reason.

As was her habit, Holly didn't object to going for a walk. She usually agreed with whatever I suggested unless it greatly upset her. Once, when planning to offer her help with her homework, I suddenly entered her room while she was talking to the ghost. Leaving quickly when she seemed about to scream.

I parked by the train station in the only remaining space. One which was likely vacated by a commuter to Manhattan who had returned home early. The station's inadequate parking was a continuing complaint in letters to the local newspaper.

As we walked up Greenwich Avenue I wondered how to begin my investigation. I felt less capable than Nancy Drew, in the ancient black-and-white movie we saw the previous night on Turner Classic Movies. I still knew nothing about Holly's life before she appeared, blood stained, at my car door. The most non-threatening topic with which to begin my investigation was probably food.

"How are the meals in school?"

"OK," she said quickly, not expanding on this topic.

I tried again. "What did you have today?"

"Veggie burger on a whole wheat bun, salad, banana."

"That sounds healthy. Do they give you a choice?"

"They had lamb roast. I don't eat meat."

I already knew this from our weeks together. Judging by the food in her house her family might have been vegetarians, but those who ate fish too.

Greenwich Avenue was only four blocks. We would quickly be at its end. I walked slowly to extend our time together, hoping that today would not contain another of my failed attempts to communicate with her.

I stopped at the window of an Italian delicatessen.

"How about a picnic? We'll buy whatever you want and can eat in the small park up the street."

I interpreted Holly's silence as being her OK. This shop was as different from an ordinary take-out as Manhattan's eminent LeBernardin seafood restaurant is from a London fish-and-chips.

The menu ran to three pages on which the ingredients of each item were described. I already knew that giving Holly a choice of more than two things was a mistake, like with many children. Then she would take forever to decide. Or not choose and resent me for doing so. The menu had at least thirty items and I helped her discard broad categories. Nothing with meat in it. Vegetarian pizza or pasta were possibilities, as were the cheese or spinach ravioli.

We decided on one serving each of the Ravioli Con Formaggio (pasta filled with four types of cheese laced with marinara sauce), and the Raviolo Con Spinaci (spinach and cheese filled pasta served with capri sauce). She added a Cherry Coke and I had coffee. Our selections were placed in a multi-colored container emblazoned with the store's name and images of the Greenwich beaches. Now well provisioned, we continued our walk.

I stopped at an art gallery's window, pointed to a picture, and asked Holly what she thought of it. "OK,," was her curt response. But I persisted and, following my mindless comments about products in most of the stores we passed, something finally clicked in her—at the window of a specialty store which sold only paper products. Holly's face became animated and she eagerly agreed with my suggestion that we enter and see if she would like to buy something.

The store exuded charm. Despite being tiny, it boasted two sales clerks. One left her seat and greeted us, energized by Holly's entrancement with the displays.

"I didn't know there were so many types of paper," I said fatuously. But Holly's obvious delight was enough for both of us as the clerk began her spiel.

"Most people don't," she said pleasantly, and offered Holly her hand. Which, surprisingly, Holly accepted. She usually resisted being touched. As they walked through the shop, Holly seemed to inhale the facts she heard.

"Paper can be divided into six categories: watercolor, drawing, print, visualizing, Oriental, and specialty. Watercolor paper is used to separate the artwork in stacks, for handwriting by calligraphers, and for book or magazine covers." I wondered if Holly knew what a calligrapher was but the clerk's enthusiasm carried the day.

"You're probably most familiar with bond paper for writing and the drawing paper you use in school."

"I'd like to buy some Torinoko paper, please."

Silence filled the store as the clerks stared.

"That's an unusual paper. Where did you hear about it?"

"My daddy liked it."

"Does he use it often?"

"No, he's dead."

"I'm her stepfather," I said quickly, to ease the situation. Then, "What type of paper is it?"

The clerk's face began to color but she caught herself.

"Torinoko means 'child of the egg.' It's the most permanent paper there is. The Treaty of Versailles was written on it. The gampi fibers with which it was originally made are now rare so most is made of kozo, or kozo with mitsumata. We have some in the storeroom. I'll get a package. We save it for those who really appreciate beauty," she added with a smile.

The paper was thick and heavy and Holly caressed the large sheets which the clerk lay on the counter. "It comes in two sizes: machine made, which is eighteen by twenty four inches without a deckle, and twenty four by thirty six inches with it. We have both in stock."

Holly pointed to the smaller size. "Can you cut it in half?"

"Of course." The clerk addressed Holly as if both were connoisseurs despite their age difference. "Though the Japanese wouldn't consider that quite correct." Both smiled knowingly at this caution.

As their conversation continued I felt a bevy of emotions. It was wonderful that Holly now spoke so freely compared with her brief answers since we first met. A memory from her past had finally surfaced. Her defenses against her unbearable pain are beginning to lift, I told myself. I hoped that other memories would follow.

There seemed no more to be gained from this store. After the purchase was wrapped, we resumed our walk and soon reached the park, near the top of Greenwich Avenue.

Chapter 32

It was more a rest stop than a park. Containing just the statue of a long dead war hero, three nearly leafless trees, and four wooden benches with small concrete tables before them. A painted checker board topped each. Except for us and the rare child who skated through to a nearby street, the park was empty.

A bleak sun reduced the chill. I placed the deli's picnic basket on the table before us and divided the ravioli.

"Where did you learn so much about paper?"

Holly kept her attention on the food, eating slowly at first, then with increasing appetite.

"From my father."

I felt encouraged. This response was three times longer than her usual ones.

"I write on pads, not special Japanese paper."

"He used that too," she added, during mouthfuls.

As we silently ate, I tried to think of another non-threatening question.

"Did your father use this paper every day?"

"Just once," she said. Her face quivered and I feared I might have pressed her too greatly but she continued speaking. "A day before...he woke me and showed the paper. 'It'll pay for your new bike,' he said."

"What was written on it?"

"Algebra: pluses and minuses. And big L's." The symbol for calculus.

"I didn't know you learned algebra in the fifth grade."

"We don't. Mommy taught me."

I waited a moment before speaking slowly. "Do you know *where* the paper your father wrote on is now?"

Holly looked confused. Her fork stood midway between her mouth and the plate. She stared in front of her for about five seconds. Then she nodded, "Mommy says I should tell you."

Her face was now relaxed and I let the silence strengthen her decision.

"Marian is hiding it." The doll which she insisted I retrieve from her house and she now carried daily. Even against the jeers of her schoolmates, to whom she explained this younger behavior with the adult explanation of "It's a habit."

Holly lifted the doll's sleeping gown. Strapped to its body with Velcro bands was a narrow metal tube. Inside this cylinder were two sheets of the heavy Japanese paper. I felt a rush of hope and wanted to hug her. These notes would certainly cause the authorities to view our situation differently. But my optimism disappeared the moment I unrolled them.

The pages were covered with continuous numbers, interrupted periodically by a comma, period, or quotation mark. It was obviously some type of code, a subject of which I knew little. But even if I was an expert, I lacked the computer resources to decipher it. The inexpensive machines at the Greenwich Library weren't adequate. This task would require many of them connected together to create a supercomputer.

With a sense of despair, I placed the pages before us.

"Do you understand it?"

She placed her spoon in the spinach ravioli, wiped her hand on a napkin, and spread the coded message on her lap.

The following is what we saw.

3253232355,

"53432355125334545554355113342,"

44114241543251221115435414325544423142454,

543253152232324244353442431323514421512342514132
4244112251,

"1143412353432242445315223254543251445114344231511
235144445124151154425343445453221142421251343355
1242431123411155544."

"5553154351514154341125512321155444325334544142445
411433151,"441142415432512151235325514135512121514
11
2344251434·1.

"44541155114341235353131253345432515442·43,"

"5453514311212351543251224212541144424444153451235
535422323,1143411253342242255143514444125334114355
44·4243·

"41534353543542543255531554321215234233141523445·1
2351112551,5453445151134243543251223451115415434·22
55·1344·451,

"5432115441424431532551345535324231323153335144211
554534331512453511131·32,

51255143355134513251112551·43
22514351·3453154435425432·34512142345432."

4453124243415432514451125334·331523115142
3242415112423444543542543254325134424322,

1143·4111151532424·442214211·54325151
1211345135512323,

354254325432513·253145155531535422323
221142435432·34531522·3223514·444

113441155315441411543432,
3355445131345154325335154533344331155
545322515422513441355123323.

Whoever said kids were fun was never a parent. They can be tiring, argumentative, or simply dreadful. Even granting that what Holly experienced would have devastated any adult were it their family which was slaughtered. Still, apart from our playing together and my reading to her at night, she was not an enjoyable child. It's hard to like a child who either doesn't speak or merely replies "yes," "no," or "I don't know." Responses which couldn't help me then.

I placed my finger at the first line of numbers and repeated my question.

"Do you know what these mean?"

Holly shook her head and turned back to the food.

A thought popped into my mind: of course she can't think about the papers. They must rouse memories of her parents' loss.

Realizing this, I began relating to her as I had with recovering soldiers in the past. Listening, watching silently, and speaking slowly.

"It is some kind of code," I began. "A message your parents knew you could figure out but another child wouldn't be able to. Do you know what a code is?"

"No."

Considering the high level education which her parents provided her I was sure she did. But arguing this point wouldn't have been productive.

"Do you like to read?" I knew the answer I wanted to hear but also that a difficult child will sometimes respond "no" to any question. That day I was lucky.

"Yes," she said, still not looking up from her food.

"When you read you're really deciphering—solving—a code. The letters are marks which you learned stand for sounds and can create words which have meaning. So when you write a letter to your friend you are really using a code which you both understand. What we must do is to figure out the secret which your parents wanted only you to learn."

Holly seemed responsive so I continued sharing the little I knew about codes.

"An easy code is mirror writing. The letters are written back to front and intended to be read before a mirror. Maybe without spaces between the words like there are none in your parents' message." Holly's eyes flickered with interest.

"Another code substitutes one letter for another. Here, it looks like your parents replaced the letters with numbers." This made sense for they were physicists who think mathematically.

"Did they ever mention any particular numbers?" Then I backtracked, realizing this was a dumb question. "Did your mom or dad ever tell you about codes?"

Holly returned to the food and I feared that I had lost her fleeting attention, perhaps permanently. But a minute later she thrust her left hand towards me. I saw food stains, bitten down nails—and a large childish ring.

"The ring."

"What about it?"

"It's a Captain Midnight decoder ring."

Success, I told myself. "How do you use it?"

Perhaps it was my elated look which aroused her further response.

"You count the number of letters in the first word on the page."

It consisted of ten numbers and many of them were "5." But knowing just this didn't help me determine their meaning. Five might mean a fifth letter substitution wherein "a" became "e," "b" became "f," and so on. Or it might mean that five should be added to some mathematical constant, perhaps the whole number of *pi* (the sixteenth letter of the Greek alphabet and also the symbol of the ratio of the circumference of a circle to its diameter—3.141592 plus), the letter substitution then being be made.

Or maybe Holly's parents meant to teach her about a cipher wheel. This is made using such children's implements as a compass, ruler, protractor, pencil, scissors, fastener, and two pieces of cardboard. Two circles are drawn, say one with a radius of three inches and the other with a radius of two and one half inches. Each circle is divided into twenty six equal sectors, one for each letter of the alphabet, which is then printed in the correct order on the top of each sector. The smaller wheel is fastened atop the larger wheel. A message can then be coded or decoded by lining up the "A" on both wheels and knowing how many spaces to move the smaller wheel and whether clockwise or counterclockwise.

I explained this to Holly, adding that though a cipher wheel could be made by children, it was invented in the fifteenth century and used by soldiers as late as the American Civil War. Yet even as I completed my description, I concluded that because the sheet's message consisted of numbers, no cipher wheel could decode it. Or none simple enough for a child to use.

I had to view the coded message with a child's mind, I told myself. Her parents meant for the solution to their riddle to be an enjoyable, educational exercise, not something which need be labored over by a team of mathematicians.

Though the message remained uncoded by the time we finished eating, one good thing was achieved: Holly looked normal. Not that her clothes, being typical of a girl for her age, ever seemed strange. But she usually exhibited an other worldly appearance by giving one or two word responses to friendly chatter and not expressing feelings. *Except* when she related to her angelic figure. But this message from her parents had grabbed her attention and at moments I felt as if I were relating to a healthy child.

I wondered how to keep this positive change in her mood. Was it wise to conceal from her the mortal danger which approached? Shouldn't she be trained to protect herself if I were killed first? These gloomy thoughts ended my optimism as we returned to the car.

Chapter 33

I wasn't popular in the English orphanage where I grew up. The other boys beat me daily until the chaplain taught me judo and how to box. He was a retired military officer who entered the clergy late in life. Being unable to obtain a traditional parish, he filled our long open position, winced at my bruises, and determined to end my torture. He also steered me to the military as a first career and encouraged me to read books by two of the twentieth century's greatest theologians, Reinhold Niebuhr and Paul Tillich.

When I decided that Holly must learn to defend herself, I longed for this clergyman's support in our hopeless situation, and against the seductiveness which alcohol still retained for me.

Holly stared as I cleared these memories from my mind. I didn't like having to speak of this adult issue. I used simple words as if, despite her high intellect, I was speaking to a mentally limited child.

"You and I are in a rough spot. The people who killed your parents and brother are nearby."

"Why don't you call the police?"

"Because they are unlikely to believe anything I might say. Maybe if we found what your parents hid and the men are looking for they would. Not now. And because they wouldn't believe me, they won't protect you. So we have to rely on each other."

"I was once a soldier," I continued tentatively.

Holly nodded and I was glad that she could stay focused on what I was saying.

"When I first fired a gun the noise so scared me that I shut my eyes when I pulled the trigger." I made an embarrassed sound and silly facial expression to lighten the moment. Holly's expression didn't change so I just went on speaking.

"But I did learn to shoot and because of that, ordinary people are alive today. People like you and Cedric and Patience." Now I tried to engage her intellect, the part of her personality which seemed least affected by the trauma she experienced.

"Did you ever hear of Niccolo Machiavelli?"

"He wrote *The Prince* five hundred years ago. It was advice for rulers on how to govern."

"Right," I said, impressed by her knowledge. "That *was* some school you went to."

"I found the book at home."

"Which only shows how smart you are, reading it at your age. Machiavelli wrote that 'war is just when it is necessary; arms are permissible when there is no hope except in arms.' I will do my best to make sure that nothing ever happens to you. But if I fail, you must be able to defend yourself."

My armpits grew moist as I spoke, remembering the sight of her dead family. The possibility of this becoming her fate enraged me. Still, I held back from what I had to say. She did it for me.

"Make my day," she said, repeating the Clint Eastwood movie line in a deadly serious tone.

"That's how it might have to be," I agreed.

"I shot clay pigeons with my mother's shotgun," she informed me.

"Then you'll certainly be a better shot than I was when I started out. At first I missed the whole target."

This wasn't true but I felt that hearing it would give her confidence. Still, I thought, to kill someone even defensively one must behave instinctively: the will for this quickly disappears. Unless one is a psychopath which Holly certainly was not. So even if Holly learned to shoot accurately, could this help her? I hoped that it would but wasn't sure.

By this point in our conversation we had reached the car. Holly didn't object to my suggestion that we stop at a shooting range before going home.

Our trip was a somber one for I hated what I was forced to do. I like kids to stay childlike as long as they can. Reading Walt Disney comics and later the Nancy Drew or Hardy Boy series. Definitely not the current teen thrillers which depict suicide, abortion, addiction, and even murder.

But just as my martial arts training had changed me from a suffering child into a capably aggressive one, Holly too had to change— If she hoped to remain alive.

The gun store's window sign, "Xtreme Safety—Firearms Sales/Rentals/Target Range," well described our need.

The store was stocked with everything a shooter could want. Steel gun vaults to store one's personal armory. Expensive jackets to hold shotgun shells for the well-tailored skeet enthusiast. Gun cleaning necessities. The rifles and shotguns stood in racks along the wall. Pistols, modern and black powder replicas, lay in locked waist high glass cabinets. Several men ogled the wares. Holly's eyes glanced over them without interest.

The clerk was a short, bearded, pot-bellied man. Except for the pistol he wore in a hip holster, he could be any mall's Photo Santa. He looked with delight at Holly, as does the marketer of any product towards their next generation of customer.

"Holly loves to skeet shoot and would like to try a pistol. Could we use your rental range?"

"Our pleasure," he said, with an even more welcome smile. "I'm Teddy and I teach the youth hunting course. They get cocoa, marshmallows, and pretzels after each class and so will you. We're trying to get more families involved in shooting. Once people see how much fun it is they'll support it. It's one of the safer sports, with far fewer injuries than cheerleading or even swimming. Did you know that college football was once banned because of the large number of fatalities?"

I wanted to end his friendly chatter and get on about our business.

"I'm ex-army. You don't have to convince me."

"Load Clear," he said proudly, rolling up his sleeve to reveal the tattoo of an American flag. Above it was the common paratrooper self-description of "bullet stopper."

I nodded knowingly. "Could we start with a .22. Then see how comfortable she is shooting something more powerful. Maybe a .380." The latter, though ill-powered for a self-defense weapon, probably had the greatest recoil she could tolerate considering her size..

"We'll show your daddy," he said, speaking directly to Holly and bending to her height. "With a little practice you'll be better than he is. What do *you* think Calvin?" The deep-chested brown-and-white Alaskan Malamute at his side recognized the tone, barked in agreement, and approached Holly for a cuddle. She hesitantly scratched his head which seemed to make this powerful dog her friend for life.

"We'll leave Calvin upstairs because of the noise. Which won't hurt us for we'll be wearing hearing muffs. Eye protectors too—these must always be worn!" he said, using that firm tone which is familiar to children.

"Police don't wear it," she said, getting into the mood of the lesson.

"They do when they practice. When shooting to protect themselves or others, maybe a child like you, they have no time to put it on. Here you'll learn the right way to shoot. For fun and not self-defense though the basic techniques are the same."

Teddy grabbed three sets of hearing and eye protectors, giving me mine and adjusting Holly's. Then he went behind the counter and carefully chose two cigar box shaped packages. "There's a ten dollar per hour charge for the shooting range. This includes the targets and use of the guns. You pay for the ammo."

I nodded readily.

We followed a long corridor to the back of the store.

"We have the latest in sound proofing and air filtration equipment. The best target retrieval system too. We give shooters the luxury which Greenwich residents insist on and all gun lovers deserve," Teddy said emphatically.

I had been to only one shooting range in America. Accompanying a co-worker who, despite his erudition, fancied himself a throwback to his Sicilian forebears. His doctoral dissertation was on using the Rayleigh-Lamb Wave to determine the acousto-ultrasonic transfer characteristics of adhesively bonded piezoceramic transducers.

That range was cramped and shoddy, as if reflecting the notion that shooters should be glad they had *anywhere* to practice their hobby. This room was impressive: apart from its ten spacious firing positions, it resembled an adult playground. The floor was covered in light pink and purple tiles, with darker alternating black and brown shades at the firing positions. The walls were pale, with trees and clouds painted on them.

Along one wall were cabinets, their doors converted by clever painting into the semblance of a country cottage with lower and upper floor windows and a peaked roof. On the other side of the room were plush sofas, club chairs, and colorful Formica coffee tables. Drink and snack vending machines were close by.

"Wow," was my only response.

"That's what people usually say when they first see it," Teddy said. "My wife's an interior designer. She renovated this space when our kids were young. We want shooting to become as acceptable a sport as it was a hundred years ago." He offered Holly his hand and they walked to the table at the first firing position. I trailed in back.

While we were speaking a man had entered the room. He settled himself at the tenth firing position, beside a uniformed policewoman who was preparing to leave.

"The last two firing booths are reserved for town police officers. We contract with Greenwich for a dollar a year," he added.

I nodded. "Makes for good publicity and security, I guess."

"Now, young lady," he said to Holly. "You probably don't know but some of the best shots are girls. Recently, in New Zealand, two ranked first and second in the college clay shooting championships. They beat all of the boys," he said with an exaggerated grin. Holly returned a small smile. Despite my earlier concern, firearms training might well have a positive effect on Holly, I thought, though not with a less sensitive instructor.

Around each shooting bay were director's chairs with padded backs and seats. Teddy seated himself in one, Holly spontaneously sat beside him in another, and I stood in back of them, listening. The other man began firing as we spoke. He was using a 9mm caliber weapon or larger judging by its size. But the blast was well suppressed by the battery operated noise canceling mechanism of our protective ear mufflers.

Teddy opened one of the flat packages he brought. Lifting the pistol from its molded plastic case, he handed it to Holly who hesitantly accepted it. The design entranced me for It was like no gun I had ever seen. It looked both ultra-modern and of nineteen thirties art-deco style, having a black inlay grip and red front and rear sights.

"What is it?" I asked, despite my reluctance to intrude on Teddy's good rapport with Holly.

He recognized the admiration in my tone.

"It's a Beretta .22 caliber Neos. The deluxe version with adjustable trigger, three sets of colored front and rear sights, and a laser engraved logo."

"Holly," he said, addressing her in a serious tone in contrast to his recent playfulness, "guns should be respected but not feared. You must always treat every gun as if it were loaded and be as careful with it as your daddy is with his car when he drives. And you must never, *ever*, point a gun at something you don't intend to shoot."

Teddy opened a small ammunition box he had taken from a nearby cabinet, removed the Neos' magazine from the molded pistol case, and inserted three .22 caliber cartridges. Then he gave the magazine to Holly and supervised her loading of seven more rounds. With his hand over hers, the magazine was then inserted into the gun. He took it from her, stood up, cocked and pointed the pistol, and fired at the target. I saw through the spotting scope that his shot was far off the bullseye and wondered if he did this on purpose.

"Now it's your turn," he said, handing the pistol to Holly. At first she appeared confused. Then, gaining control of herself, she pointed the gun at the target and fired, missing it completely.

"That's better than I did when I was your age," Teddy said soothingly. "You jerked the gun when you pulled the trigger. Concentrate on colors when you shoot. White, like when you're relaxed and watching a video. Yellow, you're holding the gun and loading it. At Orange, you're pointing the gun and focusing on where you want the bullet to hit. Then, at Red, there's just you and the target as you s-l-o-w-l-y pull the trigger. Try it again."

I watched through the spotting scope: Holly's next shot also missed the target. But then her breathing slowed and she rapidly emptied the magazine. There were four misses, three hits just outside of the bullseye, and one dead center.

"You are *great*," I exclaimed, with the exaggerated enthusiasm which children appreciate. Teddy's praise was no less effusive. I was also pleased that, though he didn't mention it, the technique which he taught Holly (Conditions White, Yellow, Orange, Red) was the traditional one intended for combat situations.

My needs weren't ignored either. In the second package was a .40 caliber Series 92 Beretta. A weapon of extraordinary durability and designated the M9 after winning the nineteen eight four competition for the United States military contract.

One doesn't forget well-learned skills, I told myself, as I loaded the magazine, slipped it into the butt, took the second firing position, and fired. I barely hit the target.

"Maybe we should have Holly teach you how to shoot," Teddy said in a loud whisper, in his continuing attempt to increase her self-confidence.

My accuracy remained poor; concentrating on the combat colors didn't help. Despite the cool temperature in the range I felt warm and my heart began racing. The thought that I was dying from a heart attack entered my mind even as I told myself that this was just one more of those panic attacks which periodically ate me alive. Despite my crippling anxiety I tried to appear calm and apparently succeeded, for when Teddy looked towards me he didn't comment on my appearance.

Within moments of replacing the pistol on the table I felt fine. Until another terrifying thought arose: how could I protect Holly if I couldn't defend myself?

The colonel interrupted this painful memory. "Did your fear of guns begin right after you killed those people in Athens?"

Chapter 34

I had become so involved in telling my story that I temporarily forgot my situation: being a prisoner in a hospital jail in Azerbaijan. So I nearly jumped at the sound of the colonel's voice though the connection he suggested was one which I long considered. "No," I replied. "My fear of guns began four months after I shot them but the psychiatrist believed both events were related. I got a medal for it."

"Yes, and a game leg too. I read the reports," he said smugly, recrossed his legs, and indicated that I should continue my narrative.

Holly's shooting lesson went better than I could have hoped and after she gorged on the cocoa and marshmallows which Teddy provided, we returned to the car. Despite my fear of guns I would have liked to purchase the one I shot but couldn't: federal law required an instant background check of all firearms buyers, including this "wanted" one, through the National Crime information Center. But the rules for the informal sale of guns were more relaxed in the neighboring state of Vermont. There, I earlier learned through an Internet search, a permit isn't needed even to carry a concealed weapon.

We arrived home a little after five. Holly's cheeks were flushed from the cold and the afternoon's excitement and she immediately went to her room. Whether to play Nintendo, read a novel, or commune with her ghost friend, I didn't know. Rather than satisfying my curiosity by intruding on her privacy, I sat with Cedric and read the

Greenwich Times while Patience taught Pat to cook. The lesson didn't sound like it was going well. Whether from Pat's lack of interest or her simmering resentment towards her mother I couldn't say.

I hadn't thought much about Pat since we left the island. Not from the selfishness or fear of intimacy which doomed my earlier relationships, but because our current overriding concern had to be our escape from the overwhelming danger which trailed us. Nothing else mattered.

So Pat and I had spoken little though I continued to rely on her for aid with Holly's personal needs. All I still knew about Pat was that she was a lawyer considering a career change; the daughter of two ministers; and had a divorced sister with children who I would meet at an upcoming Sunday brunch.

I was surprised that her parents revealed so little about her in casual conversations: how she was as a child and past family events. But perhaps, being clerics, they lived their lives on a higher plane than ordinary mortals. Or that my ideas about families, which derived mostly from movies, were as inaccurate as films are about most things.

What did I like about Pat? She was tall and I liked tall women. Hair color never mattered to me but I found her black hair attractive. I would have preferred it longer but our relationship was too young for me to suggest this. Her lack of interest in such homemaking skills as decorating and baking was a drawback. After growing up in an orphanage, I hungered to create the magazine perfect home life I never had. I began wondering if I could do this with Pat or even whether we would stay together. Maybe my current "performance problem," to which she did react with sensitivity, reflected my unconscious awareness that our relationship wouldn't last much longer.

Though apart from this there was nothing unusual about our sex life. She preferred to be on top but, considering my bad leg, this was fine with me. And she always wanted me—or made it seem that way.

"*Seem that way*?" the colonel repeated, as if my phrase had some deeper meaning.

Chapter 35

During the two hours in which I had been talking nonstop, the colonel occasionally nodded and, rarely, asked a question, but otherwise didn't react to even the most unbelievable event I described. Making him appear like the popular image of a psychoanalyst. Which he mentioned that he was in civilian life, though he was now in the military—where I knew the traditional rules of medical ethics and confidentiality don't apply.

At first I felt uncomfortable speaking to someone who didn't talk back: this isn't how people usually relate. Then I started feeling better for, as I described the recent months, my experiences started making sense. Though I never could have predicted what would happen. Nor, I'm sure, could this colonel.

At some point during our talk his search for information seemed to expand into the discovery of who I really was. Or maybe it just turned into a typical, though extended, psychoanalytic session. An explanation which would have pleased this military doctor since most like to emphasize that they are physicians first despite their service affiliation.

And we *were* on the same side in the war against terror and we both wanted to figure out what actually happened to me and Holly on that final day. Hours later I did—though I'm not sure the colonel believed my explanation. Not that day. But someday surely.

So for the moment we were this improbable investigatory team, one as unlikely as the military ever had.

But maybe we were the only one they could put together quickly even if our information might lead to the sole defense which America had against... I don't even want to think about *that* possibility.

During those hours, as we sat just a few feet apart, the colonel and I became *real* allies and I began to trust him. Which was why I let myself question him about my interrogation.

"I have irrelevant things going through my mind. Should I describe these or just say what I think is important?"

"Tell me everything. Though being able to do so derives from trust, which takes time to develop and we've just met. You'll find yourself speaking of personal matters but my job isn't to analyze you even if some happens along the way. We need the missing scientific data and to learn more about the terrorists. Facts existing in the minds of only you and Holly.

"She's still traumatized and can't talk so you're all that we have. American security is on the tipping edge but if our military has any say it's not going over. Help us and you and Holly will get home and be safe for the rest of your lives. If bullets come your way, we'll take 'em for you!"

Some of what the colonel said connected with me but I certainly didn't buy his lie about Holly being alive. I knew she was as dead as the tissue box beside my bed and the shackle which imprisoned me to it. Still, I trusted him a little. Maybe because of his self-effacing style or that he was a doctor—if he really was one. Interrogators often lie to prisoners, which is what I was despite his increasing warmth and vow.

But we weren't alone in this room. The general sitting silently in the corner could be a valuable witness if the colonel didn't keep his word. Or maybe the general was there because it is better to have two rather than one witness against a murder defendant. During their trial by military tribunal...before their execution...

I sipped from the bottle of Poland Spring Water on the side table before continuing my story. I felt shy talking about my sexual problem even though I recognized that my sensitivity was quaint considering the peril which America faced.

Chapter 36

Food became more important when our sex stopped. Pat bought two cook books with one indicating where her real interest in cooking lay for it described just about everything which could be made with a microwave: main dishes, vegetables, even brownies. The other book was very different and I think that its real purpose was to impress me. Which it did, all seven hundred pages of Craig Claiborne's *New York Times Cook Book* .

Meanwhile I tried to find new interests for Holly. To rouse her from her depression and increase her willingness, or ability, to speak in sentences of more than three words. I thought that cooking might serve this purpose. The stove did temporarily become her Nintendo and Claiborne's book her reading passion.

It was when Holly's interest in cooking Italian began that I started talking seriously with Cedric. So maybe you could say that it was an eggplant which changed things. Or, more accurately, Pasta With Eggplant. That was Holly's obsession one Saturday morning.

Now the colonel made another of his rare interruptions.

"And that was the morning you forgot to do something important," he asserted.

"Yes. How did...?"

"Just to show you that we have good information. Don't bother trying to lie."

I don't think the colonel was really concerned about that. He was just parading his cleverness like doctors love to do. I kept myself from sharing this insight and went on talking.

Eggplant are funny looking things. Possibly something about it reminded Holly of her mother for she went a little crazy that morning. She copied the recipe and Insisted we go shopping for the ingredients right away. To calm her, we quickly left the house for the supermarket.

I barely heard of eggplant and never imagined how many varieties there are. Large and oval; elongated; egg-shaped; slim, and in clusters. Black, purple, yellow or white. The other recipe ingredients were basic and available in most homes though not ours: olive oil, pasta, tomato sauce, mozzarella cheese, butter, Parmesan cheese. Because of her heavy work schedule, Patience was into one-pot cooking.

Holly was still frantic by the time we got home but preparing the meal calmed her. Peeling and cutting the eggplant into half-inch slices, browning them in olive oil. Cooking and draining the macaroni, adding the sauce to the pot and then baking all, after dotting the construction with butter and sprinkling it with grated cheese. An elaborate procedure for a basically simple dish and I wondered at Holly being able to concentrate so well considering how upset she had been.

We enjoyed eating her accomplishment. In fact, it was so good that I thought Pat might be jealous, this adding another reason to explain their growing dislike for each other. Which reflected, I earlier concluded, the normal jealousy between the daughter and woman in a man's life. Having lost her family so recently, Holly must be particularly afraid of Pat taking me from her.

"*Maybe*," said the colonel suspiciously, as if he didn't buy my theory, and the general in the corner coughed. Likely to remind his subordinate that the purpose of the interview was to gain militarily useful information, not parade his psychoanalytic insights. Apparently this message was received for the colonel didn't make another comment, except to ask a clarifying question, for the next hour.

Like I said, it was after Holly cooked the eggplant that there *was* a change—things got rapidly worse. Before, I felt bonded at the hip to Holly and Pat. Later, both were distancing themselves from me when I most needed them. I couldn't deal with the dangers we faced alone and needed advice.

First, I still couldn't solve the riddle which Holly's parents created and held the key to our survival. Second, I didn't know how to reduce the coolness between me and Pat and she and Holly, or what to do next. Except to go down fighting when the terrorists decided that the time had arrived for us to meet our painful ends.

After brunch that day I sat rigidly in the living room and stared out the window. Holly was watching a Poo bear video with Cedric. He noticed my tortured look and left her to sit beside me.

I was wound so tightly that I hungered to scream out my fears and my being clueless what to do next. But I couldn't. The more Cedric knew, the greater danger he and his wife would face. Then only a fool would let me and Holly remain at their house considering the situation we placed their family in. So I didn't speak until Cedric began talking to me. First, telling me a story. Then asking a question. Gently, like I did with Holly.

It was this talk with Cedric which saved my life.

Chapter 37

"A mother called on me yesterday," Cedric said. "Her alcoholic husband keeps her and their children on a tight budget while spending lavishly on himself. Sometimes he 'accidentally' hits her with his elbow while sleeping. Things are so bad that their teenage son promised to get a job to support the family if his mother got a divorce. What would you advise her?"

"I don't know."

"Think about it," he insisted, and I did. I welcomed any task which would stop me from worrying about my own situation. "I'd say that her family's future depended solely on her abilities. Which must be considerable if she could raise such an impressive boy. That with faith in herself she might return to school, gain training, become financially independent. And find a better husband."

"Pretty good for a scientist," he said in an approving tone. "You might be in the wrong field."

"What did you tell her?" I asked, now with more than casual interest in the woman's dilemma. She seemed as blocked in her life as I was in mine.

"I told her about despair," he said. Upon hearing this word, I felt understood and my depression began lifting. Maybe because Cedric managed to identify what I was feeling. Or, possibly, because I had just found another wise mentor, as when I met Bryll years earlier.

"Despair is the ultimate situation," Cedric continued. "When one is without hope, unable to move, and feels there is no future. Some turn to suicide to relieve the guilt and self-loathing which despair produces.

"Others try to avoid this pain by drowning themselves in work or relationships—except in those extreme situations when all hope seems lost. Yet this wrenching anxiety can enable us to find courage—but only by confronting our difficulties.

"To be courageous means to embrace life and cope with our fears, not try to avoid them and thus life itself. To lighten the occasional darkness of the present by embracing the future."

I didn't understand everything Cedric said. He was a deep guy and more a scholar than village pastor though he would have scoffed at the title. So I said only what I felt and this seemed OK. "Thanks, I feel better."

"I'm glad," he responded. "Though I don't know what's going on here. The three of you make the oddest family I've seen in some time. That Holly looks shell-shocked is understandable considering the recent death of her mother. Which explains your depression too, but not the fleeting terror in both your faces.

"I gave up trying to understand Pat when she was a teenager. Then I predicted she would become a stay-at-home mother and her sister a career woman. But her sister is divorced with kids and Pat's boyfriends bounce away from her though I probably shouldn't tell you this."

"No one is perfect," I said soothingly, though welcoming the information. Pat was a private person. Apart from the attempted rape by her boss, I knew nothing about her. Not even casual memories of her childhood in Greenwich which I would have expected to hear by now, after her return.

Our talk helped me to feel relaxed for the first time in weeks and I wanted it to continue, but not about me. Being afraid that I might let slip personal information, I asked Cedric about his life.

"Why did you become a minister?" It seemed as exotic a vocation to me as mine of army officer had been to others.

"It followed my calling from God and reading of Heidegger's rejection of Him. Still interested?" I nodded. Something in his tone must have attracted Holly for she turned off her video and listened too. Why not, I thought, she probably has a higher IQ than both of us.

"My first job was as a high school history teacher in Cheyenne, Wyoming. It was a less wealthy town then, just family owned stores downtown. People socialized around pancake breakfasts catered by teenagers, not the hundred dollar a ticket charity functions they now have in that energy rich state.

"To supplement my salary I got a part-time job as deputy sheriff. At first I thought It was the sight of an accident which changed me. A mother and infant were killed by a drunken driver and I had to inform the husband. Probably that incident was just the catalyst. After my shift ended I needed to wind down and stopped at a small bookstore. There were trays of used books outside. I picked one up and what I read made sense of what I had been experiencing as a police officer. Have you ever heard of the German word *entschlossenheit*?" I shook my head.

"The concept is from Martin Heidegger, an early twentieth century German philosopher. It means that if a person is resolute in misfortune and behaves with determination, then they are half-way to being cured. Few read him now though he deals with a modern torment: why despair is experienced and how to overcome it.

"Heidegger's philosophy rejects the need for God but for me achieving the power of self-affirmation is easier because of my unshakable confidence in Him. So it was an old book which started me on my road to the ministry. But enough of this heavy stuff. Now I must play Connect Four with Holly though she always beats me. We'll talk again."

I nodded and thought that I could not have made a more fortunate choice of hide-out than at the home of this ex-sheriff.

Chapter 38

Happy families are all alike but every
unhappy family is unhappy in its own way.
—Tolstoy, *Anna Karenina*

Having grown up in an orphanage, I learned about families from watching movies. While the more melodramatic events of film were absent from our Sunday brunch, there were resemblances.

Pat's sister had four children under the age of six, a trying situation for any parent. Their behavior added to the tension between their mother and aunt, whose conversations went like this.

"You should discipline your kids."

"When was mothering your strength?"

"Children need their father. Not a narcissist who drives him away."

"Information you gained from sleeping around?."

Holly contributed to this atmosphere with her smiles and stares, towards her fantasied ghost or from sheer craziness.

Throughout these events, Cedric gazed beatifically at his grandchildren while his wife fled as often as possible to the kitchen. My earlier depression changed into a headache. I helped Patience clear the dishes, planned my escape, and noticed a letter under the front door, Recognizing its script, I wanted to burn it unread. Instead, I took it to my room. I didn't bother excusing myself from the brunch. No one would have noticed me leave after the last interchange I heard.

Three year old Melanie: "I farted."

Her mother: "How nice of you to inform us."

I sprawled on the bed and opened the envelope. I remembered following a similar routine before reading love letters in the past and wondered at this association. Then I realized that this writer also sought an alliance.

The note read as follows.

My Friend,

I await your commitment and provide you with further ideas to consider, for these possess greater power than weapons.

From a tiny acorn a great oak may spring. This English proverb indicates my respect for your birth place, home of the greatest of scientific discoveries: Isaac Newton's law of gravity following his simple observation of an apple falling from a tree. One which is still revered in the garden of Woolsthorpe Manor, Lincolnshire, your native land.

Yet I offer you the possibility of greater riches. In pagan Rome, Caesar was God. Christians had to choose between allegiance to Him and their temporal ruler, a dilemma leading to endless strife. But Islam demands no such painful choice. Within its boundaries there is but one sovereign, one God and lawgiver. And His prophet, Muhammad, peace be on him, who conquered and ruled on God's behalf throughout the days of his glorious reign.

Al-Mutanabbi wrote a thousand years ago:
Tastier than old wine,
sweeter than the passing of winecups,
is the play of swords and lances,
the clash of armies at my command...

You were a warrior. You lived for this. Be one of us.

You need not fear for Holly's life. Though but ten years old—alone, at night, in the wilderness—she escaped my soldiers and found a fallen hero, one who was willing to shield her with his life. Such a child must be under the special protection of God and I dare not harm His ward.

One day we will meet, as brothers or enemies. The choice is yours.

Allāhu yusallimak*

Hasan

The night before receiving this letter I read to Holly a Sherlock Holmes tale. A man receives orange pips. This warns of his impending murder unless he follows orders. He refused and armed himself with a pistol only to die mysteriously.

I schemed. Maybe I could send Holly and Pat elsewhere while I, very visibly, remained, But Holly would never leave me. Some mornings even getting her to enter the school building was a struggle.

Yet Hasan really wanted her and not me. I could flee this house without her and be safe. Why risk my life for a child I barely knew? Because part of you is still a soldier, a voice rumbled within me, as I remembered a surprising lesson from years before. It was given at Great Britain's Royal Military Academy at Sandhurst and described soldierly heroism as being a form of suicide.

*May God give you peace!

The teacher raised the rarely asked question of why soldiers were willing to sacrifice their lives for others. Not included in that category was such valor as the medic who faced enemy fire to rescue the wounded or the soldier who charged a machine gun position.

The instructor concerned herself with that rarer military bravery: the voluntary, deliberate sacrifice of one's life for others when death was certain and no one would have criticized the soldier for acting differently. Examples included throwing oneself over an enemy hand grenade to protect comrades from the blast, or flying a damaged airplane into a gun emplacement to save the lives of targeted ground forces.

The speaker explained these exemplary acts as being "heroic suicides" motivated by strong group cohesion. Most of these heroes were members of small elite fighting units where a powerful emotional connection made each willing to commit "altruistic suicide" for the others. As I would for Holly, and for much the same reason, I concluded.

Finally, cradling this depressing thought, I fell asleep.

Chapter 39

In front the sun climbs slow, how slowly!
But westward, look, the land is bright.
—Arthur Hugh Clough, *Say not the Struggle Naught availeth*

By next morning the rain had passed and the sunrise again caused me to consider our survival possible.

While shaving, I thought of a story which Bryll told me during my first month at the Institute. It concerned a group of the younger scientists who were trying to discover an ultimate secret of life: how atoms came into existence fifteen billion years ago.

One of the basic building blocks of matter is called a quark. Three quarks are glued together by a particle called a gluon to form a proton consisting of two "down" quarks and one "up" quark; or into a neutron made up of two "up" quarks and one "down" quark. Think of putting together a book case: the sides are the protons or neutrons and the fasteners are gluons. Put enough of these parts together and you get an atom. Just like constructing a bookcase by putting the shelves together.

Which sounds simple except that objects as tiny as quarks and gluons can't be seen. We infer their existence from what happens in scientific experiments. So to theorize what happened at the very beginning of our solar system, a "RICK," Relativistic High Ion Collider, was used to smash gold atoms together with enough energy to produce a temperature many times that of the sun. Unfortunately, what resulted was too few of a type of particle which was expected from the explosion. Until a clever physicist suggested that some of the particles which would be expected to be ejected during the explosion were being held back by the force of their neighboring particles and so didn't appear. Thus he managed to explain the results by looking at them differently. A technique which Sherlock Holmes a century before might have advised the scientists to try.

So I analyzed *our* situation differently. Since we were small in number (only two, possibly three, if Pat remained with us), the only advantage we could have over the terrorists was intelligence. Our collective brainpower (including Holly's formidable addition) might be greater. For us to work together as an effective unit I would have to count on Holly, and also to tell Pat what I was thinking. Since my "performance problem" began I had pretty much shut her out of my life.

But about *that* I didn't know what to say. No matter how it's explained, being impotent sends a message of rejection to the partner. And talking about feelings was never my strength. So despite my intention to reconcile with Pat I continued to say nothing about our relationship. It was she who made the first move.

"Is it over with us?" Pat asked, as we lay in bed. It was just after 3:00AM, when she usually woke up. She was an even worse sleeper than me. The only woman I heard of with a similar problem was a long retired co-worker's deceased wife who had been in the French Resistance during World War II. Thereafter she couldn't sleep until morning for nighttime was when the Gestapo agents made their arrests.

In the past, when obsessed with solving a scientific problem, I often fell asleep at 9:00PM or 10:00PM, then woke four or five hours later to continue working, stopping at dawn when I started feeling groggy. With our similar sleep patterns, Pat and I made a good couple. A woman capable of sleeping all night undisturbed would value an equally conventional partner and quickly chuck me, as many did.

So I was already awake for several hours when Pat spoke. I had been trying to decode Holly's final message from her parents. And, as with my previous scientific puzzles, it maintained more of my attention than did my lover's concerns. But I had increasingly come to view this emotional tendency as a defect, and immediately put down the coded sheets and turned towards her.

"Are we over?" she repeated. "My experience has been that once sex goes, the guy soon follows."

"It's not like that with us."

"How is it?"

I wasn't sure. During the previous weeks my feelings had swung between depression and terror and finally to relief after speaking with Cedric. Now I was living comfortably in his house and didn't want to break up with Pat and have to leave. Particularly with the worldwide hunt for me and Holly by assorted bad and good guys. With these conflicting motives, it's understandable that I wasn't sure exactly how Pat fit into my life.

"Could this ambivalence have caused my impotence?" I asked the colonel.

"Save your questions for later," he replied crisply. "What did you tell Pat?"

What could I say? That my feelings toward her *had* changed? Certainly not. I said that we weren't over and wouldn't be. I hoped this statement would satisfy her but It didn't.

"Then what *is* happening?" Pat continued, her anguish making me feel even worse than before I spoke. I'd failed Julia, who killed herself with alcohol, and would likely wind up getting Holly, Pat, and even her parents murdered. Feeling completely incompetent, I fell back on saying what immediately came to mind, as I sometimes did with Holly.

"It's *not* you and how I'm saying this will probably come out wrong," I began explaining, "but I was emotionally wiped out when we met. Partly from my girl-friend's, Julia's, death, partly from the troubles with Holly, and the rest from having been unable to convince my co-workers about something really important."

My eyes locked onto the colonel's. "It was the ongoing argument over whether the W-76 nuclear warheads needed renovation."

"You told her about *that*?" he asked sharply, as the general in the corner stared in my direction. Usually he faced downwards, concentrating on my words, his shoes, or maybe just dozing.

"Of course not! Do you think I'm a moron?" I asked heatedly, feeling more insulted than threatened.

"OK. OK. Now tell me about that conversation with Pat." As I did, the general's gaze again drifted downward.

"I met Julia at my job," I told Pat. "But it wasn't a typical job and our relationship wasn't the usual. You see, she was my boss's wife and he encouraged our affair."

Both the colonel and the general now stared at me again, like Pat did. Life tends to be lived and not considered but the more I thought about mine the more I realized that this was really *some* story.

"Bryll came from a poor family. He was seventeen when his father died and things got worse. Thereafter, he saw it as his responsibility to care for his mother and sisters, who were being maintained by an uncle and always reminded of this.

"Bryll was a brilliant guy. After attending Groton on scholarship he was awarded another to attend the Massachusetts Institute of Technology where he received his doctorate in electrical engineering at the age of twenty-four. They offered him a junior teaching position but he turned it down, feeling that to support his family he needed more money.

"Using a contact from Groton, he got a job at a Wall Street brokerage house. There he used his analytical and mathematical skills to reduce the risk of investments by offsetting them with others. By his twenty ninth birthday his income was well into the six figures and he was a legend in the financial community. Ten years later, when his fortune was above eight figures, he retired from business and devoted the rest of his life to scientific research, which gave him the greatest professional enjoyment.

"Though patriotic, Bryll was the first in four generations of his family who didn't serve in the military. This, I was told by others, is another reason why he wanted to hire me for I held the military credentials he lacked.

"By the early seventies, protests against anything military were rising. Bryll believed that after the Vietnam War ended, defense research budgets would be decimated. He determined to help protect his country.

"He could have returned to MIT and worked in one of their labs but he considered their bureaucracy and petty politics wasteful. So he set up his own research facility, hiring the best scientists by paying three to four times what the universities offered, and adding luxuries which college professors only dream about: catered meals, a concierge to handle household chores, use of the Institute's planes and apartments in Manhattan and London. A leased car was a routine perk.

"He settled his group on two hundred acres in New York's Hudson Valley, near West Point's Hotel Thayer where he put up visiting government officials."

Pat stretched. "You *will* tell me, won't you."

"I'm getting there. The story takes longer than I expected," I said, and continued my explanation. Which already seemed to be improving our relationship: while I spoke, Pat began hugging me.

"Bryll was thirty years older than Julia. Both were married when they met but not to each other. He married in his second year at MIT to a socialite he met at a Radcliffe dance. Julia was the French wife of a scientist who was one of Bryll's employees.

"She was like no other woman he ever knew. Not that she was more beautiful than his wife who was tall, lithe, and stunning. But she was also often sickly, or pretending to be. Having doctors visit, and I do mean *visit,* her continually, and letting Bryll bring up their sons.

"Julia's husband was much the same though it was science and not his health which consumed him. Bryll met Julia at a reception for new employees. Things soon started between them though they kept their relationship secret for years.

"Bryll's wife likely knew something was up. He had affairs throughout their marriage and they didn't have sex since their youngest child was born. But he never became seriously involved with another woman until he met Julia. Her vivacity and dress entranced him. Like I said, she was French. And they shared many of the same interests. Both loved tennis and sailing while his wife spent her days in bed."

Now Pat's interest became aroused. "How did you learn these personal details?"

"I'm getting to that," I said, continuing my narrative, which then became both mine and Julia's story too.

"Bryll wanted to marry Julia despite the huge scandal this would cause. But she always refused, saying they should wait until his sons were grown. Incidentally, he treated her children as well as he treated his own.

"Years passed during which Bryll's wife became even less willing to leave the house. After her commitment to a psychiatric hospital, Julia's husband left her; and the Institute for a cushy job which Bryll arranged. He and Julia then began living together in an apartment in Manhattan.

"But unlike in the movies their love didn't conquer all. Bryll's sons never forgave him for the way he treated their mother and she died in the hospital. Bryll and Julia married and lived together for the rest of his life.

"As Bryll grew older he began to worry whether Julia could survive his death. He knew she would always need someone to care for her and wanted to pass this responsibility to someone he could trust. Bryll decided on me. He gave Julia to me."

Pat inhaled deeply as I continued.

"I agreed because of Bryll's great personal skills. And because I came to love him as the father I never had."

"Did he tell you what he wanted?" Pat asked.

"Not at first. He began his campaign at one of the Institute's dinners. Scientists are individualistic so our meals were buffet style to allow for the greatest choice. There was even tofu 'turkey' for vegetarians. You wanted it and Bryll would order it. He was a combined father and mother to all of us. It was the best job I ever had. I'll never find another like it.

"I'd broken up with my girl-friend and, like people say, was vulnerable. Bryll listened and I told him everything: the death of my parents, my life in the orphanage, experiences with the British army. Even about the love affair which had just ended.

"The next week he asked me to drive Julia into Manhattan for a medical appointment. She later told me it was to discuss his condition—which wasn't good.

"Bryll had Stage 4 pancreatic cancer which spread to his spine. Like every scientist, he researched anything he didn't know. His odds weren't good. One, two more years at the most. He decided that Julia needed someone to care for her after he was gone. This was the last task he gave me."

"He actually asked that?" Pat demanded to know, with the same astonishment I would have felt had I not known Bryll.

"I'm coming to that. As you can imagine, I was more than a little frightened when he called me into his office for sleeping with the boss's wife is high risk behavior at any job. But this was never mentioned. We discussed my projects, the world political situation and, again, my childhood. It was only when I got up to leave that, almost in passing, he spoke of Julia. 'I trust you to care for her when I'm gone. She won't survive on her own.' I couldn't say anything because my eyes suddenly filled with tears as I realized that he would soon die and I would be losing him just as years before I had lost my parents. A moment later I found myself ushered from his office. I never spoke alone with him again.

"Yes, Bryll knew about me and Julia. He chose me for her."

Chapter 40

Though telling my story took longer than I expected, Pat listened closely. First from politeness but soon from real interest. It was a good story though it was just one of many which I could have told. Except for being able to explain how they fit together to form my life.

"What did that love affair have to do with us?" Pat asked, in her most reasonable tone. Despite which I couldn't answer her for I wasn't sure.

"Maybe because Julia represented another of my recent failures," I suggested. "After I couldn't convince co-workers about the inadequate reliability of one mechanism and became the lousy manager of the millimeter wave project."

"What's that?"

"A sensor which detects the energy waves which people give off naturally—to see if they're carrying weapons. It's revolutionary protection against terrorists. What I've told you is public knowledge. I can't say more about it."

"What *can* you talk about?"

"Not wanting what happens to us to resemble what happened between me and Julia."

"Which is..." Pat's face took on a weary look. Apparently I can explain only scientific matters briefly.

"I failed her and my unspoken vow to Bryll. She had a drinking problem, he got her off alcohol and she was sober for the rest of their marriage. But after his death she began drinking again. Alcoholics are masters of deceit. She'd promise to stop, I'd find hidden bottles and she would promise again. I even isolated us on a cottage in the country and took away her car keys. She would get the local taxi driver to make liquor deliveries. Julia died with an empty vodka bottle at her side and I found more around the house. I didn't do her any good."

Pat listened thoughtfully. "I still think you're good for me," she said. "Maybe your feelings come from growing up in an orphanage. Some abandoned children blame themselves for their state and later, unconsciously, try to prove their unworthiness by choosing and failing with unsuitable mates. Can this apply to you?"

"It's plausible. If I'm not simply a jinx?"

"A scientist talking about jinxes," she said, but in a sympathetic tone while holding me tightly, I responded and the need for further discussion of our relationship soon ended. My impotence had clearly vanished.

Minutes later I showed the coded sheets to Pat. With her law school honed logical capacities she might see something which I missed.

"Why do you think the numbers are that important? Maybe it's a game which Holly's parents invented."

"Then why did she hide the papers. Her parents must have told her of its importance. I searched their house before I left. Not as good as a real detective but damn thoroughly and I found nothing which seemed even vaguely relevant to the parents' findings."

"Let me look at it again." Pat glanced over the sheets without much enthusiasm. "Could that the numbers range from one to five mean something? Maybe each represents a letter,"

"Unless one of the numbers indicates a divider between words."

"Stop being difficult. The first line has ten numbers so each letter must be represented by a number which is evenly divisible. One or two or five."

During the next hour we created charts to match all possible number combinations of the first line, "3253232355," against the most frequent letters.

We quickly gave up the idea that each number represented only one letter since the largest number in the message was five. Pat suggested that a letter might be represented by some formula. As, if a five is followed by a one it means a particular letter but if followed by a two a different letter. We discarded this idea too, feeling that so complex a code to solve would certainly not be given to a child of Holly's age no matter how bright she was.

Gloom descended as our pads filled unproductively.

"Holly, Holly, Holly..." Pat shook her head. Then her face lit up. "We're being dumb, probably from all the stress. The first line must be a greeting to the addressee. Her name—Holly—which is *five* letters. So each letter must be indicated by *two* numbers."

Pat's valuable suggestion caused our renewed enthusiasm and return to the task: *h* might be 32, *o* be 53, *l* be 23, and 55 be *y*. With simultaneous smiles, we exclaimed the resultant word: *HOLLY. We* quickly turned to the first line.

Which now became translated as "O_ly_o__y__o__I,"____h_____,_ho__ _h_____h_____,"

"I can see another letter," Pat said. "The first word looks like 'only'. So "n" must be forty three," said Pat. 'Let's do the next line." This read:"_n_lon_o_h h_l_on_no_n_o_n_o'_ay__n_."

"Enough for today," I said. "I'm groggy." The afterglow from our sex had so relaxed me that I briefly forgot our hours of survival being counted down. After breakfast I remembered this and behaved like soldiers usually do before combat: chatting about ordinary matters and imagining *the time* will never arrive. Pat, Holly, and I snacked on Fig Newtons as we traveled along the streets of our Monopoly game.

"I'm sometimes addressed as *president* though Pat would deny that I deserve this title," Cedric mentioned, in a self-deprecatory tone after I joined him. I had left Pat and Holly to finish the Monopoly game, hoping that their mutual enjoyment would reduce the increasing coolness between them.

"Which just meant I once presided as head of mission in a region. When used, the title indicates affection and honor though it never impressed Pat when she was a teenager. I failed in at least one clerical responsibility: to help my children become a role model for their peers. A goal no different from the teacher who wants their child to excel in school or the police officer who would particularly object to reading about their child in a newspaper's police blotter."

I continued to find it odd that Pat never discussed her childhood. It couldn't have been more difficult than for most youth considering that she was now willing to live at home, ten years after leaving for college. Then I remembered that it was Holly's angelic figure who advised us to go to Greenwich.

"Was Pat's name ever in the police column?" I asked, having sensed a hesitation during his choice of these words.

Cedric paused before answering. Apparently weighing his ethical commitment to honesty against presenting the most positive image of his daughter to her current marriage prospect. His expression indicated that both motives had won out: I was to be given some but not the entire truth.

"She tried to burn down the Greenwich Middle School." His even tone surprised me as much as the words. He leaned closer before continuing his story.

"There *was* a plot though this word conveys a maturity of thinking which none of the participants had. Pat and three girls were angry with a teacher and decided to set fire to their school. The youngest gang member was eleven, Pat a year older.

"She was the ordinance person, having brought a gallon container of gas which they later found in her locker. Their plan was to splash it over the upper floors and ignite it. This would drive the students into the stairwells which would then be set ablaze. It was an inspired idea. Many of the building's population—children and staff—might have died and the three become more notorious than the Columbine High School killers." Cedric's words implied wonderment at the horror which the behavior of children sometimes achieves.

"Why they did it remains unanswered. Being angry at their teacher was no real explanation. Thankfully, no one was hurt. We got a note from a psychiatrist stating that Pat presented no danger and enrolled her in a private school. The first one didn't work out but in the next her grades went back to "A's" and the incident was quickly forgotten. People don't want to think of adolescent girls as representing a threat, like they do of teenage boys.

"Surprising, isn't it," he said. "The early years of a successful attorney."

"It's difficult to understand a child," I observed.

"It takes time, which I have a lot more of now that I'm semi-retired. So I think about my family and read. History, theology, still the Bible, but also pastoral counseling and psychoanalysis. One recent book was by an American doctor who traveled to Europe in the nineteen twenties to be analyzed by Freud. At its conclusion, which then took only six months, Freud wished him luck in finding a woman to whom he would remain happily married. The doctor expressed surprise that Freud used the term 'luck' considering how deep his psychological knowledge was. Freud replied that good fortune was essential, for it took a long time to really know a person.

"We—their mother and I—were never as close with our daughters as we wanted though doing our best. We didn't expect them to be perfect. Just to have better lives than we achieved, which is every parent's goal.

"Yet our oldest daughter marries someone who deserves jail while her sister remains unmarried. *But* has a boyfriend with a daughter who needs a mother, so I remain hopeful."

I wasn't ready to supply my marital intention. Nor to respond frankly to his next question.

"You're running from something, aren't you?"

He accepted my silence with grace.

"You don't have to tell me—I have good street instincts. I survived working in a church in Los Angeles where gangs ran the streets though being fluent in Spanish helped."

As the silence began separating us I felt that I should say something.

"What causes you to think that I'm running away?"

Cedric eyed me knowingly. "Because you never relax. Even while watching TV your eyes scan the windows and door. And you always sit with your back to a wall—like you are now. I'm not pressing you. I'm also not as naive as my daughters and wife insist.

"If I didn't feel you were a good person you wouldn't be here. But fear can corrode the quality of thinking and lead a person into danger. Enough of my lecturing. My wife says I suffer from the delusion that my long negligible advice became more valuable with age."

Cedric rose, clapped me on the shoulder, and walked from the room. Leaving me with the uncomfortable thought that my lengthy formal education seemed not to have extended to some basic areas of living.

I felt better after our talk. Cedric trusted me without needing to know more and his was a friendly voice. His perspective also expanded my thinking, which seemed to have shut down under the stress from the danger we faced. So I again studied our situation and came to a different conclusion.

Most importantly, we didn't necessarily have three more weeks. Military interrogators often make rapid changes in a prisoners' environment to reduce their will to resist. Should I expect less from a sophisticated terrorist? With this changed perspective, I made three new decisions: to quickly obtain a *real* weapon in place of the obsolete . 380 caliber pistol I was relying on; to concentrate on decoding the note and, despite the hospitality we received, to leave this house as quickly as possible.

By that evening I felt as if I had finally taken charge of our situation and was moving again, even if not in my beloved 1953 Kaiser which lay abandoned in a parking lot.

Meanwhile, Holly continued to mope and the more I tried involving Pat in our activities the worse their relationship got. Finally, Pat said that I should stop trying:

Holly would accept her as a step-mother when she was ready and this couldn't be pushed. So I relaxed about Holly's discourteous behavior and it did improve a little.

Chapter 41

War is sweet to those who know nothing of it.
—Erasmus
...awoke to new life as soon as they tasted blood.
—Homer

My last killings saved lives, gained me a medal and, paradoxically, led to the loss of my commission and posting in the Special Air Services, an achievement of which I was justifiably proud. The SAS is Great Britain's equivalent of the American Army's Rangers and both groups are internationally renowned for their military skills.

My baptism as a hero began unexpectedly. I was returning to England from an assignment in the small Gulf state of Oman. There, I had been increasing their army's ability to battle terrorism through a standard military contract. As much as possible, I trained the recruits using the drill which I endured during my SAS training. Beginning with a three week selection process to build esprit de corps, though discharging the untalented wasn't possible except for those few who were unrelated to tribal leaders.

The first week comprised the Battle Fitness Course consisting of multiple three, five, and eight mile runs. During the second week I introduced the Ran Dance during which they carried thirty pounds over a twenty mile route. To increase stress, the following days went from 4AM to 10:30PM and involved marching up and down hills while carrying a sixty pound knapsack with the cut-off time for each day not being told. Final candidates were invited to march fifty miles within twenty hours.

Since the duties of these graduates would be on their home territory, I left out some typical SAS classes: parachuting, water operations, and medical training to enable them to cope on an emergency basis with battle wounds. Instead, the men learned the specialized weapons they would be using: the MP5 SD submachine gun with flash and sound suppressor; and the Flash Bang grenade which emits a vivid light and loud sound to disorient the enemy without killing them, providing extra seconds during which a hostage could be rescued.

I and my subordinates accomplished more than was expected. Like soldiers are always told they must do. Before leaving, we were each given a going-away present: boxes of what, except for their weight, looked like gold foil wrapped nickel sized pieces of chocolate—and turned out to be British Sovereign 22k bullion coins. Five hundred for me, worth a bit over fifty thousand dollars, and two hundred for each of my men. A tax free bonus.

So I was feeling pretty good on the BOAC flight home. Military wages for officers aren't high though the benefits—job security, pension, sense of belonging—make up for it. There was a three hour layover at the Athens airport. I planned to visit its tax free store and *imagine* what I might buy. To actually *spend* money, even that which arrives unexpectedly, isn't easy after a childhood of poverty.

The entrance to the gift shop was at the far end of the terminal, near the Delta counter. Because of the threat of terrorist attack this American airline had been placed apart from the others. This made it easier to guard though no police were there at the moment.

I wandered the store aisles, feeling gleeful that, for the first time in my life, I could purchase what I wanted without regard to cost. But like they say, old habits die hard, and I bought only a large stuffed penguin. Being unable to keep a pet because of my frequent extended travels, this seemed a worthy substitute.

As I left the store I noticed two men walk slowly by me. Later, when the police questioned me, I was asked what first made me suspicious of them. I replied that a number of things struck me as odd: they wearing heavy jackets on a warm day, their quickening gait, and their heavy rosewater scent, with which suicide bombers often anoint themselves in preparation for martyrdom. But mostly because the expression on their faces seemed "wrong." To clarify what I meant, I told the investigators the following story which I was once told.

Two Columbian soldiers were sitting in a car. It was a chilly night, the auto's windows were closed, and the soldiers gossiped as they waited to be relieved. Suddenly, a man knocked on the window. The driver rolled it down and, a moment later, the soldier sitting by him drew his pistol and shot the stranger dead. A sawed-off shotgun was found under his raincoat. When the soldier was asked what made him suspicious, he replied that the man's expression caused him to feel sure that he was about to kill them, which he was. Facial muscles are associated with particular emotions and some people are naturally gifted in reading them, though this skill can be learned.

This story had likely lingered in my mind as the men passed me for I immediately removed my pistol from my duffel bag, lay it and the stuffed penguin against the wall, and followed them. Twenty feet before they reached the Delta passenger line, both dropped their luggage and drew automatic weapons from them. The bursts of fire they sent towards the ceiling caused everyone to hit the ground.

A civilian in a dangerous situation should flee as quickly as possible. But I wasn't a civilian, was armed, and wasn't about to risk committing suicide by turning my back on outlaws firing guns.

Whether these men were suicide bombers or old-fashioned airplane hijackers I didn't know. What was clear was that I was involved in a life or death event, for me and the waiting people. Here, a person doesn't utter warnings. One shoots, and not to disable but to kill.

Where should I fire? In theory, a man with a forty four inch chest will present an effective lethal target of thirteen to fourteen inches. Major blood vessels and vital organs are usually hit when the bullet penetrates six to seven inches. Thus an eight inch penetration should inflict great enough biological damage to end a criminal attack. But this is not certain. In real life non-critical tissue such as an arm may obstruct a bullet, or an attacker may be of greater than normal size. Thus the only certain way to end a dangerous situation is with a shot to the cranial vault of the head or to the brain stem. Both present difficulties.

The head is a small, quickly moving target while the cervical spinal cord is the thickness of a little finger. Yet, though elusive targets, shots in both areas will produce an instant disruption of the nervous system and immediate collapse.

Contrary to what civilians think, even soldiers with good training—and mine is universally considered to be among the best—aren't calm during battle. A bodily reaction occurs in which the soldier responds more quickly than normal, with greater strength, and gaining the ability to tolerate more pain.

Even if the events are rapid, they may seem in slow motion. The mind responds to threat with a tunnel-like vision in which sounds and anything not essential to survival are screened out. Gunfire may not be heard as resources are drawn on which aren't ordinarily used. One becomes able to anticipate behaviors subconsciously, as if to "see it coming." At these moments, reaction becomes automatic. Mine did.

I fired a bullet into the head of each man. Then, thinking the danger was over, I pointed my pistol towards the ground. But I was wrong. In that moment I sensed movement in the corner of my eye. After automatically throwing myself onto the ground, I turned and pointed my gun in its direction. There, I glimpsed a young woman raising a short barreled sub-machine gun. Fearing that I would miss, I fired at the woman's (larger) chest target rather than (smaller) head. When she began to go down, I shot there too. I was lucky. All my bullets hit her and she was certainly dead by the time her body touched the ground. As she fell, her finger pressed the trigger and bullets sprayed the area. Two fragmented after ricocheting from the airline's counter. Shards hit me in the knee, scratched my cheek—and struck my newly purchased stuffed penguin in the foot though I didn't find this out until later. Meanwhile I lay bleeding on the ground, waiting with the others for the police to come and officially rescue us.

At first they acted as if *I* was the criminal. In the ambulance, to my astonishment, I was asked why I hadn't warned the terrorists before shooting, or had just wounded them. I stayed cool and replied that soldiers are trained never to underestimate their adversary and to kill before being killed.

Which made wonderful sense to me but I could see that the police didn't readily accept my answer. Nowadays,

Europeans worry about their taxes and pensions and try not to notice anything which could disturb their orderly view of life. Like that evil people you can't reason with exist and must be killed. And that because of my action there were now fewer threats to civilized people. I felt like adding that when you look into the eyes of victims' relatives, you get your answer about what should be done.

I might be exaggerating the hostility of those officials who were just doing their job. Next morning all but one of the local newspapers considered me a hero. While in the hospital I was awarded a medal by a Greek general and invited to lunch with the American Ambassador. I was even granted one month extra leave by my unit's commander.

These events increased the irony that, shortly after my only public honor, I was involuntarily discharged from the army and thought seriously about killing myself. Changing my mind only after long discussion with my also wounded companion: the stuffed penguin I named Patrick after my long dead father. But the War Office had no choice. A soldier who is afraid of guns must be discharged, as I had become after shooting the terrorists. And more than just uneasy: even touching a gun could make me nauseous.

This symptom could not be explained by the base psychiatrist, who was an up-from-the-shoulder, we're-all-in-this-together-lads type of practitioner. He followed the usual drill. Hypnosis to relive my trauma coupled with post-hypnotic relaxation suggestions. Convalescent leave. Even offering to refer me for a brief course of psychoanalysis though doubting this would help. In the view of most psychoanalysts, soldiers, fire fighters, and police officers are least receptive to this form of treatment.

So the doctor was forced to recommend my medical discharge. Though not a pension since my particular disability wouldn't stop me from working at virtually any civilian job. But he also did me a big favor. Knowing that I received my undergraduate degree from Cambridge University (at the working class Fitzwilliam College rather than more social Christ College), and of my high score on the BARB (Army Entrance Test), he contacted Cambridge's Department of Applied Mathematics and Theoretical Physics and recommended me for doctoral study. Which surprised them until they learned of my scores on the STEP (Sixth Term Examination Papers in Mathematics). And, that though my undergraduate degree was in Economics, I had completed most of the coursework required to take Part Three of the Mathematical Tripos, the equivalent of a master's degree. Their letter admitting me to study arrived in the same day's mail as my discharge from the army. My thoughts of suicide disappeared that day but my fear of guns persisted.

Though his treatment was unsuccessful, I *was* helped by this military psychiatrist, who was a thoughtful man. When I spoke of how illogical it was that my heroic act had led to a crippling phobia, he gave me what I found to be valuable advice.

"The mind has a will of its own and senses the changes it needs to be healed. As you've no doubt discovered, I'm no deep psychoanalyst. Just an ordinary psychiatrist who tries to get wounded soldiers back into combat as quickly as possible—a place where no sane person would want to go. Usually I'm successful but when I fail it must be for some psychological good reason.

"Your fear of guns is a *symptom*. That's a fancy word for the sign that something is wrong. Ghosts from your unconscious which have long haunted you and were imprisoned by your psychological defenses have now tasted blood and freedom. I'm not skillful enough to figure out what change they want but maybe you can.

"Periodically, lie down and let your mind wander, after asking yourself what so frightens you about touching a gun. Consider the thoughts which follow. I wouldn't be surprised if the real explanation occurred. Along with your morale and strength for the lies from your unconscious will no longer be governing you. Then your fear of guns will disappear since it will no longer be needed by your mind."

I was too upset to immediately follow the doctor's suggestion. Before leaving the army I copied my yearly evaluations. They described a person completely different from who I had become.

"He has a sober personality, a quick dry wit, and an exceptionally sharp mind. He keeps his composure, being calm and never second-guessing himself. He takes everything in its stride, thinking ahead all the time and never giving way to panic. Though able to anticipate events, he instantly abandons his plan if it isn't working. He has an absolute passion to succeed, no matter what the obstacle or who the enemy.

"When wounded, he tried to conceal knowledge of this from his men, not wanting to place an additional burden on them. His men grew to love him because they knew that if anyone could get them through it would be him. They could not imagine any harm coming to him for he had the charisma of a winner. Oddly, he was able to arouse this affection though having little interest in social banter, never speaking of other than military duties or, in particular, of his personal life."

"He is one of those rarities who can act and encourage others to act courageously on a battlefield, being an exceptionally able and gallant soldier and fierce in the heat of battle because it is his duty to kill."

I re-read these lines in the weeks after my discharge but was already a changed person. My earlier fearlessness had become a watchfulness which I was unable to turn-off, an attitude commonly described as "being paranoid." I rarely left my apartment and repeatedly checked that all of the locks were fastened. When I did go out, I stared at anyone who looked remotely like the terrorists in Athens. Noting my disturbed gaze, strangers became anxious about *me*. I also put on weight, and had nightmares in which I was in danger but unable to pull the trigger of the gun I held.

Then I remembered other lines from my final mental health evaluation. "This almost ideal soldier possesses considerable rage which has become channeled by his military training and is now well controlled by this and his formidable intellect. But his drinking is a concern, as will be his adjustment to the demands of civilian life after retirement." Which came more quickly than anyone expected.

To put these matters out of my mind, I tried to jump start my studies by reading mathematics and physics journals. But I had difficulty remembering what the symbols meant, even those which were once as familiar to me as my name and had given me as much pleasure as does the latest Harry Potter novel to a child. It was as if I had lost the ability to be myself.

I also found that losing my identity as a military officer, and thus my purpose in life, had seriously lowered my self-esteem. Which had nothing to do with money for I still had almost all of my severance pay and the proceeds of the fifty thousand dollars worth of gold coins which I sold soon after arriving back at the small London apartment I owned.

Because of my interest in economics, I always read *The Economist* and *The Wall Street Journal* whenever possible. Now being where I could easily purchase them, I spent my empty days lying on the couch, drinking beer, reading these publications, and giving in to my feelings of depression. Until, coincidentally, I read an article about the lives of some enormously wealthy Americans. They, like me, had suddenly lost their careers through no fault of their own, and with it their sense of identity. They too became depressed and avoided others until, and with some it took several years, they got off their butts and re-established their lives.

I'm not sure why the article had the effect on me that it did for it told me nothing I didn't already know about what I needed to do. But it is inspiring to learn that others who were in your dreary situation managed to get themselves out of it. Though I didn't so much as lift myself up as lay myself down and let my thinking wander over my puzzling symptoms.

Within a half-hour I realized that losing my military family had resurrected those long buried feelings of loss which followed my parents' death. And that the phobia I unconsciously created was intended to force me to change my life: to create a new family for myself, one with *real* intimacy and not just service comradeship.

Though this insight represented little more than what the military doctor had suggested, I felt so much better that I left my apartment for the first time in days and hurried to a local firearms shop. I wanted to test my theory and hoped that my phobia was now gone. But my optimism disappeared as I handled their goods. To my disappointment I found that my fear of guns, the panic and nausea which occurred when I touched one, still remained. So my newly discovered interpretation could be only partially correct.

Chapter 42

The next day my new schedule began. After driving Holly to school in the morning I sat in the Greenwich Library and tried to further decode her parents' message, leaving at ten minutes to three to pick her up. From her school we went to the shooting range for her hour of daily practice, followed by a round of the best at the town's old-fashioned ice cream parlor. After dinner came her homework, my discussion with Pat's father, bedtime for all, and my adequately performed sex, thank you for asking.

Though having the soothing effect of all routines, I couldn't fully suppress my worry. I still lacked a plan for our flight, the message which could save us still remained largely coded, and my anxiety about guns made me, at best, an inadequate bodyguard. *Unless* our enemies were so easily upset that they would flee when I vomited on them.

Pat's parents lived in a rambling five bedroom colonial. It was built one hundred and five years earlier, by the owner of Greenwich's hardware store after his late life marriage on his forty seventh birthday. Like most such unions, this relationship brought complication: in the form of a quarrelsome widowed mother-in-law. To maximize marital bliss, the bridegroom constructed for her a separate three room apartment on the second floor, complete with kitchen and bathroom, which could be reached by a back staircase. This effectively made two separate homes. While I, Holly, and Pat lived in this apartment, we ate our meals with her parents, who considered Holly a gem. Still, their religious convictions seemed to make them but reluctant observers of our unmarried union, feelings which, however, they never mentioned.

Despite this underlying friction, I was grateful for their presence. It reduced the frequency of Holly's misbehavior or, as we came to call them, her "meltdowns." Which might range from dawdling in the morning, necessitating my frantic drive to get her to school on time, to, once, she slamming a door so hard that a glass pane shattered. We were all sympathetic in view of the trauma she experienced. I told myself that, though an adult, I sometimes felt like doing the same. Being English, I tried to avoid confrontation. But when Cedric took me aside I realized that things had finally gone too far.

"Talk to Holly," he advised me one afternoon. Only with considerable effort had I managed to drag her to school that day.

"I don't know how. Being a parent isn't my strength," I replied honestly, though not saying how recently my parenting role had begun.

"I can tell you all that I know in a few sentences," Cedric said. "And if I discovered it before my daughters were born it would have saved us much pain.

"Kids will usually do what they're asked. They want to please grown-ups and to grow up. If they're disobedient, it's because they can't help it for a reason which they likely don't know or, if they do, makes sense only to them. Always tell them why they must do something so they don't feel you're trying to boss them around. If they refuse, say you're disappointed and leave it at that. The worst threat to a child is their parents' withdrawal of love. Taking away their video game or TV privileges doesn't compare as punishment.

"Holly wouldn't be acting like a baby unless something is bothering her. Tell her your concern and see what she says. Probably that's all she needs. There is a Yiddish proverb that a wise man hears one word and understands two:"

I tried to follow his advice but wasn't sure how to open the subject, having learned through my earlier communication mistakes with Holly that kids are much more than short adults.

Holly lay on her bed reading a Nancy Drew. She studiously avoided looking at me as I entered. After seating myself on her bed I said that I wondered if she was feeling alone and afraid. Suddenly my task didn't seem so foreign for I had lived with the same emotions for much of my early life. I continued improvising and hoped for the best.

"I never told you but I grew up in an orphanage." Then, thinking that she might not know the meaning of the word, I asked, "Do you know what an orphanage is?"

She said "no" without looking up from her book.

"It's where children live who don't have parents."

Now she looked directly at me. "Every child has parents. What happened to yours?"

Like most English people I feel that speaking about emotional things is taboo. We tend to use wit in its place. So it wasn't surprising that, before replying, I remembered an Oscar Wilde quotation: to lose one parent is a misfortune but losing both reflects carelessness.

"They died in an auto accident when I was two. They were only children and I didn't have any relatives. When people thought of adopting me I would behave so badly that no one would take me. I lived in the orphanage until I went to university."

"What did you do that was so bad?"

"I punched holes in walls with my fist when I got mad. Or stranger things, like painting a toilet seat black with shoe polish. When I got older I took televisions and speaker systems apart to see how they worked. I did manage to get them operating again. So you can understand why families were afraid to have me live with them."

But Holly didn't respond to my self-disclosure with her own. When I stopped talking, she returned to her reading. I watched for a minute and then asked if she would like to play a game. She agreed and we played Chutes and Ladders, a children's board game in which figures climb up ladders or fall down chutes depending on where they landed after throwing dice. The pictures on the squares indicate whether they behaved badly or well, like by reading a comic instead of doing homework. Holly didn't speak again until she was within several moves of winning.

"I had a dream this morning."

"What was it about?"

"Daddy. He put something in a box and said I'd get a prize when I found it: 'a five by five kite.' He looked sad. He said I would see him before my birthday. I started crying and woke up."

I caught my breath. "When is your birthday?"

"November twenty fourth. I'll be eleven."

No wonder the dream upset her, I thought. It predicted her death—at the end of the same three weeks we were promised by the murderers!

After leaving Holly to her homework, I retrieved the pistol from my luggage though wondering what good it would do. At the range my hand shook so badly that I would often miss not only the target but its larger cardboard backing. I consoled myself with the thought that most defensive shooting is at shorter distances than the fifty feet of the range.

Then I did what the psychiatrist suggested whenever a puzzling thought or feeling arose: to lay down and wonder about it. Why did my fear of guns persist? Were its purpose to remove me from the military and into a new career, this was long since accomplished. If the doctor was right, there *had* to be another motive—a realization or change which my mind was trying to force. But despite my long minutes of meditation, no reason arose. Which made it increasingly likely that I'd soon be dead, perhaps even before Holly's birthday. Along with her, Pat, and maybe her parents too. Then, since the doctor's recommendation hadn't worked, I confronted my fear directly.

The pistol I stole from the island cottage was a .380 caliber Colt dating back to the nineteen thirties. It was well cared for and showed no rust. The trigger, hammer, and slide functioned smoothly. But the weapon was drastically underpowered, better suited for decorative display than self-defense. Still, maybe I could use it to treat my phobia.

I opened my suitcase and reached into the zippered compartment. With each deliberate movement during which my anxiety didn't appear I felt increasing confidence. I lifted the gun and removed its magazine. Still no fear. It was gone, I assured myself. I was worrying unnecessarily.

I aimed the unloaded weapon at a painting on the wall: towards the head of a soldier who was slashing his sword at a fleeing American revolutionary. *Slowly,* I squeezed the trigger, seeking to place an imaginary bullet in my target. Then it began.

My hand shook, I felt nauseous, and worries that I was having a heart attack entered my mind. These experiences engulfed me even as I tried to convince myself that I was in good health and experiencing only anxiety, which could mimic virtually any medical symptom. But it was no good. My thinking had by now shifted so entirely from the gun to my health that to shoot while in this condition might make me a greater danger than any assailant.

I replaced the gun in the suitcase. Within moments my worry disappeared, so completely that it was as if it never existed.

I lay on the bed and wondered what to try next, staring at the English soldier in the painting. His vibrant confidence reflected mine of years before. Then I gazed out the window at the darkening sky and waited for inspiration to strike. Until, as even endangered sentries sometimes do but won't admit, I fell asleep.

Chapter 43

The bedroom was dark. Sometime during the previous hours Pat had lain beside me. I watched her breathe, put my arm about her, and snuggled close. We both dozed. When I awoke for the second time I felt better—until I remembered. Hasan and his spies who watched and waited. And the lifeless bodies of Holly's mother, father, and brother. My expression must have communicated my change of mood for Pat began caressing my forehead.

"You look like a child when you sleep. Then you wake an old man," she said.

"I am an old man."

"We're both getting old but at least we're healthy. Not like my father with multiple sclerosis."

For the moment my thinking shifted.

"Do you worry about getting it?"

"Sometimes. I'm fatalistic," she admitted with a shrug. "MS runs in the family. My aunt got it when she was twenty four. Not as badly as my father: she doesn't yet need a wheelchair. But has been briefly blind with slurred speech. Once she couldn't feel anything in her hand and the next day it burned and itched. We have much to be thankful for."

"Even with terrorists and the police after us?"

"Let me help. You're so intent on being the super soldier—which maybe you once were—that you won't let me. It's not just you and Holly but me too. Even with people hungering to kill us, our relationship is the best I've ever had and I'm not losing it to anyone!"

What should a man say when he's told this by the woman he loves? I didn't know so I just held her tighter and thanked The Good Lord, who watches over everyone including agnostics like me, for bringing Pat into my life.

Now I began to really listen to her. Like other bright people I was often accused of asking questions but paying little attention to the reply. Whether my change resulted from our desperate situation or my having found love I can't say. But I did change and, even during what I considered to be our final days alive, I felt less bleak. Maybe also because I told Pat some of my secrets and speaking about these can be healing.

Everyone had experiences they're ashamed to admit. Children's may consist of stealing, teenagers obsess over betrayed friendships, and adults fume about adultery. With me, it was what my fear of intimacy and guns had produced, though the latter was something which many mothers might wish their sons to suffer from. But this symptom had destroyed my self-confidence by ripping me from my military family and pushing me back into my solitary life.

So the secrets I shared with Pat might not seem sordid to others: being afraid of guns and only a little less of intimacy. But they loomed large for me and, after revealing them, I seemed to have greater energy. Now *we*, not just *I*, got down to the work of saving our lives.

"And maybe freedom too," the colonel whispered, as if he couldn't contain this thought.

"Yes, that too," I agreed in a softer tone, before continuing my story.

Pat suggested that we start by dealing with what we could control and not worry about the rest. That the key to our salvation still seemed the coded message. I agreed, adding that a crippled soldier couldn't be much protection. But like most women, Pat wasn't into guns. I'd have to work on that fear alone.

Having earlier decoded six of the message's letters, Pat bore down on its second line and obtained the following:

"____lo_____o_____l_____o__ _o _____o_____ o'_____.""

"Let's assume that _o is *to* and see where it gets us," Pat said. Her guess caused the second line to be interpreted as:

"_____o_____o__ht_h_____t_o__ to _____o_t____ o'_____ _____.""

"That's not much better," I said in a disappointed tone.

"If you added your energy maybe things would go more quickly," Pat replied with annoyance. She was right. I was letting her do the work yet complaining about the results. Like a typical husband, I thought..

"Let's go out of sequence and try the sixth line," I suggested. This resulted in:

"Th_t_____o___y _h__h _o_____t o___to _____, _____H_____o_____-___th.""

"The first word is probably *that*. Let's assume that *a* is eleven and try it on line three." We did.

"Yo_n____t_a_____t__o_t____tan__,"_a__th____ _o_____nd. "_tay__an__oo_ _o_th_t_n,""

This gave us another letter, the blank following *th* likely being *e*. So fifty one was *e*.

I felt irritated. "This is terribly slow, There must be a quicker way. Holly's parents couldn't have expected that she'd have the patience to do what we're doing even if she is a genius."

"Did she say anything which might be a clue? A hint they gave her."

I told Pat of Holly's dream in which her father promised her a "5x5 kite."

"That's an odd measurement for a kite. In inches it would be tiny and in feet far too large," she observed. Then she playfully hit the side of her head with the heel of her hand.

"Of course," she exclaimed. "Holly remembered something using the symbolism of dreams. The five by five kite is the five by five grid matrix which one of her parents must have mentioned. Five boxes long and five wide, making twenty-five boxes in all. It's a code used by children and has the numbers 1 through 5 on top and on the left side, while in the boxes beginning at the left are the letters A through E in the first row, F through J in the second, K through O in the third, P through T in the fourth, and U through Y in the last line. Z is an infrequently used letter and skipped."

Using her insight, our deciphering was completed in minutes. While driving Holly to school, the lines of her parents' message ran through my mind.

Holly,

"Only forty two am I", said the gaunt physicist, though his wrinkles belied his age,

"And long I sought these priceless equations to gain fortune o'er my final days."

"You need travel but short distance," said the beloved webbed friend. "Stay and look for the tin,"

"To enable the gift as it surely will, and forgiveness for any sin.

"Do not with youthful impulse leave, to seek in the great universe,

"That discovery which comes but once to each, even were Heaven generous with re-birth."

So find these formulae I hide first with the ring, and at this I bid thee farewell,

With the hope you will gain through less arduous path, my secret how atoms may together dwell.

The poem's meaning was clear. Her parents' scientific discovery was hidden and it was Holly's task to find it. Following which she would be given a prize and forgiveness for any misdeeds. The pages might be in a tin box, not far from the house on the island where they were staying. Exactly where the container was or what the ring referred to, I didn't know. Yet her parents must have believed that the cryptic elements of their message would be clear to Holly. They wanted to encourage her interest in science, not destroy it through frustration.

Chapter 44

"Did your parents ever talk to you about a ring?" I asked Holly, as we drove to her school.

There was a long pause. Perhaps from her sadness over their loss, or her uncertainty how to answer my question Not knowing why, I expanded on it.

"Maybe a ring you wear. A key ring, or a group of friends. Even a Web ring: that's where people come together over the Internet to share their interests."

"No," she responded quickly. But her answer seemed to reflect only moodiness.

Our car passed slowly up Greenwich Avenue. Mothers who had earlier dropped off their children at school were now shopping. When we reached the hardware store near the top of the street, Holly spoke again.

"Captain Midnight," she said, as if her words were apropos of nothing.

"Who?"

"Captain Midnight—an old TV show. You got a decoder ring after mailing in Ovaltine jar tops to join his Secret Squadron. He sent hidden messages which you could understand using his Code-a-Graph. The ring had a number telling which word was important."

I felt as if I had stopped breathing "Do you remember what number was on your ring?"

This question she answered immediately. "Thirty-nine."

My mind counted the words in the riddle. The thirty-ninth was "webbed."

"Does the word 'webbed' mean anything to you?"

Now her cooperative attitude vanished. "No," she said abruptly, looking out the side window and locking out my presence.

I drove to the school's rear parking lot to give us more time together. After I turned off the engine she remained seated, as if she were paralyzed. After waiting for her to unlatch her seat belt, I sensed that she wanted me to do it for her and did, though she could easily do it for herself. So I free-associated about her puzzling behavior, as the military psychiatrist had told me to do with mine. Then I sensed that by acting dependently Holly was trying to return psychologically to that happier period of her life before her family's murder.

Instinctively, I held her hand as we walked to the school. Most children her age would resist this public display of affection, afraid of being mocked by their peers. She didn't. My conclusion about her feelings is probably accurate, I thought.

I wasn't the slightest bit perceptive about feelings until two months ago, I thought. Did this healthy change derive from my experience with Holly? Pat? Her father? I smiled. Maybe it was the angel, I thought, and smiled more broadly.

Chapter 45

I changed my routine that day by cutting short my unproductive study in the library. Instead, while awaiting Holly's dismissal from school, I went to Greenwich's only firearms merchant, being determined to remove or at least to reduce my fear of guns,

Many people hold erroneous ideas about gun stores, which are just retail establishments like any other. And despite popular fantasy, they are uninhabited by illiterates wearing National Rifle Association logo on their underwear.

This shop was at the basement level of a drug store and reached by walking down a flight of stairs. Few would have expected the clerk I faced: a freckled-faced, red haired mother in her thirties whose toddlers wandered about the thickly carpeted floor. One clutched a large ring of her mother's keys. The second chased her older sister down the empty aisles. Here, no cheap "Saturday Night Specials" were sold. The lowest priced new weapon cost upwards of four hundred dollars though used ones were available for two hundred dollars less.

The clerk's fashion statement was a holstered Colt Model 1911 .45 caliber semi-automatic pistol, the preferred American military sidearm for most of the twentieth century. If she wasn't the store's owner, her knowledge of guns would have warranted hiring her.

"Can I help you?" she asked, looking torn between wanting to quiet her children but possibly losing an expensive sale.

I didn't want to state my real reason for being there: that I was afraid of guns and trying to acclimate myself to them. She wasn't running a mental health clinic. To give myself time to think of an excuse, I nodded in the direction of her children.

"Your daughters are cute. How old are they?"

"Three, four, and nearly five."

"It's good to see children in a gun store. Makes the sport seem a family activity, not one of crazed shooters whose exploits are widely publicized."

"That's another reason I keep them here—they probably make more sales than I do. Also, the cost of full-time day care in Greenwich. A thousand dollars a month per child, *plus* the cost of lunches and snacks. Paid with credit card, no checks. I guess they've been burned like we have."

"Does the owner object," I asked.

"I'm the owner. The druggist upstairs is my *husband*." She emphasized this to indicate her lack of interest in a romance.

I wasn't yet ready to explain my reason for being there and continued our chat. She seemed to welcome the diversion: except for us and her children the store was empty.

"How did you come to open a gun shop."

"Because I'm a woman, you mean? I have an MBA from Columbia. In my past life I did market research on consumer products: toilet paper, disposable diapers, even cars. When we decided that I should be a stay-at-home mom, I studied what was needed in town. A female neighbor spoke of being put-down at a suburban gun shop. They treated women customers there as badly as do some auto dealers though women buy fifty three percent of new cars and hold a ninety five percent veto power over all car purchases. I know—I did that study.

"There were plenty of places in Greenwich to buy clothes and food. A gas station with personalized service was a possibility but I couldn't get enthusiastic about washing car windows which would be the only way to distinguish my station from the self-service ones. So I studied the sale of guns.

"Surprisingly, women were frightened and had become gun buyers. There were recent rapes and a half-way house for paroled sex offenders was opened just across the border in New York. Many of their husbands work long hours on Wall Street or at Greenwich's financial center along the waterfront and they wanted to be able to defend their family alone. This isn't easy since women tend to be nurturing and non-assertive.

"That's where my shop comes in. We specialize in selling guns to women and help them to get over their fears. Our classes are free to customers and held during the day when children are in school. Look around. Does it *seem* like a typical gun store?"

It certainly didn't. Not that some, particularly the newer ones, aren't spacious. But none I saw were painted in such bright colors or had Marimekko throw rugs hung on the walls. Beside copies of prints which I last saw at the Austrian/German Institute on New York City's Fifth Avenue.

I didn't know why I believed that she could help me. Maybe because women tend to be more empathetic than men or she helped others to get over their fear of guns. But I felt comfortable enough to explain my situation, though what I told her certainly wasn't the whole truth.

"I think you can help me with my problem. We live in a deserted part of town: my wife, our daughter, and her elderly parents. I grew up in England. Shooting isn't a common sport there and I feel uneasy about it..

"Could I take your course without buying a gun just yet? I'd be happy to give a non-refundable deposit on a future purchase." I didn't add that, because firearms sales had to be cleared through the government's database, there was no way I could buy a gun from her.

She readily agreed and, with courteous reluctance, accepted two-one hundred dollar bills.

I felt better when I left the shop and that I was now beginning to fight against the danger which enveloped our lives.

It seemed ironic that, after living in the predominantly male worlds of orphanage and military, most of those now helping me were women: Pat, this proprietor/instructor. Even Holly's angel who had come to her aid when she was desperate.

I smiled as I spoke of Holly's fantasy and expected the colonel's similar reaction. But he wasn't smiling. Nor was the soldier at the foot of the bed whose forearm tattoos I noticed for the first time. Below the "meat tag," a permanent dog tag inked prior to overseas deployment, was a popular Middle East symbol: the hamesh hand or Hand of Fatima. It is also known as the Hand of God.

Chapter 46

I often spoke with other parents while awaiting Holly at the school's front door. But this was dangerous, as the wanted poster at the Post Office continually reminded me when I did errands there for Patience. My face in that picture had a clean-shaved, fuller appearance, but my size and accent weren't disguised by my new beard. Still, I enjoyed the innocent warmth of my conversations with parents, which contrasted with Holly's foul mood that afternoon.

Though answering my questions, her responses were single words in a barely civil tone—when she wasn't glaring. Whether there had been some unpleasantness at school or an upsetting dream the previous night I never learned for she disappeared into her room as soon as we arrived home. Pat being out, I joined Cedric in the book lined room which he called his library and Pat described as her former bedroom.

Instead of the ancient L-Z-Boy rocker which he preferred, Cedric now lay on a black leather couch. It was purchased cheaply from a local psychiatrist who decided he could make more money prescribing drugs than doing talk therapy.

I sat on the recliner and tried to relax as my feet rose. A thickening silence enveloped us until Cedric put down his book and turned in my direction.

"Where's Holly?"

"In her room, feeling disgusted with the world and me. Today, maybe even with you." Though of all the people in this house, Holly seemed most comfortable with him.

"Reverence is owed to a child."

"I'm too old for religion to sink in," My annoyance surprised me for I was usually tolerant with older people. Particularly those like Cedric who dealt courageously with their infirmities. 'It's mostly dominated by women," I added.

"That's true," he said equably. "The typical congregation is more than sixty percent female and women make up most of the employees and volunteers. Why, isn't hard to figure out. Many churches are sentimental and nurturing and men feel more comfortable with solemnity and ritual. Wanting spiritual rigor, not 'therapizing.' So traditional churches have more male members and others become spiritual sorority houses. Incidentally, my phrase about reverence being owed to a child doesn't come from the Bible. It's a Chinese proverb.

"But what *is* wrong with religion? It's been my life's work and if I've wasted so many years I would like to know before it's too late."

Now I backtracked. Cedric was far too nice a guy to hurt.

"I'm sorry—it's my mood today too. Apart from the little religion that was forced into me as a child I know nothing about it."

"More the reason for you to criticize and me to respond—to learn from each other."

Then, maybe because of the fragility of my life and that of those I loved, I did want to discuss religion. For unlike science, it deals with such questions as the evil which prompts murder. Perhaps I had been half in love with that which I rebelled against, I thought.

Cedric's nearly unbearable, unscratchable itch, a common symptom of multiple sclerosis, had recently returned But his eyes shone as he spoke and I remember our hours together as being a special experience.

"Religion can have a unique meaning today. Helping people cope with terror and dread, and the despair which pain produces." He gestured limply with his hand toward his body. I averted my eyes as his face contorted. To help get his mind off his pain, I asked the deepest question about religion I could think of.

"Why religion when there are other philosophies of life. Scientific objectivity, or the teachings of Plato or Sophocles."

My question succeeded. Cedric's face brightened as he shifted his body on the pillows and resumed speaking.

"My father was a minister so I had religion crammed down my throat. Not only scripture but the family's worry about what parishioners might think. A parish is a family operated business and, though every religion teaches that people are imperfect, congregations never seem to relate this fact to their leader.

"So before becoming a minister I had to prune much in my own unconscious. Including such prickly thoughts as why bother when I could get a better paying job with fewer hours working as an accountant. If I was brighter I might even have become a scientist like you," he added, with a self-deprecating smile.

"I also asked myself your basic question of why religion. Until I realized it is because religion concerns itself with the meaning of life with all other issues being secondary. There are other belief systems. Communism or fascism had similar elements but grave distortions, being radicalizations in which social and national concerns were granted ultimate importance. Mottoes like 'classless society' and 'thousand year Reich' gave these movements a pseudo-religious character, raising their far-fetched goals above individual concerns, substituting a philosophy for the individual conscience and making their horrific acts possible, even desirable.

"These 'isms' colored our lives. Now radical Islamic fascism is most prevalent but there are other totalitarian ideologies. All are dangerous because their power derives from their similarity to true religions: identification with a group and belief in a Utopian future.

"These are akin to the normal consciousness of nations. Ancient Rome represented universal law, and Great Britain the spread of Christian humanism. Governments are created to fulfill their citizens' needs but require a transcendent value to survive. If lacking, the regime may become demonic as occurred with Nazi Germany, where Hitler united power with the salvation myth of the Nordic race."

Inadvertently I yawned. What Cedric said was fascinating but I couldn't see how it related to my situation.

"What does all this have to do with terrorism?" I asked.

"Coping with multiple sclerosis teaches patience though there are better ways to gain it. I must miss the built-in audience of a pulpit." Then he smiled and made a pun, "And now I have one."

"Terrorism is the true Satanism," he concluded, "for it combines the desire for absolute power with myth, simplified laws, and the mere pretense of justice."

Chapter 47

After driving Holly to school the next day, I went to join my fellow members of the Greenwich Woman's Pistol Familiarization Course. To lower my anxiety at being its sole male member, I arrived early at the drug store and scanned news magazines. An "Insider" column sent my heart racing. I stopped fearing the women.

Ransom Note Received

An official source who must remain anonymous informed us that a letter demanding two million dollars for the safe return of the missing Dellum family was received by the research firm where the parents are major shareholders. They are also noted physicists of the Massachusetts Institute of Technology.

The rest of the article summarized previously published information about the Dellums and the vacation home from which they were allegedly abducted. My eyes froze on another detail: the fingerprints found on the ransom note were *mine*.

For a shy scientist I'm certainly getting publicity, I thought, as I carefully smoothed the cover of the magazine before replacing it on the rack. The Greenwich police had recently arrested a child for cursing, terming it "third degree verbal assault." Who knew how they might charge an adult for soiling a magazine.

I was surprised at Holly's local tragedy being given national space, old news that it was. Even if the events in her life *were* sensational. A family gone missing from a resort island; military secrets; the blood stained fingerprints of a foreign scientist. Who stood trembling before entering a woman's group. I waited until several members arrived, then steeled myself and followed them downstairs to the gun shop.

On its closed door was an orange arrow pointing down the corridor to another door. Inside was a fifty foot pistol range. The snack tray and coffee urn on a corner table strengthened my long held expectation of refreshments being better at meetings run by women. A role which is forced on them by the frequent casual interest of men in maintaining life's necessities.

The instructor/store's co-owner being nowhere in sight, I introduced myself to a petite blond. An angel with flawless skin, pale pink lipstick and nail polish; dressed in a black leather, mid-thigh length skirt and strapless gray top. I felt like picking her up and taking her home—until I remembered the engagement rings which Pat and I bought after we began having sex again. So I just introduced myself to this vision of loveliness. She already knew me.

"You're the brave Englishman," she said with a smile. "Laura mentioned you. The only man in our class."

"I am nervous, but more about shooting," I replied. Then, whether because she seemed so easy to talk to or from my need for support, I spoke openly of my difficulty.

"I'm afraid of guns. I wasn't always but for the past few years my hand shakes and I get nauseous when I hold one. I thought the class would help. Not to learn how to shoot which I already know, but to get comfortable with it."

"That's why we're here too," she said, touching my shoulder. "A year ago I was mugged at knife point in San Francisco. By wannabe or real gang members while sitting on the stoop with my girl-friend. They only got thirty four dollars from the both of us but it's scary having whether you live or die depend on the whims of others. It *so* frightened us that we moved back East though muggings happen everywhere. Afterward we vowed to never again be helpless and joined the Pink Pistols."

"What's that?" I had never heard of this organization.

"A self-defense group of lesbians and gays who are dedicated to Second Amendment Rights. Their motto is 'Armed Gays Don't Get Bashed.' Having a pistol would have made us feel safer and had we shown and been prepared to use it we likely wouldn't have been robbed or experience whatever warped plan their minds could conceive. I'm bisexual," she added in a matter-of-fact tone. "I was married but now prefer women. They're really more beautiful."

I felt that these nuggets of information would have been more appropriate at our second meeting but was glad that we spoke. I felt less tense.

My first class of the Assertive Woman's Firearms League (AWFUL being the humorous acronym by which they described themselves) soon began. Six of the other seven students were in their thirties or forties, one was about ten years older. All were expensively dressed. I can't tell a Menichetti from a Calvin Klein but do know when clothes cost a lot, having learned this earlier from Julia and later from the comments and gasps of Pat as we passed Greenwich shop windows.

While snacking on outstanding coffee and chocolate brioche, we listened to Laura's instruction. The difference between revolvers and semi-automatic pistols. That it was illegal to shoot a fleeing robber. And, most importantly she insisted, the need, whenever possible, to avoid shooting anyone lest we spend years communing with an expensive attorney.

Considering my extensive firearms background, I expected to find the class boring. Instead, I became so involved that I temporarily forgot my fear of guns. My previous classes were military and in Great Britain so I knew nothing about the permitted civilian use of deadly force in America.

After lecturing for a half-hour, Laura joined us for coffee and was asked a personal question. "Do you carry a gun when you're away from the store?" In response, she removed from her jacket pocket the smallest pistol I ever saw.

"It's a 9mm Kahr PM9 with a black polymer frame and matte stainless steel slide. It comes with two magazines, each holding six or seven rounds. The larger is a little longer so you can wrap your pinky around it. The gun is only four inches high, a little over five inches long, and under an inch in width. It weighs less than seventeen ounces unloaded and fires the first shot double-action. What does that mean? Why is this an important feature in a semi-automatic pistol?"

All hands except mine shot up: I still felt nervous at being the only male present. After receiving the correct answers, Laura responded to another question before she ended our break: why she carried so small a pistol.

"If a gun is heavy you'll always find reasons not to carry it and a gun in your drawer at home can't protect you elsewhere. And so long as your assailant believes that you're unarmed you have an advantage.

"I was trained by a former police instructor who carried a much smaller pistol: a two shot .22 caliber derringer which would fit in the palm of the smallest hand here. He carried this gun because, 'during a robbery the cop gets shot first!'"

We spent the rest of the class practicing loading and unloading a revolver and a semi-automatic pistol which were passed around. Laura first demonstrated and then had each student repeat the procedure while the rest of us watched. I was last and despite my military training she followed the same routine with me. Laura spoke of the awkwardness of learning a new skill: "remember how hard it was the first time you inserted a tampon." After laughs and embarrassed smiles in my direction, I accepted Laura's apology with good grace.

Before dismissing us, she reminded the women to bring their newly purchased pistols to the next class, when they would be shooting at a realistic target: a mugger who looked exactly like me! I joined in the group's laughter, her comment being far less caustic than the male chauvinist comments I heard throughout my life. Her understanding squeeze of my hand helped and she whispered that I should remain when the others left. The women sauntered slowly from the range, seeming entranced by their newly found power and being reluctant to leave.

"How do you feel?" Laura asked, after the last student left the room.

"A little better. I don't know how I'll do at the next session: my hand shook when I loaded the gun."

"I noticed your tension. That's why I made my tampon remark though it was meant for the others too."

"It was OK. I felt more comfortable than I expected. They tolerated my inadequacy better than most men would."

During the silence which followed, I felt that Laura was deciding what to say. To make her pause seem natural, she offered me more coffee and the remnants of the biscuits.

"Alison told me about your fear of guns. Many woman fear guns too. They resist being strong and assertive which a gun can symbolize. It also enables them to defend themselves and not have to rely on a man. Some women fantasize how their life would change if they were a man. Being able to walk down the street without averting their eyes when someone stares, and not having rude comments made about their body. But to be powerful conflicts with their major role of being a nurturer. These issues can't underlie your fear of guns. When did it begin for you?"

I considered how much to tell her until concluding that, if my information were suitably disguised, she still wouldn't know who I was and might even help solve my problem. Certainly my insights and those of the military psychiatrist hadn't. Perhaps a maternal gun expert's could.

"It started while I was in the military. After I shot some terrorists before they killed others."

It was promising that Laura didn't respond immediately. She seemed the type of person who didn't speak unless they had something meaningful to say. I awaited her comment expectantly. She looked away and shook her head, as if trying to clear her mind. "Were you ever afraid when you were in the military?"

"A little anxious when I learned something new. Like how to disassemble a weapon or use a parachute. But I never felt fear even in combat. I followed the procedures we learned which is what good training makes possible."

Now that same triumphant glint appeared in Laura's eyes which would appear in the military psychiatrist's: before he informed me of an interpretation.

"The military is a dangerous place," she began. "I think you had been afraid for a long time but until that moment of great danger when you battled the terrorists, you managed to avoid awareness of your underlying fear. Afterward, this long buried emotion burst through and produced your phobia.

"It sounds like what happened to my father. He once supervised window washers in skyscrapers and was never afraid of heights. One day, when he was high up in Manhattan's Municipal Building,, he saw an employee outside a window with his safety harness unfastened. My father froze and couldn't move. When he regained control, he motioned the man to come in and fired him. Then my father quit his job and got another doing repairs in an apartment development. He never could tolerate heights again, not even to climb a three foot step-ladder. This made no sense to me until I took an abnormal psychology class in college and asked the teacher about it. He described my father's behavior as being a classic counter-phobic reaction: doing what you most fear in order to try to master it.

"Maybe it was something like that with you too. You were always frightened and joined the army to overcome it. While there, you operated on automatic pilot until the incident with the terrorists. Then your anxiety broke through and became symbolized in your fear of guns."

Her words percolated through my mind. When I finally did react, I burst out laughing. Laura became angry.

"I'm sorry," I apologized. "I'm not laughing at you. Your explanation was unexpected yet feels so right that it makes excellent sense. Like they say, it takes a woman though I don't mean this in a disparaging way."

"I know you don't and hope that what I said helps. But even if my interpretation was correct, it doesn't mean that your fear is now gone. The mind is conservative and allows itself to change only slowly."

"But why did my fear begin after I shot the terrorists? Why not a year earlier?"

"Maybe then you weren't ready to cope with your underlying conflict. That's what my psychology teacher replied when I asked him the same question about my father," she added with a gentle smile.

I felt much better after leaving Laura. Though a layman, she turned out to be a more than adequate therapist for my problem. While driving home I concentrated on her interpretation: that I joined the military to change my basically fearful nature. Then, after becoming an authentic hero, this emotion broke through to force my change into a scientific career for which I was better suited. Though there are bright scholarly soldiers, they have an important quality which I always lacked: an authentic interest in military matters.

I once read about a sportswriter who hated sports. During a fishing trip, he tried to join in the male camaraderie by telling a football story with feigned enthusiasm. Then another in the group, a celebrated prizefighter, questioned him: "You have no real interest in sports. Why pretend?"

I was never asked a similar question in the military for most soldiers aren't as perceptive as was the boxer. But it would have found me more speechless than the sports writer whose pretense was probably essential to keeping his well-paying job. I would have made much more money in a non-military career.

While driving home, I felt that I had regained my stamina. Like the military psychiatrist told me: it takes a lot of energy to keep feelings buried and much power is freed when this is no longer necessary.

Chapter 48

Everyone was happier that evening. Holly did her homework without prodding and later helped Pat to wash the dishes. This was virtually the first cooperation which Holly had showed her since we arrived in Greenwich. Patience joked as she bustled about the kitchen, pleased that Cedric's multiple sclerosis symptoms had lifted and he didn't require his wheelchair that evening.

"What should we drink to?" Cedric asked at the dinner table, raising his glass of pomegranate juice, the current health food rage. Its high antioxidant level allegedly reduced the level of free radicals in the blood leading to optimal health.

"What?" Cedric repeated, extending his glass in Holly's direction. Her face stiffened, she hesitated, and I feared that she was about to repeat one of her recent nasty remarks. But after peering into a corner of the room, Holly's face relaxed and she spoke in a sure, clear voice, unlike the whining tone we endured in recent days.

"To God, who will protect this house from evil," she exclaimed.

Her comment surprised all of us except Cedric. Pat's mouth gaped until she slowly touched her glass to her lips. Patience smiled broadly and, after joining in the toast, left her chair to kiss the top of Holly's head. Who accepted this intimacy though she usually recoiled from being touched.

Cedric looked pleased and began one of his theological lectures—to which his wife reacted with barely feigned enthusiasm. Also being a minister, her husband's words perhaps seemed a continuation of their working day. Pat looked annoyed, as do most adults when their parent expounds on a familiar topic and presumes their interest.

"Holly," Cedric spoke softly, as if both were alone and the rest of us merely bearing witness. "You're speaking with the voice of a prophet. Do you know what that is?"

Holly eyes locked onto his. "Like pro-phe-tic? I can read the word but don't know what it means." Then she spontaneously left her chair and leaned against him. Perhaps wanting to sit in his lap like a child but knowing that to do so would cause him pain from his inflamed nerves.

"A prophet is a very good teacher," Cedric answered "Though instead of explaining math and science he advises you how to live your life. There have been many teachers but only a few prophets in human history. Moses was the first.

"He didn't want to be a prophet and even argued with God, who chose him, saying that he wasn't good enough for the job and wouldn't be able to do it. Which was to take a group of Hebrews from the only life they knew, being slaves to the Egyptians, and changing them into free people in their own land. Why do you think this would be hard for Moses to do?"

Holly thought for a moment. "Maybe the Hebrews wouldn't believe him. They'd think he was crazy."

"Right," Cedric boomed, as if he were speaking to an entire auditorium instead of four people. "That is exactly what Moses told God: they ain't gonna believe me and who should I say sent me?" Cedric chuckled and Patience and I smiled. Pat scowled.

"But God didn't make Moses' job easy since He wasn't easy to understand. Like when he said that His 'name is Nameless,' by which he meant that he didn't have a name like ordinary people but instead is *the* God, the creator of action and history.

"Moses argued and argued about how he wouldn't be a good prophet. Just as you sometimes do about helping to wash the dishes" (here Cedric added a smile). "But like most parents, God wouldn't take 'no' for an answer. When Moses said he was a lousy speaker and predicted that people wouldn't listen to him, God answered that his brother, Aaron, who was a good speaker, would go with him and speak for him. Thus God created the idea of a priesthood: Moses would be the prophet with knowledge from God while his brother would be the priest who could explain what God, as he told to Moses, wanted people to know. Which can be dangerous because...?"

I had no idea but Holly did and I was floored by her insight: "A priest who speaks in the name of the prophet might not be telling the truth because they may want to be a prophet themselves."

"Holly, you are an amazing child—a treasure. You are so right. And that's why no person who wants to be a prophet can be a real one because God will only choose a humble person and Moses was 'the most humble of men.'"

This meal, which began like an ordinary family dinner, had inexplicably changed into something very different. I envied the bond between Cedric and Holly and awaited their every word for it seemed they were speaking not only to each other but directly to me. And this scene contained a natural drama of which Cedric and his wife were unaware: that we in this house were defenseless against murderers who watched, and waited.

Cedric continued speaking, though his voice briefly faltered. "God gave Moses the power to make miracles, to convince his people to believe him. When the Hebrews left Egypt the Lord 'went before them by day in a pillar of cloud to lead them along the way, and by night in a pillar of fire.' It must have been quite a sight. But the Egyptians didn't give up easily for they didn't want to lose their slaves. So Moses used one of His great powers: "Moses stretched out his hand over the sea; and the Lord drove the sea back by a strong east wind all night, and made the sea dry land, and the waters were divided. And the people of Israel went into the midst of the sea on dry ground, the waters being a wall to them on their right hand and on their left. The Egyptians pursued, and went in after them into the midst of the sea, all Pharaoh's horses, his chariots, and his horsemen...then the waters returned and covered the chariots and the horsemen.' So the Hebrews were saved from the people who tried to hurt them."

During the ensuing silence I felt as if I were alone in the immense universe. A feeling which continued until Holly asked Cedric, "Why did you become a minister?"

Cedric briefly touched her hair, conscious of her unease at being touched. "Because I was suffering," he replied, in an even but revealing tone. As if her question concerned a painful experience he had tried to forget for many years until the memory finally become his friend. Cedric's voice labored and I sensed the evening's sermon, if that is what it had been, was ending. "We've both suffered. Your mother died and, as for me, I'll tell you about it when you're older. We both had to leave our homes to find new ones."

"If God is so powerful then why does He let people suffer?" Holly asked.

"Because, most of all, God is freedom. That gift which he gives to all of his children. Enabling them to rise above their fate and, through good deeds, become more alive than they were. Leading to the End of Days and coming of the Messiah, when people will have become all that they can be. Suffering hurts yet without it there can be no change. But God understands. We are His children and He hears our cries and sometimes—*sometimes*—He feels stirred towards mercy and sends an angel to help."

While he spoke, Cedric's eyes seemed to glow. Now, he being obviously exhausted, they dimmed. Holly hugged him and I too felt close. As the light from the chandelier momentarily dimmed, the distance between us seemed to shrink and his words throbbed within me.

The brightening of the chandelier broke the spell. With this we changed back— into the usual. Holly, quiet, isolated herself fitfully in her chair. Patience fidgeted about the plates of food which Pat merely played with. But, oddly, my terror had disappeared even as I tried to reject the only explanation which entered my mind. That, perhaps just temporarily, Cedric had managed to convince even as irreligious a person as me that the Heavens would protect us.

Chapter 49

Though math and science were easy for Holly, her spelling tended to be erratic. A problem, she informed me, which had long existed. This was blamed by her parents on the modern educational philosophy which fostered inadequate structure in Holly's private school education.

Her previous school originated one hundred and twenty years earlier, as a Congregational establishment to educate women. In the nineteen fifties a Montessori preschool and boys were added, along with an entrance exam which eliminated all applicants except for children in the upper two percent of the intelligence population, those scoring an IQ above 130. Here, children didn't fight or use drugs, courses like Chinese and calculus were routine, and many students (including Holly) voluntarily worked on personal projects for hours after the school day officially ended. Her mother appreciated the school but recognized its flaws. "She said my spelling would always be creative," Holly added, after sharing examples of these one evening.

"The Jews were a proud people and had trouble with unsympathetic genitals."

"The seventh commandment forbids admitting adultery."

"Those with only one spouse are called monotonous."

So most of the help I gave to Holly was with her grammar and spelling which, despite my own scientific leaning,,had been drilled into me at an early age.

When we were done one evening, Holly went to her room to read an old book which her school principal gave her, a classic which had been discarded by the Greenwich library during its yearly sale. It contained illustrated stories about a mythical American family, the Peterkins. The author, Lucretia Peabody Hale, had never married, and came from a noted American family. Her seven brothers and sisters included a cleric and the author of *A Man Without A Country*; the Consul General to Egypt at the time of the opening of the Suez Canal; and one of the first females to travel the world alone and then write of her adventures.

First published in the eighteen sixties, these stories gained a wide popularity because they mocked the stifling aspects of Victorian culture and enabled Americans to laugh at themselves. In each story the Peterkins struggle helplessly with common family problems: what to do when salt rather than sugar is placed in tea; the difficulty in moving a newly purchased piano indoors; how to get their horse to move—until a stranger suggests they untie him from the hitching post.

I understood why these stories attracted Holly. The confusion endured by the fictional Peterkins might well have described her own feelings. Besides which every story had a happy ending. Each problem was ultimately resolved—by The Lady From Philadelphia whose fresh and clear insight always saved the day.

Holly particularly enjoyed one story, "The Peterkins Snowed-Up." In this tale, much as we had been, the Peterkin family awoke to find themselves isolated. The water pipes and milk were frozen and high snow drifts made leaving the house impossible. Their food and coal were nearly gone and, after a breakfast of ice cream and coffee, they entertained such ideas as chopping a new, unblocked door in the side of the house, and slaughtering their pet pig for food. Until they heard a voice behind them: that of the butcher who was making his delivery and had entered the house through the side door. He had been unheard because of the noise which the family was making. He said that the storm ended a half-hour earlier, the road was now clear, and other deliveries would also be as usual.

Implied in this story was that if the family had just slept late they could have saved themselves from unnecessary worry. Or, I thought, frightened people sometimes become so confused that they miss critical information.

Chapter 50

Recent events—the gun instructor's explanation of my phobia, Cedric's religious comments, Holly's belief in aid from spiritual forces—motivated me to act. I shared my plans with Pat.

"It'll take at least a week for us to get away. Check maps and find somewhere close enough to drive. My financial accounts were frozen. I hate to ask but how much money can you lay your hands on?"

"Enough," she said, putting her arms affectionately about my neck. "We're together and that means sharing the good *and* the bad. I can draw electronically from my brokerage account. Can I help with anything else?"

I thought for a moment. We would be vulnerable until we left. But less if the doors and windows had the security they should. Which meant putting dead bolt locks on the doors and steel pins through the window frames to prevent the windows from being opened. I could also install a wireless alarm onto each. These were now widely available in hardware stores. "Tell your dad that you've read about a rash of burglaries to explain the security improvements I want to make. Considering his recent frailty, I can't imagine him refusing. Don't say that."

"I can still be tactful with my parents. I'll say that even God expects people to help themselves—and without the acid tone which he'd expect from me."

"Like during dinner."

"It wasn't very different from many who grow up in a clergyman's family," she shrugged, "except that *both* my parents were clergy so I always had them and *two* sets of parishioners watching us. When I was older I got as far away from religion as I could. That's why dad so cherishes Holly. If she came years ago he would have traded both his kids for her."

I knew she was joking. It was clear from the way her parents related that concern for the welfare of their children was central to their existence. I still wondered what yet unspoken childhood experiences had created Pat's deep anger and resentment.

Despite these feelings, Pat prepared the ground so well that, when I suggested improving the house's security, Cedric readily agreed. Adding, with sly humor, that "neighbors might interpret this as reflecting a spiritual crisis: my distrust of God to protect us from evil."

Wanting to make a congenial response, I said, simplistically, "people can behave like animals." This led to another of his lucid sermons.

"That's not true, " he began, "for evil is a specifically human experience. Animals lack consciousness and so cannot be evil. God's compassion is based on his awareness of man's tendency towards both good and evil. After the flood—you *do* know about that don't you?" he asked, tempering his reference to my spiritual ignorance with a comic tone.

"Noah?" I offered.

"Excellent!. After He destroyed the world the Lord told Himself, 'I will never again curse the ground because of man, for the imagination of man's heart is evil from his youth; neither will I ever again destroy every living creature as I have done.' In the Book of Genesis if you want to read further.

"Man has an evil impulse for which the Bible uses the Hebrew word *yetzer*. But this word can refer to both evil and good feelings, *yetzer ha-ra* and *yetzer tov*. What results depends on the human imagination. Good thoughts can reduce one's tendency toward evil, and there is a basic capacity for good. Thus people have the ability to choose: 'the crooked will become straight....though your sins are like scarlet, they shall be as white as snow.'"

I was intrigued by Cedric's perspective. "Then why are some people evil?" I asked, having a more than theoretical interest in this subject. "Surely knowing that its outcome is disaster they would choose otherwise."

"Because their hearts have hardened," he explained. "Why did Pharaoh continually seek to enslave the Hebrews though being repeatedly warned that it would lead to his destruction. Because his heart had hardened and he no longer had the freedom to choose. A remedy which God could provide but did not. To return to the topic of our dinner conversation, this is why we need prophets: to steer people into making wise decisions. Which they may choose not to. Some people are lost to the point of no return and God does not interfere.

"A few people are free of evil impulses but most have good and evil tendencies though some are controlled by evil. *Facilis descensus Averni est.* The descent into Hell is easy.

"Nations can be evil too. If the merit of its citizens outweighs their sin, that country is righteous. If evil predominates, the nation is wicked. But only the Lord can accurately balance merit against evil.

"Repentance and good deeds can change the course of fate for God's compassion is ever-present. As was written in Isaiah, 'I was ready to be found by those who did not seek me.'"

Chapter 51

...that the lights by which we steer will bring us all safely to anchor.
—Winston Churchill

Being ignorant of the peril we faced, Pat's parents considered my concern with security to reflect an English eccentricity. The last murder in Greenwich, of fifteen year old Martha Moxley for which a relative of the late Senator Kennedy was convicted, had occurred thirty years before, they informed me.

But every soldier knows that survival is the result of careful planning: eighty percent of battle consists of preparation. So I corrected the weaknesses in our security perimeter. Fastening each door and window and checking they stayed that way for even the best lock is worthless if left open. Pat or I would have to monitor them continually.

Defense also meant knowing what to do if someone did break-in. I made plans for dealing with that too, as best I could in the short time I had.

Creating a security room, to which we could flee if invaders gained entry, would have been ideal but impractical since it required my willingness to notify the police. Nor, within my time constraint, could I have fenced off the property or convinced Pat's parents to purchase a watchdog.

Once, while in Edinburgh, I stayed at a hotel where a security conference for public housing managers was being held. Having no set plans for the day, I entered the room and sat in the back row. During a break, I identified myself to the speaker as being a military officer on leave. We chatted, learned that we had been stationed at the same base, and were warmed by this instant camaraderie. One of the best perks of a military career is having friends who live just about everywhere. He spoke enthusiastically about his current work and I enjoyed listening to him, as I do to most experts.

"Sometimes we're called in after the fact," he said. "To explain how something happened and what could have been done to prevent it. Recently, an American lawyer tried her best to protect herself.

"She was no tosser*. Having lived in Baltimore, the murder capital of America, she wasn't about to take chances and followed the best security advice. Replacing her thin wood panel door with a two inch thick hardwood one and having the panels filled with concrete. Installing a Ring-and-bar Pin Tumbler lock, which is impossible to jimmy and far better than a lock with a wedge shaped or square tongue. Protecting the windows by placing locking pins in each."

"Sounds like she did a good job," I interjected, as he paused. It soon became clear why he hesitated to share the ending to his story.

"A neighbor walking his dog saw her arrive home a little after midnight. Apparently she had a drink and watched TV in the living room before going to bed."

"*Apparently?*" That seemed the operative word.

---

*slang for *an ignorant fellow*

"So the forensic people said after they found her. A neighbor first ignored a noise. When he did call the police she had been dead for hours. She had been raped and had a 'trophy' taken: her nipples and the surrounding skin. To avoid leaving teeth marks or because the rapist was kinkier than the usual ones."

"With all her precautions, how did he get in?"

"By using the simplest technique: coming through the bathroom window which contained ordinary frosted glass. He covered it with wide adhesive tape and then pressured the glass with a rock until it broke. The tape deadened the noise and prevented large pieces of glass from falling."

We didn't speak for a few moments. Maybe we should have toasted the woman with our coffees though this would have seemed melodramatic and too cheaply commemorate her undeserved fate. Letting our silence honor her seemed more fitting. I asked a final question.

"If doing all the right things don't provide enough protection then what do you teach in your classes?" I received a weary smile.

"How to buy time and decrease probability. You'd be amazed how quickly one can get past even expensive locks. At every locksmith convention there's a lock picking contest, often with a new model which is advertised as being pick proof. Some are opened in seconds.

"A burglar, which is what a rapist is first of all, isn't interested in what little he can get from most residences. So the typical home thief is an unskilled teenager whose inexperience and anxiety make him dangerous. What the police most fear is a skilled locksmith who is also a rapist or murderer. Such a person could enter almost any home, quietly and unknown. Thankfully, one who is willing to learn about locks tries to avoid violence while those tending towards it won't put forth the study effort.

"I teach techniques which gain the resident time to call the police and get to their security room. It also increases the probability that their neighbor's less secured home will be the target."

Remembering this conversation, I checked all the doors and windows and found they could be forced with just a screwdriver. An intruder bothering to bring a jimmy—a small crowbar which fits between a door or window and its frame and is used as a lever—would have even less problem breaking in. While extensive structural changes were beyond my ability, help from a clerk at the local Home Depot gained me what I needed.

The front and rear doors and their frames were sound but many of the screws were loose. I replaced these with longer, self-tapping sheet metal screws which were threaded all the way to the head. Then I added sliding dead bolts, and door chains with welded rather than cheaper bent links; and replaced the supplied three quarter inch screws with longer ones. I made sure when installing the chains that there would be only a one inch clearance when the door was opened so an intruder could not insert their hand. Then I added a wide angle peephole for further protection. For the windows, which were of the old double-hung variety, I installed key-operated locks.

These simple but effective improvements were finished by the time I left to pick up Holly from school. Though they would not protect against determined intruders, breaking in would now make noise and gain us time to prepare our *active* defense. But for this I needed a heavy duty weapon, one like those owned by the women in my shooting class. However these were barred from official purchase by all fugitives—which now included me.

I was really stupid, colonel, for feeling confident my plan would work. Still, even Eisenhower said that making plans is most important for the *process* itself. Any plan might have to be quickly discarded when disaster struck. But the process of thinking about the event will enable the faster construction of a different and more effective plan.

Though considering what happened, probably no plan I devised would have changed the course of events. I would not—could not—believe what turned out to be true. Nor, I'm sure, would General Eisenhower, who was a much better tactician than me.

Chapter 52

There can be no reasoning with an incendiary bomb.
—Franklin Delano Roosevelt

While driving to Holly's school I again felt grateful for Pat's parents. Other hosts would have been outraged by a guest's seeming paranoia about security or their child's obsession with an angel. But they readily accepted Holly and me with all our peculiarities. Their warmth comforted me even as our lives advanced towards the lethal destiny I feared.

I parked in front of the school building and stood with the waiting parents. All but one were female. For weeks the other father had tried to chat me up about male things. A former policeman, he gained early retirement after his non-shooting thumb was injured and his wife graduated from law school. Gossip held him in low regard for his pension was considered a scam and he continually sought a girl-friend from amongst the other mothers. My only bother was his occasional puzzled interest in my accent.

After I brushed off his friendly overture, he spent his waiting time, until his four children arrived, in more fruitful chatter with a newly divorced mother in our group.

The children from the elementary school were dismissed at three. Five minutes later, after seeing other children in Holly's class leaving the building, I became alarmed by her absence.

Fearing the worst, I entered the school and walked warily toward the principal's office. I stood and listened outside one closed door. Then I heard a noise from down the hall and froze. Holly was standing tall and determined in a corner, holding an upraised hockey stick. Her whispered, rapidly spoken words explained. "One of them was at the window": a murderer of her family.

The hallway looked deserted.

"Let's get out of me," I said, wanting us outside among other people.

Holly's color returned as she snacked on the Health Valley snack bars and apple juice I kept stowed in the car. Nothing reduces a child's crisis faster than eating I had learned.

I put my arm about her.

"You're still a child but have dealt with what most grown-ups couldn't, and so well that we're still alive. You're smart and brave and ready to fight grown men with guns and I feel honored to know you. Soon you'll only need a hockey stick to play the game." Then, more softly, almost as benediction, I added a line spoken by an American general a hundred and fifty years earlier during the American-Mexican war. "Rise, veteran...for you have been baptized in fire and blood and have come out steel."

I feared that my speech, similar in tone to those I gave to soldiers years before, might have been beyond her years for while I spoke she remained staring, as if seeking something nearby. But her words indicated my error and gave me further thought.

"I'm not afraid," she said. "Mommy told me this morning that I needn't be afraid." Now she hesitated before adding, "and that she wasn't still angry with me."

Holly's face radiated such certainly that despite my skepticism about angels I couldn't help but believe her. I wondered what her mother might have been angry with her about but then wasn't the time to ask. I got down to basics.

"Where did you see the man?"

"In my home room during grammar. I looked out the window toward a helicopter's noise and saw him."

"Why do you think he's the same man?"

"Because he *looked* the same," she burst out, as if feeling that I didn't believe her.

"I'm not doubting you for a moment," I said soothingly. "But it would help me to know what he looked like."

Holly's face contorted as she dredged up a painful memory.

"He had a black mustache, thick glasses, and wore a white baseball cap. He looked angry. I opened my mouth to scream and he ran." Holly looked away, not wanting to talk anymore.

"You did fine," I said, and turned to a less upsetting subject. "Where did you get the hockey stick?"

"From my classroom."

As the Impala's two hundred twenty horsepower engine burst into life, I suddenly had an idea. "Let's get away this weekend. How about going to Vermont to buy maple syrup?" And a pistol, I told myself, for that state had lenient gun laws. A sporting goods show, outside which guns could be purchased without government paperwork, was now running in Burlington.

Though both are politically liberal states, Connecticut and Vermont differ economically. Connecticut is wealthier, having many high earners working on Wall Street or in newer, even more luxurious offices in Greenwich and Stamford. The state also has large research facilities, as of the drug manufacturer Pfizer, and industrial facilities at New London's submarine base.

But Vermont is a poor state whose conservative attitudes only recently became diluted by migrants seeking a cheaper life style. Though willing to move north for the sake of lower living costs, they kept their liberal attitudes. And, being affluent, opinionated, and vocal, they had greater influence than their small numbers would otherwise warrant.

While the newcomers' legislative goals were popular—for who could object to better roads, schools and available health insurance—their desire to raise taxes to achieve these aims created protest among long-term residents. But another of their imported ideas, gay marriage, caused little concern. It exemplified Vermonters' core belief that the government should not infringe on the individual's right to be left alone. Which included having minimal restriction on the ownership of guns.

Unlike virtually every other state, Vermont law does not require a permit to carry a gun. Any adult may do so, openly or concealed.

My Internet skimming of Vermont's brief gun laws had taken only a minute. They concerned: the prohibition of guns in schools and institutions; their use during a crime, and the use of a silencer (which carried a twenty five dollar fine!). Of greatest interest to me was learning that while pawnbrokers and retail merchants were required to record firearm sales, no paperwork need be filed for their casual sale by residents.

Children's lives are structured by adults. Ask most any child what they'll be doing on the following day and, if not attending school, the likely answer will be, "I don't know." So Holly didn't object to my unexpected suggestion that we travel to Burlington. Which, she probably sensed, was farther away than nearby Stamford where we saw a movie the night before. She also wanted more distance between us and her family's killers.

As the miles increased our rapid flight became a calming thing, my antidote to our continuous terror.

Chapter 53

After our first hour on the road, Holly broke the silence. "I have to use the bathroom."

"We're twenty minutes from the next rest stop. Can you wait?"

"No," she replied quickly, and I knew that I had to find a bathroom—fast.

"OK, I'll see where we are." I glided the car onto the shoulder of the road and reached for the Rand McNally Atlas. In addition to maps it contained the location of all WalMarts. One, which certainly had bathrooms, was off the next highway exit.

I told the good news to Holly whose blank look and squirming caused me to fear that we wouldn't make their facility in time. Or if we did that the line to enter the woman's bathroom would extend yards outside the door, a common sight which always embarrassed me.

Pat told me of a product which could help to solve this problem. Something she always carried with her. Until recently it sold only in Europe but it was now being imported for American women. A funnel like device made of plastic or corrugated paper with which a female could urinate while standing up. Using this was far quicker than sitting on the toilet. "It doesn't work well without some such thing," Pat remarked casually, while reading a news item about it.."I've tried peeing while squatting and one gets wet all over." It seemed eminently logical to provide female soldiers with this device too though because a product is valuable doesn't mean that military bureaucrats will buy it.

With these relevant thoughts, our car screeched into the WalMart lot. I parked as close to the entrance as possible and we rushed inside. The greeter smiled, gave his "Welcome to WalMart," and thumbed directions. I felt relief when Holly entered the bathroom and wondered if real fathers became as frantic when facing this common problem. Perhaps with experience they confronted the situation calmly.

"Everything all right?" I asked her a few minutes later.

She nodded, and I remembered other practical matters which I had forgotten in our flight from Greenwich. To call Pat about our trip; buy clothes for Holly and me; and to find a motel for the night. We would arrive in Burlington after the gun show closed for the day and I wouldn't be able to make my purchase until the following morning.

"Let's eat. We'll shop later," I suggested. The Panera restaurant next door seemed a good bet.

Holly was in that intermediate age of youthful customers. No longer a child who nagged their parents for a snack because it contained a toy, she now had her own shopping style. Which was to be expected for, while accompanying them, she had used her parents' credit card for purchases since she was six.

Holly had begun sharing stories from her life. Some evidenced her assertiveness. Once, when taken for a haircut, she insisted, "I want my hair tipped." The stylist replied, "I don't know how to do that." To which the then four year old Holly responded, "Well get me someone who can!"

We had bonded since our first meeting, when I washed the blood from her hands and face and committed myself to her safety. But I still felt more like a courtesy uncle than parent and continued to express my demands tentatively, lacking the biological authority of a father.

So despite our closeness she had issues which I avoided raising. Though I knew that, if we managed to survive and remained together, I would someday have to speak with her about them. Like her sexual development.

Could her increased moodiness reflect an early pubescence? Were I her true father I could learn from her mother if she was "developing": breast buds and pubic hair. But Holly's continued coldness toward Pat made this impossible, leaving me to wonder.

Holly was now increasingly talkative about her parents. I planned to explore this area and hoped that the information I gained would lead to the solution of their riddle.

Like WalMart, Panera was a source of comfort, familiar in its muted colors and greenery. Taking her time, Holly finally ordered turkey and tomato on a cinnamon-raisin bagel. Adding a glass of milk and refusing any of the extraordinary deserts available. I silently applauded her concern with nutritious eating and copied her choices, replacing cinnamon-raisin with whole-wheat.

The food arrived. Because the bagel was too large for her mouth, she ate the filling with a finger and munched on the bagel. Something babyish and not aesthetically pleasing but sensible. Far better than the grosser eccentricities of some scientists I had known. Like the renowned physicist who refused to flush the toilet and hired a maid for this among her other duties. I sensibly made no comment about

Holly's eating behavior before leading our conversation into serious matters.

"Have you eaten at Panera before?"

"When my father didn't want to make us lunch. He brought his laptop and read e-mail while we ate." Panera offered the benefit of free wireless Internet service.

"I checked my e-mail only every few days. Hate the spam one gets."

"He complained too."

Holly was now speaking in the ordinary tone which a normal child uses. So I risked asking a personal question and hoped that it wouldn't produce her angry silence as these often did.

"Something puzzles me. You said your mother told you that she wasn't angry with you. What did you think she might be angry with you about?"

Now Holly did shut-down but only for a minute. Not, I sensed, because she didn't trust me but because her relationship with her mother had been private and one she may not have shared even with her father.

"Playing with her makeup. I put some powder on my brother—like they do with TV announcers. It spilled on the rug and I said he did it and I wouldn't clean up the mess. My mother did though I think she knew what really happened." When she stopped speaking her eyes were filled with tears.

A teenage busgirl, clearing a nearby table, interrupted us..

"How old is your daughter?"

"Ten." Holly replied for herself.

"I have two younger sisters and a ten year old brother. One day after he was *really* impossible we took a vote on whether to sell him or our dog. The dog won so I said it would have to be two out of three and we never voted again. Going far?"

"To Vermont," I answered.

"Vermont is glorious," she said. I wondered at her extravagant adjective but my guess that she had a boyfriend there was wrong.

"My parents have a summer cottage on the water. There's something about the water. No matter how upset you are, you see it and become healed. You can feel but not conquer its power. It has no destructive pride or ambition, only...enchantment."

I didn't know what to say. To term her words "poetic," as they were, might appear mocking and not the praise which was my intention. So I just smiled. Which Holly attempted but didn't quite succeed at. Smiling doesn't come easily after one's family has been murdered.

The busgirl moved away.

Holly sipped her milk. "Why are we *really* going to Vermont? Not for maple syrup. You can buy it in Greenwich."

"Like I said, you're a smart little girl."

"Smart or little?" Her sass surprised me. Maybe I had been underestimating her capacities and the degree of psychological healing which had occurred..

"Not for the maple syrup," I admitted. "Vermont has lax gun laws. The pistol I found on the island isn't powerful enough to protect us. We're going there to buy another. Soon we'll travel somewhere and be safe."

"When can we stop running?"

That's a good question, I thought. "When we know what your parents were trying to tell you in the riddle.

Then the government *must* protect us because what happened will make sense to them."

"It'll never make sense to me," Holly said, with greater thoughtfulness than I had given her credit for.

"No, not like that."

There seemed no more to say. Before leaving, I left two dollars for the busgirl. Though her language deserved more, I was afraid that leaving a bigger tip would encourage her to become yet another impoverished poet. .

Chapter 54

Hand-in-hand, we weaved our way past families departing WalMart. Buying essential clothes quickly and then going to the food section for snacks. Holly chose peanut butter filled pretzels, coconut covered marshmallows, Strawberry Twizzlers, and Fig Newtons. While waiting to pay, she added *Teen Vogue* and *Seventeen* to our cart..

Shopping lifts one's spirits, I thought, as we left the store and walked toward the car. The flier was visible from twenty feet away. "There's something on the windshield," Holly observed. "Probably a car wash," I replied, and couldn't have been more wrong.

It was an ordinary eight by eleven sheet, folded into thirds. I involuntarily caught my breath as I began reading,

> *Your life is a sum of breaths,*
> *Death comes each moment nearer,*
> *Your path is laid,*
> *By one who does not jest.*

Though the note was unsigned, my immediate reaction was fright: the terrorists had found us. Why didn't I notice their pursuit? But even as the adrenaline coursed through my veins, I reread the note, became calmer, and...smiled.

While at university I spent many hours in the library stacks reading works ranging from World War Two infantry magazines to translated poetry. I recognized these words. They were stolen from a poem I unconsciously memorized for it, like all good poetry, seemed to speak to me personally. Written by a renowned Iraqi poet a thousand years before, it read,

> *Your life is a sum of counted breaths*
> *With each breath that passes*
> *a part of life is lost*
> *That which gives life brings death every moment nearer,*
> *and your caravan is led by one*
> *who will not jest with you.*

Our enemy's plagiarism made them seem less fearful.

"What is it?" Holly asked. I re-folded the sheet and placed it in my pocket. "A car wash," I replied, attempting a casual tone towards this repeated pledge of our deaths.

I considered. Though seeming senseless, there *must be* a logic to the murderers' behavior. They hadn't killed us because they needed the information which they thought that Holly possessed. Then why not torture her for it as they had her mother? Because what didn't work with an adult surely wouldn't with a fragile child. Better to let me do the digging and provide the answers they wanted.

Other questions persisted. Since they were already doing a good job of frightening me, why did they send this poem? To tighten the screws? And were they following our car or had they bugged it with a tracking device? These were now so common that parents bought them to monitor their teenagers. For a layman like myself to remove a tracking device would be near impossible: they were so small and easily concealed that I might tear apart the car without finding it. And this was with the commercial models, not the tiny ones used by intelligence services.

I drove at the exact speed limit to avoid being stopped by police. While trying not to obsess about whether particular cars were following us, Holly opened the package of Fig Newtons and my worry changed to the effect of the sticky sugar on her teeth. A ridiculous thought, I realized. It was likely that we would both be dead long before her cavity would develop.

The traffic grew sparse as we entered rural Vermont.

"Tell me when you see a sign for a motel," I instructed Holly. "I'm tired of driving. Maybe let you do it for awhile."

"I know how to," she said unexpectedly.

"How did you learn?"

"My father let me drive in the supermarket's lot. Early on Sunday, when no one was around."

Though I was joking to lift her mood, I took her information seriously. It was safer to have more than one driver. I could be wounded or worse. Considering the danger we faced, her ability to drive might come in handy. But not that day.

"There's too much traffic on this road. I'll let you drive in the morning," I promised.

Chapter 55

Deposition—Civil Action Against the Pine Rest Motel in the Deaths of Jason and LindaAnn Brillent—(Civil Action No. 1999-CV-0407; Document Number 12) Letter Written By Detective Ronald Alloway, Orinoco, Maine Police Department, Addressed to Retired Detective Harold Marwin Mathrup

November 14th,
Dear Win,

I was sorry to hear about the deaths of Lorene and her husband. A child's death is particularly painful since it's so out of sync with how things usually are. But at least their kids have you and Ellie. We'll talk at the Department's reunion in Orlando in December (you're coming, right!?).

I need your help with the Brillent killings, our first since you joined the force in 1970. The push is for an arrest NOW. The case got much publicity in the East; probably little in Salt Lake City so I'll summarize the basics.

Brillent was a thirty-eight year old Canadian scientist. He was visiting Orinoco to help North East Paper with the more environmentally friendly technical process which they're installing. He's divorced and was accompanied by his ten year old daughter. Both occupied a room on the second floor of the Pine Rest Motel on New Crescent Road. It was built since you left and is better than the town is used to. Though not a Sheraton, it has DISH TV, power showers, high speed Internet access, and free

Box use. But *not* an electronic entry system, old fashioned room keys being used.

The bodies were found by a maid on the afternoon of their expected departure. Brillent was bound to a chair, gagged with a sock overlain with duct tape. There was bruising on his face and cigarette burns on his chest. His daughter was tied to the bed, naked and spread eagled, also gagged. She had cigarette burns on her chest and thighs but wasn't sexually assaulted. The room had been searched and possessions were strewn around but apparently nothing was stolen. Three hundred sixty two dollars, credit cards, and jewelry were found.

The deaths occurred about ten hours earlier, or 4AM. Both died from .22 caliber gunshots to the temple, execution style with the barrel just inches from the body. One adjoining room was empty. The other was occupied by a local couple who noted nothing unusual on the previous evening except for several loud words (they being newlyweds, this is understandable).

The woman had left her bed in the early hours of the morning to use the bathroom. She heard voices from the hall and the phrase was so striking that she remembered it. "Believe in the day of judgment." This was said in unaccented English but the reply was in a foreign language she didn't recognize.

An Internet search found these words to derive from an old Persian poem, part of the following couplet:

They seem not to believe in the Day of Judgment
That's why they change the Words,
they misinterpret God's work.

The department's current thinking is that this was a cult killing done by religious freaks. How does this explanation sound to you?

Our youngest (now four) is driving Karen crazy. She says he's getting more like me every day!

Best,

Ron

Deposition – Civil Action Against the Pine Rest Motel in the Deaths of Jason and LindaAnn Brillent – (Civil Action No. 1999-CV-0407; Document Number 13)
E-mail addressed to Detective Ronald Alloway, Orinoco, Maine Police Department From Retired Detective Harold Marwin Mathrup

November 19th,
Dear Ron,

Thanks for the kind and supportive words. We will meet in Orlando. It'll be great touching base. I shouldn't miss Orinoco considering how much more Salt Lake City offers but I do. Maybe it's the adjustment to retirement for a workaholic like me, or that retiring isn't good for anyone. I'm interviewing for a job with a local department.

We heard nothing here about the Brillent murders. It seems a strange one for Orinoco. More a big city case though I remember a similar murder in Vermont about six years ago.

A mother came home from her waitress job to find her husband and eight year old daughter dead. Both were naked and tortured (also with cigarette burns), though here the girl was sexually abused. Small belongings were missing: her diary and the father's Michigan State sweatshirt.

There was a foreign element here too: a German word written on the wall in the child's blood. Police believed it was intended as a red herring and that the attacker was someone local. Fingerprints and DNA typing were gained from town residents who volunteered but none matched the crime scene evidence. As far as I know this case was never solved. Several organs were taken from the child indicating a cult ritual.

But your case seems simpler. It's likely that the Brillent murders had nothing to do with a cult and didn't involve robbery since the money and credit cards were untouched. Both the man and girl being tortured is unusual but not unknown in sex crimes though deviates usually have interests specific to one sex.

I'm thinking that maybe they tortured the Brillent father for information and, when this didn't produce results, they worked on his daughter. But what could a paper scientist know that would be so valuable—*unless* he was involved in illegal activities. Or both may have been victims of mistaken identity, the right place/wrong time scenario or vice versa.

Thanks again for your sentiments and your case info—it felt good to use my brain again.

Win

Chapter 56

Holly's choice of the Holiday Inn was a good one. There is much to be said for the safety and cleanliness which the chains usually provide. I've always considered the celebrated charm of bed-and-breakfasts, with their reduced privacy and too often casual plumbing and heating, to be overrated.

This Holiday Inn was predictable, Upon registering, I was asked the usual questions and gave the expected replies: we were father and daughter staying for one night. Our room had two double beds, a giant TV, a hair drier, and unisex robes to substitute for those we forgot to buy at WalMart.

We arrived at the motel a little after 7PM. I hadn't sighted any pursuers though the possibility of our car being bugged made that fact irrelevant.

"Would you rather take a nap or get something to eat?" I asked Holly.

"I'm not tired," she said, meaning that eating would be OK, Holly communicated indirectly. I had by now learned that if neither of my proposals met her objection she would not make a tantrum after I chose either. If she did object to one, it automatically meant that the other was acceptable.

Her preference for vegetarian food was more logical, it being far superior to the typical American and British diets of fast, fried foods. But she wasn't rigid and also ate fish, which I liked too. So we found plenty to choose from at the motel's restaurant, where I again went along with her choices. A salad, Insalata Mista (mozzarella cheese, plum tomatoes, artichoke hearts and green olives on mixed greens). An appetizer of humus and pita triangles. Then jumbo shrimp with broccoli and pasta, tossed in lemon, garlic, and olive oil. She rejected the waiter's offer of the desert tray but ordered a sixteen inch whole wheat crusted pizza (veggie pepperoni; veggie sausage; mushrooms; red onions; red peppers; tomato sauce, part-skim mozzarella cheese) for later snacking in our room.

I was awed by her appetite and hoped that this, and her increased willingness to speak of her family, indicated her improving mental health and that we would now make headway in interpreting the riddle.

Holly *was* calmer once we settled back in our room. Maybe from all she ate or because dangerous Greenwich was far away. So I brought out her parents' message for another try, while she lay on her bed scanning *Seventeen* and munching on Strawberry Twizzlers.

"You very smartly discovered that the 'ring' referred to your Captain Midnight Decoder Ring and that 'thirty nine' indicated the thirty ninth word which is 'webbed.' What do you think 'webbed' might mean?"

Holly mumbled inaudibly.

"*Excuse me,*" I said. My anxiety caused me to fantasize wrenching the candy and magazine from her but I controlled myself.

"I said," she began, in a tone dripping with what parents describe as 'having an attitude,' "that it might mean *the Internet*. Otherwise known as the *World Wide Web*."

"But it speaks of a '*beloved* webbed friend.'"

"Kids *love* their computers."

"OK. Other thoughts?"

"Spider's web?"

"Who loves a spider?"

"How about an animal with webbed feet—a bird?"

"It might be," I said, with interest. "Maybe the hiding place is an outdoor bird feeder."

"My mother hated animals. I pleaded for a dog..." Holly turned back to her magazine. I placed the two sheets holding the riddle on the night table and shut off the light above my bed. We had gotten as far as we could this evening and maybe ever would. But the riddle *must* have a simple explanation. One which could be discovered only by Holly, a girl who was as bright as her parents and shared their personal experiences. No other youth could give me the answers I needed.

I soon fell asleep but was jolted awake a few hours later. In my dream I was on the second floor of an English mansion, being chased by immense spiders which I sensed but could not see. Just before they caught me I reached a door, flung it open, slammed it shut, and ran mindlessly into the dark room. And straight into the sticky threads of a spider's web from which I couldn't break loose. Another door then opened and a man slowly entered. He wore a fez and pushed a cart containing torture instruments: pliers, knives, shock box, blowtorch. His thick eyeglasses glinted in the light as he approached.

When I frantically awoke, Holly was still sleeping in the adjoining bed, though not for long. A little after 2AM I woke again and found her lying beside me, covered in a blanket which she brought from her bed. She described her nightmare to me the next morning, while we ate in the Holiday Inn's rustically named Breakfast Barn.

"I was in the kitchen. My mother was cutting cookie dough and my brother spilled his juice. I asked my father to take me to a Star Wars movie. He looked sad and said that soon we'd be together. Will I live to grow up?" Her tone was intense, a quest for hope. But I was a scientist, not a cleric.

"Did you ask Cedric what he thought?"

"Yes, and I told him the truth: that my parents and brother were killed and you're protecting me."

Had she informed Cedric of this earlier I would have been angry but during our weeks together I had come to trust him.

"What did he say?" I asked.

"He said that to love involved the greatest sacrifice and because my parents had loved me so greatly they were now angels who would return to help me." As Holly spoke, the harried look left her face. Inexplicably, I too felt calmer.

Minutes later, after gazing at the small boy at a neighboring table who reminded Holly of her brother, she told me something else. An assertion which logic insisted I must deny yet I could not. A prophecy which chilled me but gave me hope. For Cedric also believed that the Lord had sent me to conduct Holly through this world and so I could not fail.

Chapter 57

The gray morning matched my mood. Though some events made sense, I still felt as if I were enveloped in a logically implausible novel.

The torture and murder of Holly's mother, father, and brother had a clear goal: to obtain the priceless equations. As did the demand for Holly's innocently acquired knowledge. But I couldn't understand why the three bodies—which I saw at point blank range and were certainly dead—had been made to disappear. Nor why one would want to create the pretense that her family still lived.

Yet, being a scientist, I remained committed to the scientific method of investigation, believing that what was adequate to explain the workings of the universe should also suffice for events in our small lives.

Holly stared at my face. "You look upset,"

"I'm just trying to figure out what to do next," I responded. I wanted to protect her from further distress but also knew that the information she might provide could be crucial to our survival..

"What was your father like?"

Holly's eyes watered. "He worried about us a lot. When my mother was taking out a splinter from my brother's foot, he joked to stop my brother from crying but looked more upset than him. He was always making jokes and some were terrible."

My next question seemed irrelevant even to me but I was operating in the dark. "Do you remember any of his jokes?"

"What do bears do at Niagara Falls?"

"What?"

"Go over it in *bearrels*?"

I laughed.

"My friends called the joke 'retarded.'"

"We both have silly streaks. What did your father do at home?"

Holly ran her tongue over her lips. "He worked most of the time. Using his calculator and writing. Then he'd read to us from comics in his Disney collection or play with us. He would crawl with my brother to see who could reach the door first but let him win. My parents argued about him not shaving on weekends."

Holly's father was a guy I would have liked though I couldn't see how the information I was gaining helped our situation.

"What was your mother like?"

"She usually said 'no' so I asked my father for things first."

Her family seemed the typical American one where fathers give in to their children more often than mothers. I tried one more question.

"What did your father most enjoy doing with you?"

"Reading. We read to each other since I was three. My parents thought a child should be able to read before they start school. I'd read a page and he would and then my brother would try. He had to sound out words." She changed the subject. "What are we doing today?"

"There's a gun show a few miles away. We'll look around, then practice shooting if there's a range nearby. Do you like target shooting?"

"I'm not good at it, am I?"

"You're like every beginner at any task. You read better now than when you started, don't you?"

"Yes."

"Shooting is the same."

"The noise scares me."

"It can frighten everyone. Even soldiers, who are around guns a lot."

"Does it scare you?"

I waffled. Then wasn't the time to tell her of my fear of guns.

"People have ups and down. Though I pray you have an 'up' day when you drive us around the parking lot." I expected she would love doing this and wasn't wrong for her face brightened into the first grin I ever saw on it.

We had breakfasted early so it was barely 8AM when we went to the car. The night before I parked as close to the well-lit front entrance as I could, feeling this would be safer. But it was too public a spot for Holly to drive from. Though tall for her age, she was obviously not a teenager and I feared that a well-meaning guest might complain to the police. So I drove us to the parking lot at the rear of the building before turning off the engine and changing places with her.

When Holly was seated on the driver's side with her seat belt fastened, I lowered her head rest for a better fit and explained how to move her seat forward so she could comfortably reach the pedals. Following my instruction, she turned on the engine.

"Show me how you hold the wheel and which pedal is which?" I asked.

"Gas, brake." She indicated these with her right foot and placed her hands on the steering wheel in the proper position.

"OK. Now put your right foot on the brake and release the parking brake with your hand." The intent look on Holly's face barely concealed her excitement.

"You're doing great. Now move the gear shift lever to 'drive' and *lightly* press on the gas." Like most new drivers, Holly depressed the gas pedal firmly and the car jerked forward. Then she panicked and slammed on the brake, thrusting us against the seat belts.

"You're doing great," I repeated. "But you must *touch* the gas like your foot is a feather." She did, and the car went smoothly forward. Holly drove around the parking lot for the next ten minutes, which I felt was long enough for this lesson. The experience seemed to give her confidence. I hoped it would translate into her greater comfort with shooting that morning.

Chapter 58

We arrived at the gun show a little after eight. It was being held at a large warehouse-like building on the county fairgrounds. In the parking lot, beside their cars, were people selling guns and shooting supplies. Some had one item for sale; others could have equipped an army squad. To my surprise, Holly was far from being the only child or even girl there for many had brought their family for a day's outing. Small amusement rides and soda/cotton candy/fried dough vendors gave the setting a carnival atmosphere, one far from the unsavory aura which other than expensive, custom crafted firearms arouse in England.

We walked slowly past the wares. Holly's presence lent the appearance of innocence to my illegal quest. Here, there was no hard sell. Both sellers and customers were shooting enthusiasts and shared the camaraderie of all who believe themselves under siege. A feeling which became reduced in recent years as gun control initiatives lost favor in Washington.

I stopped midway down one row and lusted after a classic car which I immediately recognized as a 1953 Hudson Hornet. Though having only a six cylinder engine, it was once virtually unbeatable on the stock car racing circuit. My mood was also lifted by the Springfield Armory pistol which lay for sale before it, on a folding table covered with a blue and white checkered cloth.

"A '53 Hudson, isn't it?" I asked, wanting to establish our bond as car lovers before raising the issue of a gun purchase.

The owner smiled. He was short man in his early sixties. His dark brown mustache didn't match his thinning gray hair. The tattoo on his forearm was also discordant for stacks of *Harvard Business Review* lay on the table before him. One was open on his lap. He's probably a military veteran and retired executive or academic, I told myself.

"You know cars," he said.

"Mine is a '53 Kaiser." One I would likely never see again.

"With the gold hood ornament?"

"Yes."

"They're rare—where did you find it?"

"Outside Seattle. Where it was driven daily for most of its life."

"Lucky," he said. The word seemed to have a special meaning for him.

Holly's face held a look of excruciating boredom. "This might interest you," he told her. Beside the pistol lay a foot high stack of old magazines which were also for sale, each in a see-through vinyl folder. Atop was the November 27, 1937 issue of *Life* with its cover photo of a wide eyed one year old boy. The man reached underneath and handed a comic book to her.

"Maybe your daddy will buy it for you."

His tone was odd and I sensed that he would be willing to sell it for virtually nothing despite its significant collector value. For this comic was not of the usual rectangular shape but oblong, and in a pocket book format. Though the cover page, like all Donald Duck comics, had a drawing of Donald overlain with the story's title. "Donald Duck and the Pirates" was written in flowing script across it.

Holly's eyes filled with tears. "Daddy loved these," she said haltingly.

"She's not my daughter—her parents was murdered," I explained.

"Take the comic. My present to a brave girl," he said, and his face held an unexpected look of anguish.

I took out my wallet. "I'll buy it. How much?"

"Free. It was my son's. He died on 9/11. Worked at the World Trade Center and was returning to college next day. He loved New York and felt that when he looked through the Center's windows he could grasp the nature of the world. But he couldn't."

We huddled, Holly and he joined by grief and I by empathy for what they endured. She hadn't moved since mentioning her father. I took the comic from the man's hand. For me to insist on paying would be tactless but I would give him more than he asked for his pistol.

Down to business: the Springfield Armory .40 caliber twelve shot semi-automatic pistol. It looked unused as it lay inside its open original packing carton.

"It's a beauty. Why are you selling it?"

"We're moving to Manhattan to be closer to where my son's body disappeared. It would take six months to get a permit to own a pistol there."

"How much do you want?"

"Three hundred."

"I'll make it four hundred if you throw in the ammo and show me how to load it. I seem to remember this gun being peculiar in that respect."

"Thank you," he said, nodding his head slightly, recognizing that I shared his sadness and anger at how the government had failed to protect his son..

I gave him the money. He moved the three boxes of ammunition on the table in my direction and removed the pistol from its carton. Which also contained two magazines, an instruction manual, and a safety lock: a thin steel cable which, when inserted through the cartridge ejection port and out the magazine well, prevents the gun from being fired. There were, as I expected, no uncomfortable questions about my state of residency or identity.

"It's a wonderful weapon, particularly with a child around," he explained. "It has *three* safeties, all of which are automatically 'on.' A trigger safety, so the gun can only be fired if a lever is depressed. A grip safety which stops the gun from firing even if the trigger is pulled. And a striker block safety which prevents the gun from firing until *both* the grip safety and trigger are depressed.

"The loading *is* a little different. First, you insert the empty magazine into the magazine well until you hear a 'click.' Then you pull the slide back, remove and load the magazine, reinsert it, and release the slide stop lever. This will automatically load a shell from the magazine into the chamber. Try it."

I did and it worked smoothly. Remembering our perilous situation, I asked Holly to try and she readily agreed. I gave her an empty magazine. She repeated the correct procedure while listening carefully to his cautions.

"Never rely on a gun's safety mechanism. No matter how good it is, it's still mechanical and no substitute for common sense. Be sure of your target before you shoot; and never climb a tree or cross a ditch with a loaded gun."

We lingered a few minutes and received an invitation for dinner with his wife and other son. I was noncommittal, being unsure how our day would develop, but was grateful for his offer of friendship.

We left, carrying our purchase in a plastic bag imprinted with what I was told was the motto of both an early American Revolution flag and the 1st Navy Jack, "Don't tread on me." This indicated the American colonists' courage and fierce desire for independence.

Having accomplished my goal, the rest of the day was free. I suggested we walk through the fair. The line at its entrance moved quickly.

Just inside the building were tables offering information about membership in a local gun club and various civic organizations. Along a wall were the usual food vendors of sodas, hot dogs, and regional delicacies containing maple syrup. After deliberating for an unseemly period, Holly settled on a maple vanilla ice cream cone. Its three scoops steeped precariously as we strolled the aisles of racked firearms.

In the back of the building was an exit door on which was tacked a sign, "Shooting Range—Do Not Enter Without Eye and Hearing Protection." These were available for rent at two dollars a pair.

"Let's try out our gun," I suggested to Holly, and rented the gear for us. She finished her ice cream quickly, showing less annoyance towards my request than she usually exhibited.

Beyond the door was an empty field which had been set up as a firing range. The targets were set at a distance of fifty feet. Too short for rifle practice but the purpose of the range was to try out guns and not serious target work.

Four of the positions were in use, with a variety of classic weapons. A Model 1896 "Broomhandle" Mauser which conveyed Ruritanian grace and was carried by the bodyguards of Chinese warlords in many nineteen thirties movies. An Artillery Model Luger pistol with eight inch barrel and attached thirty two round drum magazine and shoulder stock. A .38 caliber Colt Detective Special, the ultimate snub nosed film noir revolver. A nineteen fifties . 22 caliber Whitney Wolverine pistol, of strikingly futuristic design and resembling a Space Patrol blaster.

To escape the noise, Holly and I fled to the last firing position. Each was equipped with a small table, spotting telescope, and stack of explosive bullseye which spatter large yellow spots where it is hit. I pinned one of these to the target, returned to the firing stand, and offered my newly purchased pistol to Holly. She carefully loaded it and pointed the gun downrange.

Though light for a pistol of this large caliber, it was heavier than the gun which Holly was familiar with and her hand momentarily drooped upon grasping it. But she gamely gripped it tighter and, adopting the shooting position she was taught, breathed slowly before squeezing off a round. I looked through the telescope: she missed the target completely.

Holly looked chagrined, as if sensing the result before being told. "I'm awful," she said. "Not so bad," I responded, "at least you could load the gun. I once loaded a gun backwards." Her face relaxed as I began my story. I was pleased that, before facing me, she had correctly placed the loaded pistol on the stand with the barrel facing away from us and towards the target.

"In America many children learn to shoot but in England things are different. I never touched a gun until I joined the military."

"If you didn't know you liked guns, why did you join the army," Holly asked. The same logical question I had often asked myself.

"I never quite figured that out. Maybe from reading poetry about war, or the romantic sight of soldiers parading in their battle dress," I said seriously. Then added, with what I intended to be a comic tone, "*Are you going to let me tell my story?*"

"OK, OK."

"The first time I was at the range I was having a hard time fitting the cartridges into the rifle's magazine. After I finally forced them in, the sergeant asked me, 'You're not going to use that magazine are you?' I gave him a dumb look and he continued, 'You put the bullets in backwards.' You didn't do *that*. Try again."

This time Holly hit the target, but high above the bulls-eye. Maybe, I thought, she was instinctively closing her eyes and jerking against the gun's expected recoil before pulling the trigger. These are common mistakes among beginning shooters.

From down the firing line a man came to join us. He carried the classic Wolverine pistol which I had admired. He watched Holly shoot and then spoke to her in a soothing fashion.

"My daughters got involved in target shooting to get more time alone with me. They had the same problem as you: being afraid of the blast and closing their eyes before pressing the trigger. So I said they should imagine themselves as space cadets who were protecting their family by shooting a monster. They learned to shoot with this gun, which looks like something out of a Star Wars movie. Alright if she tries it?" he asked me. I quickly agreed. My efforts weren't helping.

I don't know whether it was the smaller caliber of the Wolverine or the man's reassuring story but Holly's shooting improved. Now she hit the bulls-eye repeatedly, each of her accomplishments arousing our cheers and her hesitant grin.

"Mind if I make another suggestion," the man whispered to me as Holly blasted away.

"I'm retired from the State Police and taught shooting for thirty five years so I know what I'm talking about. She's too young to fire such a large caliber gun. Won't have enough arm and hand strength until she's fourteen or so.

"Get her a Wolverine like she's shooting now. Rex Applegate, an expert who should know, said it was the 'best pointing little .22 pistol' he ever handled. The original has been out of production for fifty years but it's being re-manufactured with a high-strength polymer frame by Olympic Arms. Despite the small caliber it's good for self-defense. The best gun is the one you can shoot well."

I knew he was right. But I saw no other Wolverines being sold outside the show and couldn't buy one from a registered gun dealer.

It was lunch time when we arrived back at the Holiday Inn. Holly entered our room first, I having given her the key to encourage her independent behavior. So it was she who noticed the envelope addressed to me which had been slipped under the door. It held a single sheet of paper and the type of message I had come to dread.

And as the thief stumbled back into the depths of the prison, the people commenced whispering one to another saying,

> *"How dare this heretic man steal the sacred vases*
> *of the monastery?*
> *What conceit devours this Western fool to steal*
> *the sacred vases of the monastery?"*

> *"Oh tell me our fortune," asked the young warrior,*
> *"And whether we should pray,*
> *"Or waste our time in idleness until our olden day."*
> *"I should not tarry," said the wise old seer, "for I*
> *see in my mystical globe,*
> *"That there remain but few days of your life on*
> *earth, till it comes to an unexpected close."*

This note was unsigned like the last one but I knew who had sent it.

"What is it?" Holly flung her jacket onto a chair.

"Too high a bill," I responded.

I didn't relate much with Holly for the next hour: even when it is poetically expressed a death threat chills the mind. But something about the message puzzled me. So after considering it throughout lunch, I asked Holly. Though still a child, she had some adult perceptions.

"This doesn't read quite right. Can you figure out what's strange." I folded over the message to conceal its frightening last line and placed it next to her plate of maple waffles.

She read the lines slowly. "It's weird. Some of it is like poetry but the rest isn't. Or not Western poetry since it doesn't have our rhyming scheme. The later lines do but the earlier ones are Persian style, with a rhyme and repeated refrain. This is bad poetry, not like Gibran's." She wrinkled her nose and added, as if feeling uncomfortable at her precocity, "We're studying world poetry in English."

Of course, I thought, the writer had mixed Arabic and Western formats. But why? From carelessness? To communicate multicultural familiarity and infer a sense of superiority over his victim? Combining these writing styles made as little sense as did the easily discovered plagiarism in their last message. No matter how I considered the matter, our enemy's behavior seemed illogical. But maybe the agents *weren't* from Iran or even from the Middle East. Could they they represent drug kingpins, who control the levers of power in several South American countries and feared extradition to America?

Stay calm, I told myself, even as the anxiety coursed through me.

Chapter 59

We checked out of the Holiday Inn after lunch. The pistol and ammunition lay snug in the trunk beside a dozen whole wheat loaves from the Vermont Bread Company. This favorite of Cedric was often unavailable in the local supermarkets and could be frozen for extended use.

Scattered flakes fell but no serious snow developed. We reached Greenwich late Sunday evening—where things seemed unchanged. Despite the overhanging threat, I was glad to be back. Holly ignored Pat after responding to her parents' greetings, and the image of the wicked stepmother in countless children's books came to mind.

I valued Pat's logical thinking so as soon as I could get her alone I told her of the latest terrorist notes. They upset her even more than me.

"It's craziness," she insisted. "Combining the two writing styles doesn't make sense. If they want to kill us why wait and send letters? They didn't hesitate with Holly's parents."

"I don't think they planned to murder them," I explained. "They needed information and did what they felt they had to do to get it. Their deaths and that of their son may well have been unintended.

"You see, the secret which everyone wants isn't a simple number. It's a lengthy series of equations which aren't easily remembered. This may leave Holly as the holder of the key to the kingdom. And who would she be more likely to help? Me, or the murderers of her parents and brother? Torture would just drive her crazy, not increase her ability to solve the riddle.

"The people we're dealing with aren't fools. They recognize that they need our help and are turning up the screws—until we get away. Have you found a place for us to hide?"

"New York City," Pat said eagerly. "It's easiest to get lost in a big city where people mind their own business. A law school friend will let us use her two room apartment. For five months while she's in Europe. If they're giving us three more days, we'll leave in two—on Tuesday."

"Let's make it Monday after Holly gets home from school. We're not dealing with the most trustworthy people."

"Monday, then. We'll reach Manhattan in an hour and a half and celebrate with food shopping at Dean & DeLuca."

Then, like prisoners who count the days until their release, I tallied the hours until we reached safety. Not that all of our problems would then be over. There was still my suspected involvement in the kidnapping of Holly's family. Who I knew were dead even if their bodies had disappeared.

But if they were hidden by the police, what could be the reason for this bizarre behavior? What important motive might be involved?

I would have liked to be able to accept Pat's idea that what was happening reflected simple craziness. Better still, a daydream from which I hadn't awoken. But of course I couldn't.

Chapter 60

And how can man die better
Than facing certain odds
For the ashes of his fathers,
And the temples of his Gods.
Macaulay, *Horatius*

Everyone was jittery that Sunday night. I ranted at unlocked windows and Holly whined at even the most reasonable request—when she wasn't acting *more* babyish.

Pat reread the messages from the terrorists with a sense of disbelief, probably wondering at how her yearning for love had led her into this nightmarish situation.

Even Cedric's usual buoyancy was gone. When I questioned this, as tactfully as I could, his explanation led to another of his lucid perspectives on living.

"My multiple sclerosis made me experience things differently. Some people say their illness was a blessing in disguise but I never did. There are easier ways to learn a lesson. When your body is failing you relate to time differently than when you are in good health. Each hour becomes a day, particularly when the pain is great. You draw more into yourself and fear even the normal twinges which all living creatures experience.

"Which explains *my* irritating behavior but not everyone else's. Pat's, I'm used too. She was always moody. As a teenager, she'd go from crying to laughing and back to tears within minutes. Once she blamed it on her period to which her mother responded, 'Nonsense. You've always been like this.'

"Now you and Holly are behaving the same. She's better than she was so something else must be influencing you. I won't pry—your lives are your own. But for mercy's sake I do wish you'd tell me what you're all so upset about. A sick person needs *some* predictability from those around him."

Scientists are rarely impulsive: the process leading to their creative outbursts is deliberate and orderly with each new concept reflecting an imaginative attempt at discovering unity in the variety of nature. Like finding out that the hydrogen bomb and the sun have an identical underlying process.

Which made my response to Cedric so unusual. Without thinking, I quickly told him the truth though whether this reflected my need for reassurance or a fresh viewpoint I wasn't sure. And I managed to describe the mess we were in with surprisingly few words.

"Three months ago I was an ordinary guy with a job and a classic car I loved even if they couldn't love me back. One night, as I lay drunk in my car, Holly appeared. She was blood stained, traumatized, and pursued by those who attacked her family. I went to help but was too late. They were all dead. When I later returned to her house their bodies had disappeared, leaving just faint blood stains to show where they had been.

"Holly and I have been together ever since. Running, hiding, and then more running. Threatening notes from the murderers began arriving a few days ago. They demand her parents' equations, which could make possible a revolutionary military weapon. And they're convinced that Holly knows where the formulas are hidden.

"Your daughter became involved as accidentally as I did and once in there seems to be no way out. *Except* for us to gain enough bargaining power—by finding out where the data is—to force the authorities to listen seriously to my story. Incidentally, my fingerprints were found at the crime scene and I was an expert killer in the military before my psychiatric discharge.

"Living with us puts you and your wife in the same danger we are. That's why we're leaving tomorrow night."

After I finished speaking, Cedric lay silent for a minute. He now spent his non-sleeping hours lying on the chaise-like sofa. But the upset which I had expected to see on his face from the troubles I brought into his home was absent. To my surprise, he looked relaxed and excited. His eyes crinkled—and I'm not exaggerating this—with near mirth.

"Pat was always odd so that she would involve herself with other strange people doesn't surprise me. Americans become publicly known by being exhibitionist but the British manage to produce true eccentrics, who are sometimes also geniuses. Being English and a scientist may make you one of them.

"Your story is so crazy that it might well be true. If a hard-nosed lawyer like my daughter believes you then who am I not to. But you should have told me the truth when you arrived. I might have been able to help, even if your experience has all the ingredients of great suspense fiction: danger, an important secret, the need to make moral choices. Sherlock Holmes, John Grisham, and Ian Fleming all in one. John Buchan too, though he's been little read since early last century.

"When you reach my age, death no longer terrifies. So however things turn out, I'm glad you came to our home. Even if (now he made a small smile) what you brought turns out to be the final puzzle of my life.

"As a child I learned how to reduce a fraction to its smallest term. Please don't embarrass me by asking how for I'm ashamed to say that I no longer remember. But what this exercise taught me, though the task itself has been of negligible value, was the need to strip every problem down to its essentials before seeking an answer. One must distinguish between an *impression* and a *corroborated fact* to see things clearly.

"An impression is an event which isn't yet verified. That you saw dead bodies which you believe later disappeared is an impression. Holly confirmed this by seeing them too so we can consider these deaths to be facts. Why some would wish to conceal this is puzzling. Yet it must be crucially important for such a cover-up is no little business. Apparently these people have their own game, as do the murderers. Possibly both motives are the same. Sure you're not writing the screen play for a DePalma thriller?"

I shook my head at his rhetorical question.

"No? I didn't think you were. Now I'll digress a little. Lately it's been harder for me to get off my personal issues and you've likely already realized that I enjoy having an audience.   "Perhaps what's driving you—apart from the powerful desire to live—is curiosity. The same motive which religious folk have, though ours concerns what the human purpose is and how people should live their lives.

"I won't try to impose my beliefs on you except to tell what I discovered through my own suffering. Which occurred with such monotony that my soul continually shrieked the question of its purpose, which I finally understood: to enable me to grasp the beauty of the universe. For which I had to abandon myself to that impartiality created by God, leading some to suffer and others towards joy."

Then, with a look of contentment, Cedric slowly closed his eyes and fell asleep.

I felt unsettled that night. Once I even laughed hysterically. As combat soldiers sometimes do when they feel surprised at having survived. I was afraid that something might still go wrong during the remaining hours, before we left this idyllic town which had become our prison. After wandering aimlessly about the house, I sprawled on a chair in Holly's room and watched her play a computer game with amazing speed and coordination. The sight relaxed me and I dozed off, being awakened in the middle of my dream by a roar from her game's music.

Like the aftermath of many dreams, I remembered just a piece of it: a soldier screaming the words "broken arrow." My first associations were that these words symbolized my recent sexual impotence or the romantic difficulties of my earlier life. Neither interpretation felt correct. Then I remembered something from my days as a soldier which did.

During one training exercise we were visited by a retired American Marine who had been made an honorary member of our SAS unit. This was a well deserved tribute for he had received America's Navy Cross and only the Medal of Honor ranks higher. While with us, showing pictures of his granddaughter in uniform, he looked a wimpy guy. But decades earlier he was a master in hand-to-hand combat and able to kill in a heartbeat.

During a break he described a terrifying war experience, though downplayed his role in it as true heroes always do. He began his tale with a line from his favorite movie, the old Alex Guinness comedy, *Kind Hearts and Coronets*: "It is so difficult to make a neat job of killing people with whom one is not on friendly terms."

After the death of his commanding officer, this Marine rallied and saved his men from being overrun by North Vietnamese soldiers. His unit suffered terrible losses while repelling the enemy's repeated attacks throughout the day. The Americans were aided by massive artillery support and airdrops of water, food and, most important of all, ammunition.

On the following dawn the North Vietnamese struck again in their massive human wave formations, blowing whistles and screaming. Oddly, some even smiled and carried their rifles on their backs. Machine guns mowed them down within yards of the perimeter. Then the sergeant radioed a coded message to base camp, "broken arrow," meaning that his unit was in danger of being overrun. Whereupon every available American plane in the entire theater of war—old single engine propeller driven A-26's loaded with rockets, napalm, and cannon; helicopter attack gunships; jet fighter aircraft; even B-52 heavy bombers from Guam—were sent and lay stacked from one to thirty five thousand feet, awaiting their chance to attack. Under the ensuing barrage of air power the enemy ranks broke and the American unit was airlifted out that afternoon.

I considered my dream, Holly's dead family, and the danger we faced. Then I felt compelled to do something even as I recognized that it was crazy. Though this act couldn't help us, it shows how hopeless I felt about our survival. But I knew it would frighten Holly so, with effort, I did something else. Yet even this caused her to stare.

My first desire was to yell several words out the window. Instead, I picked up the phone and whispered them into the unheeding dial tone. The words which a desperate soldier had screamed decades before and brought deliverance: "Broken arrow, broken arrow, broken arrow."

After hanging up the phone I wondered, not for the first time, if I had gone crazy. I was losing my last shred of self-control, the essential element in our protection against...*them.*

Chapter 61

Pat and I were watching an old movie, *The Sweet Smell of Success*. The film told of an unprincipled gossip columnist, his rottener hanger-on, and their willingness to engage in the worst nastiness to achieve what they wanted regardless of its effect on others. Both the acting and writing were superb, with one interchange summing up their characters: "I'd hate to take a bite out of you. You're a cookie full of arsenic." As occurs in most Hollywood films, decency and love won out in the end.

"The moment I saw you I felt content," Pat murmured, as we lay close. "This is the best relationship I ever had."

"It is for me too." I kissed the top of her head. "What happened in the others?"

Pat paused for so long that I didn't think she would reply until she did. "There weren't that many except when I slept around as a teenager. I began one long relationship with an older guy just before college. It ended a month before we met."

"Lucky me," I said, feeling envious though, considering my many affairs, I knew this wasn't logical.

"You don't have to be jealous," Pat said, sensing my reaction. "He's married and to his work too so it never could have lasted. He helped me grow up so you might say that he did you a favor."

"Does he live in Greenwich?"

"Still jealous," she murmured with a smile, running her hand through my hair. "No, he travels a lot. I have no idea where he is."

Now the colonel interrupted me. "'The moment I saw you I felt content.' Did you believe her?"

"Why wouldn't I? Though I did wonder since she looked wary when we met. Not so taken with me that she *felt content.*

"That's a great line but it wasn't hers," he said with finality. "You should have read Emerson."

Chapter 62

On Monday I finally relaxed. By nightfall we would be safe in Manhattan.

After driving Holly to school, I parked in the center of town and walked along Greenwich's four block business district. Apart from the gun dealer and deli owner, I had little contact with residents during my months there. Yet, just as in the past, I felt the need to say goodbye before leaving. Which was odd for my presence was unlikely to have been noticed. Long before, I realized the motive for this unnecessary behavior. That it reflected my yearning for the real home I lacked since entering the orphanage. But this goal required intimacy and not just familiarity with shop keepers.

Still, I followed my usual pattern. Buying a bagel and coffee in the deli and mentioning my relocating. Which news the owner accepted calmly. The gun store owner expressed greater interest.

"You're an odd guy," she said. "You look like a redneck except for the accent but you listen and feel deeply though it makes you uncomfortable. Stay safe. Here's your graduation present." With that, she kissed me on the cheek and gave me a car decal. Its slogan was understandable considering that her job involved self-defense. "I did not mean to be killed today": the dying words of a seventeenth century French nobleman.

My final goodbye, really an expression of thanks, was to the town's librarian. During my brief stay I had come to value that institution. Then I returned home.

Though officially retired, Pat's parents consulted to other churches. Often about the messy situation created by a too frank sermon or when other tensions erupted.

While passing Patience's office I overheard her reassuring comment: "parishioners are like that." Down the hall was Cedric's office. It served as his bedroom when his multiple sclerosis attacks exacerbated and he had difficulty negotiating stairs. "I get strange symptoms," he told me soon after we met. "Eye pain and blurred vision. Or seeing flashing lights when I move my eyes or hear a sudden noise. Once, while counseling a man who was depressed because of symptoms from his Lyme disease, I felt a burning and itching in my arm—neuropathic pain the doctors call it. As I became more involved with *his* problems *my* pain disappeared.

"Pain is an odd thing," he continued. "Two people can have identical anatomical injuries but only one becomes disabled while the other functions normally. The spirit is what counts."

Now even Cedric's spirit was low. When we arrived in Greenwich, Pat told me of a communication using their bedroom door between her parents. If open, it meant that Cedric was feeling well and wanted to talk. If the door was closed, he was having a bad day and feeling the tug of the disease which, though not fatal, was then tearing him apart.

Pat said that at first her mother resented the door being closed, seeing this as a barrier between them. Until she realized that Cedric needed it this way in order to renew his courage, for which he required that his wife not see him at his worst. So she developed her own way of coping by behaving optimistically and cheerfully no matter how she felt.

For the past month the bedroom door was closed more often than not. I would miss this courageous couple and valued each remaining moment with them. When I spoke with them that day I could not have borne the pain of knowing that it was the last time I would see either of them alive.

Chapter 63

The large coffee maker was one-quarter full when I filled my cup. Though not big coffee drinkers, Cedric and Patience kept the pot full for their counseling clients and the occasional villager who arrived spontaneously for a "spiritual fix."

"Isn't' it harmful?" I asked, thinking of research on the effects of caffeine. "Decaf," Patience responded, "And I doubt that anyone can tell the difference from regular though mine isn't as good as Starbucks, which seems the only store in town to always have a line. What's important is the sharing: first coffee, finally feelings. To speak openly requires trust which takes time to develop.

"Some want only to pray together but even that takes time. While praying, it's best to use mental pictures of people and not words but most haven't achieved that spiritual level. So thoughts written by others, 'cook book prayers,' can be valuable. They focus our mind and words which others wrote can eventually become our own. Reminding us of things we should ask for and providing a ceremonial element. Until they become empty of authentic feelings and intentions..." Patience didn't finish her sentence. Instead, she tilted her cup and emptied the black dregs onto the saucer.

The five soiled cups on the tray in Cedric's study indicated that he had a busy morning. Because of his pain, Cedric was having difficulty sleeping so I hesitated to wake him when I entered the room. Instead, I sat facing him, as if I were another of his counseling clients. The noise from a helicopter overhead awoke him.

Cedric saw me sipping coffee and smiled. We sat in silence until the mantel clock on the bookcase struck two thirty.

"No one comes later," he remarked, beginning to get up but quickly falling back onto the chaise lounge.

"How are things going?" I asked. His health was obviously poor.

Now the smile left his face."The pain, or my conclusions about it?"

I leaned back and sprawled my legs, aware that involving his mind would relieve his pain. "Both, if you will," I responded.

"OK. As a scientist you know that many questions lie beyond the legitimate scope of the scientific method. Yet even in science, things may seem clear but remain mysterious. The nervous system of the tiny worm, Caenorhabditis elegans, has been completely charted but no one understands how it functions. It's the same with pain.

"I'm not so naive as to believe that pain is a divinely ordained punishment. Too many evil figures have lived long healthy lives. So after I was diagnosed with multiple sclerosis I asked myself the popular question: 'why me?' And then I concluded the usual: that my illness was purely accidental. An unhappy product of those genes, habits, and experiences which form a life. But, being religious, I considered my answer incomplete and thought some more. That's the only benefit of being ill: it gives you time to think —when the pain isn't too great and the medication doesn't knock you out!

"Finally I discovered the value of of pain and illness. They strip illusion from our life and put us up against the real universe."

I was intrigued by his concept, having struggled with my far less serious but chronic knee pain over the years. "And what then?" I asked. "If illusions are given up what does one have left? Isn't that person without hope?"

Cedric smiled gently before answering, until another spasm rent his face. "No, for unless one rebels against the facts, a person can adjust to their existence. Even, perhaps, find religion. Life-long atheists have come to terms with suffering by raising essentially religious questions. Pain is God's way of making our life less agreeable, of removing our illusions and making room for Him."

Though I didn't want to argue I couldn't accept Cedric's ideas. "Why would a deliberate God spread misfortune on worthy people to increase their insight?"

"No one can argue that pain isn't terrible," he replied calmly. "Who can forget a crippling back ache? Though it doesn't compare to the agony of an abscessed tooth which itself pales before the gnawing from certain neurological conditions.

"But what's my use in telling you this for we all know it. Just as we sense the truth of the ancient doctrine that one can become perfect through suffering. Pain must exist in order for there to be something to be feared. It increases our ability to love and for the best of reasons: because others are human and like us. Thus do we gain fortitude and humility." Then, with a self-deprecating smile, he added, "But pain does hurt!"

The convulsion which crossed Cedric's face led into his extended coughing. My pretense that I didn't notice wasn't quick enough.

"Just a cough, there'll be many more," he said, though he now seemed weaker than in recent days. "Don't forget to Invite us to Holly's birthday party."

Chapter 64

All bureaucracies evaluate prospective employees though few as extensively as the military. So well before my first day in the British army all of my records from my orphanage and the schools I attended were studied. This, and the results from the enlistment tests I took, told them that I was very bright (having an IQ of 167 where 100 is average) and had excellent manual dexterity. I also had particularly good spatial relations ability. This enabled me, after rotating an object in my mind, to know exactly how it would look. Just like most engineers can easily do. This information was also evident from my high grades in the engineering classes I took but few in the military trust a civilian's opinion about anything.

Most of these results would have been beside the point except that their combination was unique enough that my file came to the attention of the commander of the 33 Engineer Regiment based in Carver Barracks, Wimbish.

This colonel didn't have an easy task. His mission was to maintain a ready complement of soldiers in the most feared and nerve-racking of all the military jobs: disposing of unexploded bombs. So he was continually forced, personally, to try to convince soldiers into volunteering for his unit.

Being naive, I was easily flattered by his compliments during the dinner at his home. For whatever reason, he really wanted me. Maybe because my IQ was so high though, as the testing psychologist told me, too smart soldiers tended to do poorly on some tasks. Then again it might only be that, being tall and muscular, I possessed the popularly applauded appearance which he felt that all of his soldiers should have.

So on a delightful summer evening I and seven other recent university graduates, six men and a woman, found ourselves having dinner with the colonel, his wife, and their dark haired twenty year old daughter. Gossip held that she was in the final stage of an affair with her married college instructor.

Being certainly the poorest and likely the hungriest of those present, I was anxious to eat but had no idea how to negotiate the lobster before me. A dish notably absent from the orphanage which raised me and being far too expensive during my university years.

Thus I sat, famished but ignorant of how to courteously approach this food, while the others kept their hands in their laps and exhibited rapt interest in the colonel's description of his unit's heroic past.

After the British Army's suppression of a civil rights march in Northern Ireland in 1972, thirteen Catholic civilians were shot dead and an IRA bombing campaign began. But their early attempts, using crude match-lit fused bombs, were dangerous mostly to themselves. The bomber had to be close enough to their target to throw the bomb and there was always a chance that it would explode prematurely or the fuse would go out.

The IRAs next big advance in bomb making came with their use of batteries, clocks, and electric detonators. This led to the army's increasing success at defusing these devices, and the IRA's addition of anti-handling mechanisms so the bombs would immediately explode if tampered with. Thus a continual cat-and-mouse game developed between bombers and bomb disposal personnel.

Some ingenious military ideas, as covering a car bomb with foam to limit the blast's effect, weren't completely effective. Others, using a remotely controlled arm and small explosive or gun which fired water to disrupt the bomb's mechanism, became widely used and saved many lives.

One of the colonel's horrific stories was also funny. In the late nineteen eighties the IRA began using homemade mortar bombs, firing them first at police stations and army barracks in Northern Ireland and later at government buildings in England itself. In February, 1991 they aimed three mortar bombs at the Prime Minister's residence at 10 Downing Street. Two of them didn't explode and the task of their defusing fell to the head of the London Bomb Squad. He placed one of the bombs between his legs and tried to remove the fuse. Then screamed in agony for his testicles felt like they were on fire: the bomb was red hot. So while working, he would periodically jump up and put snow into his pants before continuing.

It was during this story, while we laughed at the colonel's punch line of the "burning balls," that mine began tingling. They were responding to the gentle probing fingers of his daughter who sat beside me.

Why did I *now* think of this long past dinner, I asked myself, as I left Cedric's sleeping form. The answer came when I remembered another story which the colonel told that evening. About a bomb disposal officer's worst nightmare: when a civilian's life is at stake and soldiers must risk theirs, there being no time to put on a protective suit or to use a robot.

"A hostage, often a woman and sometimes a baby too, would be tied within an explosives laden vehicle or building. To save them, the soldier had to disarm the detonator, the small explosive that sets off the main charge.

He must also search for the presence of a secondary bomb and booby traps, *while* keeping the hostages calm. Once they are freed, robots can be used to complete the job." As I listened to this incident, I momentarily forgot not only my worry over the proper way to eat a lobster but also the supple fingers of the colonel's daughter which wandered over my groin.

"It looked like it would be another boring day though nothing was ever completely normal just north of the Irish border where the IRA controlled the community. There was always this incredible loneliness no matter how many soldiers accompanied you. Low hills, stone walls, and concealed gunmen if it was *that* kind of day.

"A phone call reported a woman yelling that her car was booby-trapped. She was tied in the front seat along with her infant, who was the only calm one. The IRA's tactics had changed. When we introduced robots, killing soldiers became harder so they would lure them into an ambush where a bomb was sometimes the least of the dangers.

"This woman, the Protestant wife of a local shop owner, was kept quiet by telling her that she would be gotten out safely but shouldn't move. Within a minute, the wire connecting the bomb to the driver's door was cut, the passenger's side door was checked and found to be clean, and the woman was told to get out that way. All ran, the baby in the soldier's arms, and the robot did the rest. When the soldiers were leaving, they came under rifle fire.

"Once, a car bomb was disarmed but a second was missed and triggered remotely, by an IRA man across the road who had been watching. It blew a soldier ten feet into the air. When he landed, a towering sergeant rushed forward to see if he was alive and knocked him down again.

The soldier took the rest of the day off. Later they found a third bomb which hadn't exploded.

"You need luck and the ability to tolerate people who are convinced that you may be a bit mad." We joined in his smile despite the unease which his stories aroused.

"Bomb Disposal is a good unit but not easy to get into and that's how it should be. During some training, ninety percent of the students wash out. In one class no one passed. The work sounds lethal but it isn't that dangerous if you know what you are doing and can think flexibly," the colonel concluded.

The anecdotes, food, and stimulating attention I received from the colonel's daughter made for an exciting evening and I did volunteer for the unit. But tests don't tell everything. After my basic officer education, I became part of the sixty eight percent of my class who flunked the training. My fault was that I became so intrigued by the bomb's mechanism that I didn't work quickly enough. A tendency which led to my failure with the colonel's daughter who, after dinner, granted her attention to a more quickly reacting future officer.

There were similarities between what those soldiers felt and I now did, I thought. Likely it was this which had caused me to recall those old stories. We both tolerated loneliness and danger though they had the backup which I lacked and I had no downtime to relax. Not if I hoped for us to remain alive.

But only a few hours of terror remained. Soon we would be hidden amongst Manhattan's anonymous millions. Then Hasan's vow of our doom would be irrelevant, as if it didn't exist.

Chapter 65

The difficulty, my friends, is not in avoiding death,
but in avoiding unrighteousness;
for that runs faster than death
—Plato

While waiting to pick up Holly from her final day at school, I lingered in the kitchen. The room which told the most about a home's inhabitants and which tended to fall into one of three categories.

The kitchen might be simply a place to prepare food, with other family activities occurring elsewhere. Or it was a room where the meals were both cooked and eaten. But sometimes the kitchen was the real center of the family where everyone congregated. This room had obviously filled that need.

It was big, as were most kitchens built in the late eighteen hundreds, though the fixtures and appliances had been replaced in the nineteen fifties judging by their style. The room had brick walls and light green planked floors. The cabinets were ornamented with flower appliqués and all of the furniture was of wood including a large stand-alone chopping block. This kitchen led into a formal dining room which was seldom used.

Another reason I lingered in the kitchen that morning was my thought of our future living quarters: the borrowed two room apartment in space starved Manhattan, which had only a cooking alcove.

Feeling bored, I began reading Cedric's notes for the religious book he was writing. It was in sermon format, entitled "Mortal Thoughts," and handwritten on lined yellow paper with purple ink. An odd color combination, I thought, but perhaps these had come immediately to hand.

The Word of God

Our life has meaning because we are part of the fabric of the eternal universe. Those who gain this awareness are, as Plato described, no longer bound by the shadows of the cave but free to experience Ultimate Reality, which is part of the Reality of God. This task cannot be approached through conventional words or sounds for God does not speak in this way. But only by trying to understand the power and infinite meaning of His Word.

The Word of God is not as one person speaking to another but of God revealing Himself to Himself, God as a living element.

The Word of God is transcendent and as old as religion itself.

I read the next sections with increasing interest.

Inescapable Sin and Triumphant Grace

Familiar words may be misunderstood and none more so than Sin, a word which gains its power from the depth of human experience. We frequently agree that "all men are sinners" yet deny this applies to us. Our sins are minor and not those of criminals or despots. Yet Sin is the overriding issue of our time.

To sin is to separate oneself from one's nature, from others, and thus from the essence of Being. Because humans endure separateness it grants us, alone of all the living creatures, knowledge of why we suffer. Because our fate is to be alone and unable to know the full complexity of others, this being a task which is beyond even the deepest of loves.

The greatest sin is to consider those of another religion or ethnic group unworthy of life and to rejoice in their death. Yet cruelty toward others cannot exist without self-hatred. And this sin which separates our angry, hostile feelings from our conscious nature abounds today.

Because of Sin, our separateness, we live apart from the mystery of our existence yet are bound to it—as we are to others. So, being separate but bound, we sometimes feel despair and emptiness: Sin, in its deepest sense.

But Sin can be overcome with Grace: the feeling of being accepted despite our separation from others and from our nature. Our being alone, without God.

Grace is not forgiveness or magic. It is gained by finding the courage to transform suffering into a meaningful experience.

Grace cannot arise through simple means: believing in the Bible or by gaining control over our faults though these may occur following its experience.

Grace cannot be demanded or deliberately sought. It may happen, or not, when our life is filled with pain. When we are more greatly separated from ourselves and others or have hurt another deeply and can no longer tolerate our weakness and rage. Then, perhaps, a voice calls: "That which is nameless and greater than you accepts you." And following that moment of acceptance we experience Grace. When all is different and alienation disappears. For this, no deep knowledge is required, merely assent.

Through Grace we become capable of understanding and accepting others. Realizing that though they may differ we are all part of Being, and have been reunited once more.

Through Grace we accept ourselves because we have been accepted by something far greater. We lose self-hatred and become surer of the eternal meaning of life as we experience that peace and wholeness after Grace has vanquished Sin.

Human Depth and Existence

To be religious is not merely to attend an institution or read a sacred text, but to be deeply concerned about who we are and the place of man in the scheme of things. Which requires that we look within and relate to religious symbolism with equal depth. The Bible story of the Fall of Man is not about the behavior of a single couple but is instruction into what can occur when there is estrangement from one's basic nature.

And surely the concept of God must be granted depth too. For He is far beyond a thing whose existence may be debated, as are humans in their spirit.

It is from the loss of this dimension that the need for religion arises. The hunger to go beyond being a thing to be marketed to and to grapple with such matters as emptiness and guilt and honesty and the demonic. To be religious mandates a commitment toward depth.

Society's current distress reflects its struggle wherein the symbols of religion are accepted while their meaning is ignored. By neglecting this tension we avoid personal growth through our struggle with an inescapable truth: that, though alive, we move towards our death.

The Prophetic Word

If the worth of things is measured by their price, how should the words of prophets be valued?. It is said, in Isaiah,

> The world itself shall crumble.
> But my righteousness shall be forever,
> And my salvation knows no end.
> Should these words be revered today?

It is to present generations which prophets speak. Insisting that the fruits of science and prosperity can bring one closer to God but not be Him. That peoples who sought only material progress found destruction, and never greater than in our century.

To be a prophet involves pain for no one wants to foretell the crumbling of their existence. Nor do prophets enjoy being attacked, reviled as a pessimist and worse. Yet, always, a few have such courage and make pronouncements with such power that they are heard. Because they speak not from themselves but from Him, having been told that, though the world may end, the Eternal persists and, at the boundary of their life, the Infinite becomes visible and Salvation becomes possible.

Thus these prophets, though also human, can face their end calmly. For they have seen beyond the *temporary into the Eternal, and recognize that they belong to both.*

I placed these papers down, wanting to discuss them with Patience, to warm my soul in her company. The door of her office was ajar. Probably her last patient had already left, I thought. Her work was usually over by early afternoon. She then napped before involvement in her latest project: editing a collection of nineteenth century recipes for the fund raising cookbook of a local church.

I stepped softly and opened the door further. Patience lay on the sofa, which was set next to the wall and opposite the windows. I considered whether my need was serious enough to rouse her. Then my hand froze on the doorknob as the fact of what I was viewing penetrated my mind. A confusion of emotions ran through me: loss, pain, terror.

The small wound in her forehead was large enough to have killed her. A silencer must have muffled the sound for the noise from even a small caliber bullet would have startled everyone in the house.

Cedric was disabled, I reminded myself, and rushed toward his office, behaving like a foolish civilian. The soldier I had been would have first gotten his gun from upstairs. But effects of my past training did remain and I grabbed the first potential weapon I passed: a metal candlestick holder. Thus I approached Cedric's office with this heavy fixture upraised before me, like a protective talisman.

Cedric was collapsed on the floor, the bullet having struck him as he lay on the chaise lounge which he then rolled off. The stain from his blood still spread slowly along the carpet. He and his wife must have died just minutes before, while I sat reading in their kitchen.

Suddenly I remembered Cedric's—prophetic—words at our last meeting, before this death which was so unworthy of his life: "If we never meet in this world again, God grant that we may meet in the next."

What I did then wasn't what soldiers do in the midst of battle: I prayed, though being long unpracticed.

"Lord, they were good people," I pleaded, "Take them into Your Kingdom. Give them rest, and help me to destroy these demons I must." Then I wiped my eyes, turned away from his body, and went to war.

Which was when things finally came together for me. Over the past months I had been bewildered and paralyzed with fear. Afraid of even the smallest change with some new threat being aroused. Like a brain-dead boxer: worn down, too dulled to care, giving up and awaiting only the final blow to bring him peace. Lacking even the courage to openly meet defeat.

But from this profound depression another emotion now arose: overwhelming rage during which I became a soldier again. Not that I had ever fully lost the capacity for war which, like other practical skills, never completely vanishes. With this change came other thoughts. First, from Plato: that only the dead have seen the end of war. Then that which was printed on the decal given to me by the woman gun dealer and I now paraphrased. A firm resolve: I will not die today.

Following which a heightened sense of awareness occurred. I felt calm but alert; remained outwardly focused, yet seemed to gain energy from the battle which approached. Aristotle would have described my feeling as being the joy which accompanies the use of innate abilities. The *Tao Te Ching,* as my having achieved the state of *wu-*

wei, or effortless effort, for I was now moving in concert with nature.

But it was the whisper I heard, in Cedric's voice, to which I granted the greatest authority. It said in a sure and deliberate tone, *"Today, you will fulfill your Destiny."*

Chapter 66

What is hardest of all? That which seems most simple:
to see with your eyes what is before your eyes.
—Goethe

Candelabrum in hand, I walked slowly down the corridor. Testing each step lest the old wood creak as I closed with my enemy. Who awaited me, and where Pat might still be alive. Seconds passed. Five. Ten. Fifteen.

Now I noticed, seemingly for the first time, an embroidered hanging on the wall.

> *As on a staircase go in grace,*
> *Carrying the firelight in your face,*
> *Beyond the loneliest star.**

Go in Grace, I told myself softly. "*Go in Grace,*" an ancient voice echoed in my ear.

I strained to hear odd sounds but, apart from the noise of an occasional truck, silence pervaded the house. Perhaps the murderers had fled, I hoped, though not really believing this.

*G. K. Chesterton, *The Ballad of the White Horse*

Patience and Cedric were irrelevant to their goals but were killed. Pat would likely be viewed as a problem and murdered too. Only Holly, and perhaps me, would be permitted to live temporarily. Maybe her love for me would be thought useful as incentive. She would help them or I would be shot. Though, if proving a hindrance, I would be killed as quickly as the others: to eliminate another witness to their crimes and unnecessary risk.

I tuned out these intruding thoughts, knowing that those who survived combat *act,* and on partial information which is usually the only available.

There were five bedrooms upstairs. My enemies could be in any of them.

More seconds passed during which I listened. Still, I heard nothing. Until, when halfway down the corridor, the sound of a cough arose from the living room.

I cautiously opened its old fashioned sliding door and peeked within. There, to my astonishment, Pat sat calmly, gazing out the window onto the front lawn. She can't know about her parents, I thought, and quickly entered the room.

Pat smiled when she saw me. I wondered at the cigarette she held, having never seen her smoke. She had often told me that she hated smoking.

Before I could speak, I suddenly collapsed to my knees as a taser's electrical charge disrupted my nervous system. Powerful arms gripped my body and lifted me into a chair to which my hands were fastened with duct tape while another strip sealed my mouth. My shock was the greater for Pat viewed these events without concern.

During these involuntary movements I experienced rather than saw my captors. Their strength was evident. To lift my dead weight of two hundred pounds, which the shock from the taser barbs produced, required formidable muscles. Both men, though far shorter than me, were broad enough to make full-back on any football team. The coordination of their actions indicated experience with their present duty.

I already knew how a taser would feel from what an American soldier once told me. While home on leave and drinking heavily, he had gotten into a scrape with a bartender.

"My body went limp as the fifty thousand volts went through me. I yelled but had no control over my movements or the words which left my mouth. Within seconds, though it felt like minutes, I lumbered to my feet, feeling a burning sensation on my skin where the taser barbs penetrated. I also felt hyper-wide-awake, like after you drink a lot of coffee. Probably from all the adrenaline flowing through my body. I was 'out of it' for a few hours but then was OK, though quieter than usual."

I felt the same incredible pain, unlike any which I had experienced, and sensed time in slow motion and great confusion.

The taser barbs were removed from my leg and chest. Like my past drunken acquaintance, I felt the same burning where they penetrated. My next perception was the sight of my pants and the floor. My head faced downwards and felt too heavy for me to lift.

The words of my captor were low and seemed to be coming from a great distance. Gradually, as I became more conscious of someone speaking to me, I raised my head. A man sat opposite me.

When people are asked what a terrorist looks like they often describe a person of Middle Eastern appearance with an unkempt beard, disheveled clothes, and a wild look in his eyes. This man was nothing like that.

His eyes were blue and his face reflected more Northern Europe than the southern lands. The thought went through my mind that he might be of Circassian origin, one of the oldest indigenous peoples of the North Caucasus region of Russia. Though many became Christian in the sixth century, their religion gradually changed under the Ottoman influence until most were Islamic by the mid-nineteenth century. Yet these were Sunni of the Hanafi school who tended to be non-fanatical, emigrating under the pressure of Russian conquest as far as Denmark and the United States.

I wondered what mixture of ancestors granted this man his appearance, and under whose religious teachings he found his fanaticism. What made him especially dangerous was his deceptive appearance. Considering the care and costliness of his clothing, one might easily believe him to be a TV news anchor or a successful lawyer. The severity of his black suit was lessened by its light gray pinstripes and the color of a regimental tie. A restraint reflected in his soft voice, which expressed concern for my pain that, he insisted, derived from my own deeds.

"The world's pain is caused by disorder," he intoned. "By those who remain unappreciative of the Teachings, as do you.

"Knowing that you have no family I offered you mine. Which you rejected, preferring to waste your intelligence and courage to prop a dying society. One which pays their hair stylists more than scientists: six hundred dollars an hour. I refused to believe this monstrosity until receiving the bill. But I too have faults. I indulge women and paid this sum so that my niece's hair might be cut by the expert who serves Hollywood stars. It shames me to admit that I even recognize their names though a soldier must know their enemy in order to defeat them.

"My real foes are those who peddle such culture, not you! I invite you again. Be my brother. What is this child to you? She is not of your blood and is useful only for the information she holds."

His soft words warmed me until I considered their nature: the false allure of totalitarianism which eliminates the pain of autonomy by removing it. The love he offered would grant me everything except that which matters most: the right to be free.

I didn't shake my head but he read the rejection in my eyes and stopped speaking. Then he raised the suitcase beside him onto the sofa and removed from it the usual tools of torture: a shock box with wires and clips; a cattle prod for insertion into sensitive orifices; a blowtorch, pliers and knives. My thinking recoiled from what he might do to me. Far more, from how he might torment Holly.

I visualized her leaving school with her classmates and their speech of childhood matters. She would get a lift home, or take the bus when I didn't pick her up. Being small, they wouldn't need a taser to bind her.

Then would come *the* question: the hiding place spoken of in her parents' riddle, the location of the formulas for the Holy Grail of warfare. And when she failed to answer, from confusion or ignorance, the searing pain from heat and electricity were inevitable. But perhaps psychological methods would first be used: showing her the bodies of Cedric and Patience, and perhaps mine. Or revealing the ultimate betrayal: having Pat, her stepmother, perform these unspeakable acts.

It's odd how steady the mind becomes while awaiting one's doom, I thought, as all chance of my escape seemed absent. Though I doubted my ability to tear my bonds, for duct tape is difficult to rip in even ordinary situations, I did try—and failed. While minutes passed on the large grandfather clock, each bringing Holly closer to her doom.

I found some play in the tape binding my wrists. Maybe by stretching it I could slip my hands from the chair arms. Then grab the heavy metal candle stick holder beside me and smash it into the head of one of my captors while grabbing for his gun. An unlikely but not impossible feat when I was in peak physical condition fifteen years earlier. But now? Still, I did loosen the tape. Until Pat noticed and remarked, "he's trying to get free," and the atmosphere became more charged.

"He's not needed—-shoot him," her boss instructed.

The clock read twenty of four as I realized that I would be dead in a moment. Still, I resisted this with all of my strength and continued to twist my taped wrists.

My captors enjoyed watching my futile efforts, the sense of grandiosity which a person gains when they control the length of one's life. But I knew that dying was easy. It was living which could be painful, like Holly's slowly extinguishing potential. I tried to rouse somebody from outside of the house by battering my head against my shoulder and making soundless cries.

My captors smiled until, tiring of the sight, my well dressed enemy again ordered Pat: "Shoot him." Which perhaps disappointed the two thugs facing me, who also held pistols. But maybe Pat still loved me for instead of raising her pistol she hesitated. Then she stared toward the open door and froze. Everyone did.

It was just before she fired that I heard it. A voice which reverberated through me and seemed both of this earth and beyond. Moaning and panting and grunting. On and on it came, in low and high notes, until ending in a scream of agony and deliverance. A cry enfolding the process of creation. The tale of a being arising from its animal ancestor to become improved, more human, holier — Holly: the next advance in human evolution

The large second hand of the grandfather clock had stopped and I remembered the ancient scientific belief before Einstein disproved its validity: that time was God's watch, beating at a steady rate no matter where in the universe you were.

A final prayer for Holly and me. If we must die today, let us die together.

Then the world exploded and darkness enveloped me.

Chapter 67

Classification: Secret

INTERVIEW BY CAPT. L. HEALY, U. S. NAVAL
CRIMINAL INVESTIGATIVE SERVICE (NCIS) OF
MELISSA D.WALSH, PRINCIPAL OF HAYES
ELEMENTARY SCHOOL, GREENWICH, CT/December 11,
2003

Captain Healy: "Tell me about Holly's last day at school."

Ms. Walsh: "The day she was tortured and murdered."

"Yes."

"Holly was just one of our more than eight hundred students. I passed her occasionally in the hall but rarely had contact with her."

"We're interviewing all who knew her and the students she was closest with."

"Alright. Every morning I greet the children at the main entrance when they arrive. So they know that their principal cares and isn't a faceless bureaucrat."

"It surely inspires them too.'

"I hope so. I think it's worth my time. As usual, Holly arrived that morning with her father. He drove her to and from school. Was paranoid about she being kidnapped. That doesn't sound crazy now."

"You couldn't have known."

"She seemed fine that last morning. She was never a problem: the smartest student we had in years. Wanted to be a physicist like her parents. Most children her age don't even know the word. A statement like that you remember. Her mother is dead too.

'My life closed twice before its close-
It yet remains to see
If Immortality unveil
A third event to me.

"So huge, so hopeless to conceive
As these that twice befell,
Parting is all we know of heaven,
And all we need of hell."

"*Excuse me?*"

"Emily Dickinson—*Parting*. Holly looked stricken when I first read the poem to her but it became her favorite."

"How often did you speak with her alone?"

"Rarely after her first week. I never had reason to. She was a perfect student."

"Did anything odd happen on her last day? Something that stands out in your mind. Take a moment to consider this."

"During lunch she...*stared*."

"How so?"

"It happened at times. I noticed it on her first day. She suddenly became distracted like something aroused her attention. Then she peered directly in front of her and smiled, as if toward a friend."

"A friend…"

"That last day…in the lunchroom…she seemed to be arguing with her vision. That was new. Then she resumed eating."

"Was she sitting with someone?"

"Just Marian."

"What's her last name?"

"Doesn't have one—she's a doll. Holly got teased about carrying it in her backpack but the comments didn't bother her. She said it was a habit. A grown-up word. Sometimes she seemed much older than she was. Probably because she was so bright."

"Did you see her later that day?"

"I drove her home after her father didn't show up. That was unusual. He warned me against letting her leave with anyone else so I didn't feel comfortable sending her with another parent. During the ten minute ride she began *staring* again. She had me stop the car at the corner but didn't want to leave. Finally she did. I should have gone with her. I knew something was wrong by the way she walked."

"How did she walk?"

"Slowly—as if she were approaching her execution."

Chapter 68

The soul that had believed and was deceived
ends by believing more than ever before.
Virginia Moore, *Psyche*

"It was the strangest scene," the colonel began explaining. "No one could figure out what happened. You were tied, gagged, and bleeding. Holly lay on the floor beside your chair. Nearby were four dead terrorists.

"With all that blood we thought everyone must be dead. But you had barely more than a scratch and Holly was breathing normally. We learned more later, during her interviews under hypnosis.

"She's alive? Holly is alive?" I gasped. My fantasied image of her dead face, superimposed on her mother's torn body, had haunted me throughout the day.

"Of course. I told you she was OK this morning. Did you think I was lying?" The colonel's voice exuded fake injured innocence, though in a softer tone than anytime earlier that day. He tossed the tissue box from the night table onto the bed. When I finished sobbing and wiping my eyes he continued his explanation.

"When you didn't arrive at the school to pick her up, she was driven home by the principal. Then she entered the house by the back stairs and went looking for you."

"She always came in that way," I interjected. "I'm sorry. Please go on."

The colonel didn't speak for a minute and an odd look came over his face. As if he was trying to decide whether to tell me something. Then he did, perhaps having concluded that any information which I gave him would compensate for what he revealed. Learning what *really* happened having become more important than security considerations.

"Holly heard a noise, probably your scuffle. Then she tiptoed downstairs, saw the two bodies, and went to your room. Where she lay in a fetal position on your bed, with her thumb in her mouth and her eyes closed. We had all the rooms wired for sound but only your room for video too. So we saw and heard everything which happened there but still couldn't figure it out.

"Holly was the only person in the room so it must have been she who spoke. But her thumb had remained in her mouth and the voice we heard was that of a mature woman who chanted what sounded like a prayer in some foreign language. None of our modern linguists could translate it but the Classics Department at Princeton did and explained why they failed."

"Why?" I asked, feeling like an explorer whose thinking was being forced by events to go beyond conventional explanations.

"Because her dialect hadn't been spoken for nearly three thousand years. It was a type of Aramaic, the language of the ancient Near East. The tribes of Aram and Israel had a common ancestry and the Hebrew patriarchs spoke in Aramaic. The term itself is derived from Aram, the fifth son of Shem, the firstborn of Noah, who lived in the fertile valley of Padan-aram. Hundreds of years later the language of the Jews changed from Hebrew to Aramaic. This became the language of Jesus and the tongue in which Christianity spread throughout the region."

Now he drew papers from his briefcase and spoke unfamiliar sounds.

"marya hwee lee 'adhora,
marya hwee lee 'adhora,
mit:-t:ol drighlâyhon lweeshtaw raht:an
wristârehween iméshâdn dma zâk-kaya,
wkhamneen lâdhma wâmt:âsh-shéin
nâwshathhon,
wâthwarkhon âkh 'âl ala néthé wma dathé lâykon
uls:ana w'aq:tha,
marya hwee lee 'adhora
marya hwee lee 'adhora."

He read the translation without waiting for my question.

"Lord, be thou my helper,
Lord, be thou my helper,
For their feet run to evil, and they are swift to shed
pure blood,
And they lie in wait, they hide themselves to
shed blood,
And your destruction comes as a whirlwind; when
distress and anguish come upon you,
Lord, be thou my helper,
Lord, be thou my helper."

"When her chanting stopped, she commanded in English, in a soft tone filled with regret: "As you have loved me, you must help me with this important duty.""

"A moment later, Holly began moving again. She opened her eyes, took her thumb from her mouth, and cocked your gun—taking an extra magazine which she placed in her pocket. Then she walked from the room with a blank expression on her face. And four terrorists quickly died.

"So who else was in the house? Who spoke those words?" the colonel demanded. "Holly remembers little from the time she left your room until she touched your bloody face. Just colors going through her mind: White, Yellow, Orange, Red."

"That's the combat shooting technique she learned from the range instructor. Condition Red represents the highest degree of danger before shooting begins."

The colonel continued speaking as if he hadn't heard me. "On one recording there's a piercing, unearthly scream followed by four shots in as many seconds. A cry like doctors hear from the parents of a dying child when a miracle is needed and words are thrust toward Heaven. Did you scream?"

"You saw that I was gagged when you came in."

"Right, you were gagged," he said mockingly, as if he hadn't really seen it.

"Holly has no memory of screaming. She does remember touching your face and believing that you were dead since her hand was stained red like after she touched her mother's body. Then she fainted. Which is how we found her: unconscious, with a still warm .40 caliber pistol by her side, at a death scene which made no sense."

"Why not?" I asked. "She was lucky in her shooting. It happens with beginners."

Now he questioned me rapidly like a prosecuting attorney, still using that tone which implied that I must be lying.

"What is the probability of a ten year old shooting a high recoil .40 caliber pistol four times in four seconds and getting four head shots at a distance of twenty feet? You couldn't do it at your best! Who screamed? You were gagged. There was no reason for any of the terrorists to scream. Holly didn't. So who else was in the house?"

I considered what he said. He was right: another person *must* have been in the house. Yet there could be no one, except... I shrank from stating the only possibility.

"Were other fingerprints beside Holly's on the gun?"

"Only yours."

Then an even bigger look of disbelief came over his face. "What is it?" I asked.

He shook his head. "Holly wasn't just laying on the floor," he said. "She was sleeping and not with the expression of horror which you'd expect to see on the face of someone who just killed four people. She looked peaceful, even content.

"Her head was on a pillow from the sofa, a doll was clutched in her arms, and she was covered with a blanket from her bedroom. The scene resembled a painting by Norman Rockwell—except for the blood spatter and guns."

"Some kind of miracle," I said.

"You could call it that—*if* she fired those shots. But who brought the blanket and doll and covered her? You— the only other living person in the room—was tied up. All of the terrorists were dead and no one had entered the house except them."

"Perhaps her mother did," I suggested softly.

"She was dead and gone—you saw her mangled body," he said angrily, but seemed shaken by my conclusion.

"Certainly dead, maybe not yet gone," I added.

The colonel didn't respond. He thought and stared and thought some more. Then he sighed and dropped the matter. But I knew what he was thinking: *there was no other explanation.* A doll, pillow, and blanket mysteriously arrive to comfort a traumatized child. Who, despite the horror she experienced, sleeps contentedly, as if she had been deeply comforted by someone. A scream which no one present made. A mother returns from the dead to steady the aim of her only surviving child and to save her life. I didn't believe any of it, yet there was nothing else I could believe. Which, I sensed, was what the others in the room were thinking too.

The silence between us continued and I suddenly remembered a story from the Bible which Cedric had told me. Hagar, wandering in the wilderness with her infant son, Ishmael, their water exhausted, left the child under a bush and sat at a distance. "Let me not look on as the child dies," she thought, and burst into tears. "God heard the cry...and an angel called to Hagar and said, 'Fear not...Then God opened her eyes and she saw a well of water. She went and filled the skin with water, and let the boy drink. God was with the boy and he grew up...'" and became a warrior.

Finally the colonel stood, indicating that the interrogation was over. But *my* unanswered questions remained.

"How did you find me?" I asked.

He smiled. "A school teacher recognized you from a Post Office wanted poster. On the day when you forgot to use the Cover-Up, leaving the scar on your face from the Athens shoot-up visible. Just a few questions: I have paperwork to do. The government survives with it, you know."

"Who really was Pat?"

"Not who her parents believed her to be. She never was a lawyer or even graduated from college. *Some* of what she told you was true. She did stab someone before meeting you but it wasn't her boss. A good agent tries to keep as close to the truth as possible when lying. She dropped out of college to become the mistress of Hasan, the genius of a terrorist who we long heard chatter about but could never locate or even get a picture of. We continued watching her but lost all of you for awhile when you left the island.

"We stirred the pot to boiling by hiding the bodies and writing threatening notes. With all that pressure something had to blow. We hoped when Hasan heard about these things he would become so unnerved that he would feel he could no longer trust Pat's view of events and come out into the open. Which was what happened. He traveled to peaceful Greenwich to see for himself what was going on. Where we waited for him.

"We could have stormed the house earlier but had to be sure he was there. Remember, we didn't know what he looked like and didn't learn how valuable Holly was until later. You can blame that on another of our communication foul-ups."

I was angry that Cedric and Patience were murdered and Holly placed in danger to smoke out this terrorist though I knew that in modern warfare there were no non-combatants. But I ignored my anger, having more questions which needed answering.

"How could Pat be involved with the murderers of her parents?" My mind boggled as it tried to make sense of her behavior.

"One of the horrors of trying to understand killings is that you are forced to learn more about people than you ever wanted to know. When people feel unloved and unlovable they'll do anything for it. You should be able to understand that.

"Hasan was a gifted recruiter and an excellent trainer. Remember how soon after you met she used the pronoun 'we.'" This is called 'forced teaming,' It's a sophisticated maneuver intended to establish trust by showing that you both share the same situation."

Despite my feeling, with justification, that I had been an unperceptive idiot, I simplistically objected to his conclusions even as I knew them to be valid. "But she had such a beautiful smile."

The colonel sighed, perhaps feeling that he was speaking to a five year old. "The best way to simultaneously charm and mask emotions is with a smile."

I stopped objecting as a worry entered my mind. "How is Holly?"

"Physically, she's fine. Psychologically, that's another matter. To save your life and hers she had to kill four people. Hopefully, she'll never recover that particular memory. Take good care of her. During her testing yesterday she scored an IQ of 198. That's higher than even yours which makes her more valuable to the U.S.A. than you are." His smile indicated that he was making another of his small jokes.

"How about me?" I asked. "Am I normal?"

This answer was slower in coming.

"I've read the files about you. Since childhood you've been searching for a real family. And for love too, like all of us. But you were so hurt by the death of your parents that you grew up being terrified of closeness and commitment and fleeing from them.

"There is research that children brought up in orphanages have lower levels of certain hormones: vasopressin and oxytocin. This interferes with the comfort which normally develops between children and their caregivers. That's the biology of it but I wouldn't push this. What's more important is that you gave up searching for intimacy. Instead, you sought fulfillment in military and scientific activity. Being unable to find it there, you kept looking until you finally did discover it: by committing yourself to the survival of a child who you grew to love."

While considering what he said, a question burst from me: "Would Pat have killed me?"

The colonel paused before speaking, as if he was concerned about the impact of his answer on me.

"I don't think that's what you really want to know," he said. Which was true, but I couldn't ask *that* question. So he did it for me.

"You want to know whether Pat loved you and if you're lovable. From what you told me I think that she loved you as much as she was capable of loving anyone. But I'm not the best person to ask: love was always a mystery to me.

"Asking whether you are worthy of love tells us more about your childhood than who you are now. That Holly came to love you after your short time together provides the only answer you need.

"People need families. Something you never had and she doesn't anymore. You two will make a good family. Call me if you have more questions." The colonel removed a business card from his shirt pocket and dropped it on the bed. Then he grabbed his beret off the edge of the table and left the room, with a more relaxed gait than when he arrived five hours earlier.

While we were speaking the room had quietly filled with soldiers. Probably those from the taping room first, followed by others who heard gossip about what I was saying. They looked uneasy, as if they hungered to believe my story but weren't quite able to.

Then something unexpected happened. As soon as the colonel left the room the soldiers, each in turn, came to my bed and shook my hand. Perhaps they felt that touching me would make my narrative more believable and strengthen their faith. Soon all were gone.

The general approached me last. He gripped my shoulder and murmured, "good soldier." Which, of course, we both knew that I hadn't been. For it was Holly who saved our lives. With her mother's help of course.

Then the general too left the room, leaving me alone with my thoughts. And I never saw these soldiers again.

Epilogue

No more harsh reveilles will disturb his peaceful rest.
—author unknown

It's been three years since Holly and I passed through the flames. When the government had no more use for us they pensioned me off, created our new identities, and sent us to a small American town located hundreds of miles from any major city. To keep me busy and out of trouble, I was given a job teaching physics at an expensive boarding school.

It's not a bad life. We live in a house on the grounds and Holly attends classes as a day student. This was a deal breaker. Now she wouldn't separate from me even to go to school. But the faculty understood after being told some truths (that her mother and brother were dead) and enough fiction to make sense of her other oddities. Like insisting on eating lunch with me daily, and carrying a doll in her knapsack.

One fact I considered it best not to share is the Global Positioning System chip which had been implanted in her shoulder. This enables her to be quickly located—hopefully while she is still alive—if it ever becomes necessary.

Our ready acceptance at this school likely reflected the scarcity of qualified science teachers—and Holly having a higher IQ than any student there. She's also one of the prettiest though she ignores the boys who flock about her.

"Mommy says that I'm too young to date," she explained.

"Whatever you both feel is best," I responded.

Yes, Holly still talks to her mother's ghost, a figure which Cedric more properly termed an angel. But not everyday. Just when she's particularly uneasy, or feels that her mother would enjoy learning of an event. I used to worry about this but no longer do having concluded that while I'm not smart enough to prove that angels exist, I am sure that her presence helps Holly. So it helps me too.

I also decided that because Holly and me are such odd creatures, maybe there is an overarching design to human existence which brought us together and may someday bring others into our lives.

We just had our fifth play date with the school doctor and her son. She's a young widow and her boy is the same age Holly's brother was when he was...when he died. Though usually ignoring children, Holly relates to him as if he were a younger brother. She even lets his mother nurture her. Late one Saturday afternoon, as the four of us lingered in the local diner, Holly suddenly stared in front of her, nodded, and giggled.

"Mommy is pleased?" I whispered. Holly smiled enigmatically but didn't say anything. Thus our play dates have continued.

Last month we received two presents from the head of a government agency. The first was delivered by FedEx in a flat box: two small, powerful pistols. It was suggested that we keep them handy. The note read, "Our cover story about your deaths fell through. They're searching for you."

The other gift was happier and delivered by a suit clad man driving a black SUV. It was the guard dog which Holly played with during our interrogation. This German Shepherd was now officially retired from the Army, complete with his discharge certificate *and* a small pension—which must have taken some bureaucratic doing to get. Holly held out her jacket from that time and, after a brief sniff, the dog jumped on her and they embraced as if they had never parted.

A few days later I telephoned the colonel, wanting to ask him about a recurring dream I developed and for Holly to touch base with him. I dialed the phone number on his long unused business card but found that it had been disconnected. I managed to get his last address through the American Medical Association. From them I also learned that he wasn't an Army colonel but a Marine Corps Reserve brigadier general. He had died two years earlier, well before I overcame my ambivalence about calling him. So Holly and I wound up visiting his widow.

She didn't live in the white picket-fenced house I expected but on the eleventh floor of an apartment building in downtown Minneapolis. I was surprised by her willingness to meet with strangers but she explained that many had called to express their sorrow. Her husband was killed by a sniper while walking in Basra, together with an Iraqi psychologist he was training in psychoanalytic techniques.

"'Controlling the unconscious is the key to peace,' he always said. But then he would add, 'along with a powerful military.' It was his third tour of duty in Iraq. He didn't have to return but he volunteered. He was a Marine and felt that the soldiers there were also his family and he wanted to be with them."

Then she paused before continuing, as if being embarrassed at what she was about to reveal. "When I visit the wounded Marines in the hospital I sense him walking beside me," she said, and I nodded.

Holly and I ate apple strudel and listened to her memories and didn't say anything. Which seemed alright with the general's widow. Finally, just as we were leaving, she asked how we came to know her husband.

There was so much I could have told her that I wondered where to begin. Until, while looking at Holly, I suddenly understood that what happened was really very simple.

"When Holly was desperate, her mother returned; and when Holly needed healing, then your husband was sent too."

As I spoke, the room suddenly brightened despite the chill which entered it, and Holly's face became radiant as it had in the past.

One day, while I sorted through a pile of unopened mail, Holly sat beside me reading the latest issue of *Seventeen*. A letter without return address held a sheet of paper and single typed word upon it: DAYGLO. I showed it to her.

"Your parents' formula worked," I said.

"They knew it would."

"Maybe when you're older you should be a scientist too," I suggested.

"OK. After I graduate from West Point like you did."

I didn't correct her factual error though I always believed that my training at Great Britain's Royal Military Academy at Sandhurst was superior to that which America's West Point cadets receive.

"To defend freedom like your parents did?"

Before Holly replied, a look which managed to be both childlike and sophisticated passed over her face.

"And Captain Midnight too," she said. Which is how things now stand.

So if you ever find yourself in a small dusty town. A place where the convertibles outnumber the pick-ups, the diner's coffee is as good as Starbucks', and the school's football team lost again last year though no one seemed to mind.

And you happen to see an aging German Shepherd and tall, very pretty teenager. Accompanying a limping man whose hand slips into his jacket pocket when a stranger approaches. Then you just might have found us. For despite terrorist threats we live, content and unafraid.

Somewhere, in this still free and democratic America. At the foothills of the mountains. Under the Western stars...

Note: In considering these events I am struck by how little actual proof there is. The general is dead, his small unit has been disbanded, and the bodies are gone. All of the files have been shredded and whatever deliberately vague reports still exist are already yellowing. Besides, who believes government accounts nowadays anyway?

But I ask none to believe me. That Holly exists is enough evidence for me. I have already witnessed her extraordinary nature and abilities. When she grows into a woman and bears children, they will deliver the proof of these events: people with greater intelligence and spirituality than have heretofore walked this planet. Providing hard evidence that the human species can improve. I hope they will have Holly's bravery too.

At that time, in the not too distant future, others will understand why Holly was so valued—and loved—that some were willing to risk all for her safety.

Appendix A – Declassification Document for *Ghosts and Angels*

Classification: Secret

Date: 23 August 2005

TO: A. R. Hastings, Director
Office of Information Declassification, Department of Defense

From: P. L. Smythe, Senior Declassification Reviewer
PLS - Office of Information Declassification, Department of Defense

Re: Request for clearance of autobiography — *Ghosts and Angels*

This decision is a close call. While the book could aid America's War on Terror by educating citizens about our enemy, it also includes information which it may be unwise to reveal. Examples follow:

(1) Existence of the secret American facility in Azerbaijan used for anti-terrorist operations. Yet reporting this would also have the favorable effect of strengthening public belief that our struggle against terrorists has support across civilized nations, these countries recognizing the danger of hunting monsters but the greater danger of not doing so.

(2) Certain cutting edge weapons research. But hints of these activities have already been printed and trying to put these genie back into their bottles would seem futile. Moreover, learning of ingenious American

accomplishments (using suitably vague terms) would raise morale while not adding to that classified information which, unfortunately, has already been publicized.

For these reasons I recommend that approval to publish *Ghosts and Angels* be granted, with the following changes:

1. Technical formulas must be deleted;
2. The identity and locations of active duty and potentially endangered individuals must be disguised.

I suggest that the spiritual elements in the book be removed and the work be marketed as *fiction*. We don't want Americans believing that their Department of Defense is relying on *ghosts and angels* to protect them!

Classification: Secret

Date: 25 August 2005

To: P. L. Smythe, Senior Declassification Reviewer
Office of Information Declassification, Department of Defense

From: A. R. Hastings, Director ARH
Office of Information Declassification, Department of Defense

Re: Your recommendations concerning *Ghosts and Angels*

1. Clearance for publication of *Ghosts and Angels*, following the revisions (1) and (2) contained in your memorandum of 23 August 2005, is granted.

2. Flippancy toward spiritual matters is *not* DOD policy. You are herewith directed to attend the next Faith

Sensitivity Workshop which will be held on ten Tuesdays beginning 5 October 2005. Each session lasts eight hours and begins at 7:45AM in Room 1472 of the Main Building. A reading syllabus and examination schedule are enclosed. Bring a bag lunch; coffee and soft drinks will be provided. Successful completion of this program will maintain your eligibility for the Exempt Employee Bonus Award in the next fiscal year. Enjoy!

APPENDIX B

January 23, 2004 - Closed Briefing – United States Senate Select Committee on Intelligence - Operation Fallen Eagle - Appendix 14

TOP SECRET - REPRODUCTION OF THIS DOCUMENT OR COMMUNICATION OF ITS CONTENTS OUTSIDE THIS COMMITTEE IS FORBIDDEN UNDER PENALTY OF LAW (50 USC 421, 601a,b,c)

Transcription of audio recording – October 14, 2003. Speakers are Dr. L., a physician, and his wife. Dr. L is a contract employee with the Noxwell Investigative Group, an organization based in Boston and covertly funded by the Central Intelligence Agency.

<u>Dr. L.</u>: "I should have stayed with my uncle's company."

<u>Wife</u>: "Sweetie, you went to medical school because 'engineering is *soo* boring.'"

"And because of what happened to Jonas."

"Being let go after that prank you both did?"

"I wasn't fired only because I was a relative."

"But you love being a doctor."

"Until yesterday."

"Baby, you're crying. What's wrong?"

"My consulting job."

"Well, quit it."

"We owe a hundred eighty nine thousand dollars in student loans. Forty thousand of mine is forgiven following each year of my four year contract. When I spoke of leaving early I was told that I could be drafted into the army."

"There *is* no draft!"

"There is for doctors with critical skills, I was assured."

"I never heard of a job like that."

"We needed the money."

"Where were you yesterday? I had to cancel sixteen patients and the flu clinic too."

"Doing an autopsy on a child and his parents. Two died from a single bullet wound but the woman..."

"Was she shot too?"

"She was tortured to death."

"Raped?"

"He got enough pleasure from causing pain."

"So? You've worked on crime victims before. Why was she so different?"

"Because of the expression on her face...and that there was no blood left in her."

APPENDIX C

January 22, 2003
MEMORANDUM OPINION
USING UNITED STATES MILITARY FORCES TO APPREHEND TERRORISTS DOMESTICALLY – THE ILLUSORY CONSTRAINTS OF THE POSSE COMITATUS ACT WITH PARTICULAR REGARD TO THE APPREHENSION OF THE TERRORIST KNOWN AS "HASAN"

Drafted by the United States Department of Justice at the Request of the Information Analysis and Infrastructure Protection Division of the Department of Homeland Security

Background - The Present Danger

One hundred years ago the distinction between police and military operations was clearer. Today, one or several individuals may transport such biological, chemical, or nuclear weapons that the national survival becomes imperiled. An important question is whether military forces can be used to neutralize foreign terrorists who operate domestically considering the constraints of the 1878 Posse Comitatus Act which forbids the use of such forces for domestic law enforcement. And, in particular, whether these soldiers can be used to deter the activities of the terrorist identified as "Hasan," whose real name and physical description are in dispute. He is believed to be a tall, Western appearing individual who was once educated in the United Kingdom. The following information was gained from multiple sources, some of which have been unreliable in the past. But whatever his identity, this individual presents a grave danger to the safety and security of the United States.

Hasan was born into a working class Shiite family living in Kuwait City. His father, a citizen of Pakistan, worked as a mechanic for Kuwaiti Airlines. While there he married a Kuwaiti and they had five children, Hasan being the second. His mother and a brother were killed in an auto-truck collision in 1991.

Hasan's father was not initially religious but became so in his mid-thirties after being assaulted by Sunni Muslims. These were followers of mullahs from the Wahhabi school of Sunni Islam. They were members of an extreme fundamentalist group called the Salafis, the origin of whose rage dates back more than thirteen hundred years.

Following the death of the Prophet Muhammad in AD632, two camps of Islam developed, both believing themselves to be the True Faith. The larger, Sunnis, consider the first three successor caliphs to be legitimate whereas the Shiites (who make up most of the population of Iran) believe that Muhammad's son-in-law, the fourth caliph, was the only true successor of Muhammad. Over the centuries this religious split led to great tension between the groups. Salafis believe that all Shiites should be killed to purify the earth of their heathen beliefs and have criticized the Taliban and Al Qaeda for their "temperance."

Hasan was a bright child and did particularly well in his mathematics and science studies. But he was not well liked because of his domineering and menacing air, and his tendency to become enraged when things did not go his way.

Tired of being treated like second class citizens in Kuwait, when Hasan was eighteen his father moved the family back to his native land of Baluchistan, a remote barren area in the southwestern part of Pakistan. Here, most of the residents still lived a nomadic life, in huts and tents along with their animals. A greater contrast with modern prosperous Kuwait could hardly be found. Nor could the activities, Baluchi tribesmen being long involved in warfare against the Soviet forces in Afghanistan, in factional disputes, and in the large scale smuggling of arms and drugs.

However, Hasan sought an education and was sent by his family to study in Great Britain where he gained training in electrical engineering and micro-electronics. This knowledge enabled the later miniature bomb making activity which became his trademark. Because of difficulties presented by the British Data Protection Act, further information could not be obtained.

About this time, Hasan married the daughter of a high ranking official in Iran's Ministry of Intelligence and Security (MOIS). This organization is also called VEVAK and is the successor to the earlier Ministry of Security (SAVAK) which had its own notorious past.

In 1953, with the assistance of the Central Intelligence Agency, the government of Dr. Mohammad Mossadeq was overthrown. This coup was intended to stop the planned nationalization of Iran's oil industry and a possible shift of the government leftward within the Soviet sphere of influence. In place of Dr. Mossadeq, the Shah-an-Shah (King of Kings) Mohammad Reza Pahlevi was restored to the throne of Iran. SAVAK was then created to eliminate threats to the new regime. Its first head, General Teymur Bakhtiar, was dismissed in 1961. He was assassinated nine years later because of his perceived threat to the monarchy. His successor, General Pakravan was fired in 1966 and replaced by General Nassiri, a childhood friend of the Shah. Despite this, Nassiri's telephone was tapped by SAVAK agents who reported directly to the Shah.

Throughout the 1960s and 1970s SAVAK ruthlessly crushed dissent by torturing and executing thousands of political prisoners. It had fifteen thousand full-time personnel and thousands of part-time informants. Many SAVAK officers served simultaneously in the military and there were close ties between these organizations.

Major General Hosain Fardust, another childhood friend of the Shah, was Deputy Director of SAVAK until the early nineteen seventies. He was then made Director of the Special Intelligence Bureau which operated within the palace but was independent of SAVAK. Initially created to arrest members of the Communist Party, the Bureau grew to monitor all aspects of political life including the behavior of Iranian students who opposed the Pahlavi rule.

SAVAK had the legal authority to imprison people indefinitely without trial and operated its own prison system throughout the country. Its torture methods included electric shock, beatings, inserting broken glass and boiling water into the rectum, tying weights to the testicles, and extracting teeth and nails. Among the prisoners who underwent torture and execution at the Komiteh Prison was Hasan's sister. She was arrested while visiting relatives in Tehran. Hasan was reported to have fainted upon viewing her mangled body.

Following the abdication of the Shah in January, 1979 there were widespread reprisals against the officials of SAVAK, which was dissolved by Khomeini after he assumed power that year.

SAVAK's successor agency, VEVAK (Vezarat-e Ettela'at va Amniat-e Keshvar) began, in the mid-nineteen eighties, to rehire former SAVAK agents to help the Islamic regime crush domestic dissidents and to provide knowledge of Iraq's Baath party. Though similar in operation, the philosophy of VEVAK was far different from its royal predecessor. Both sought to maintain absolute control over Iran but VEVAK possessed the additional goal of extending their brand of Islamic rule, initially to all Muslims and eventually to all humanity.

With the aid of VEVAK officials, Hasan succeeded at his original goal: to create a bomb which, being undetectable by x-rays, could be easily smuggled past security and onto any airplane. He converted a digital watch into a timing device and hid the liquid nitroglycerin explosive in a contact lens case using cotton wool as a stabilizer. Two nine-volt batteries powered light-bulb filaments to spark the explosion. All this equipment could be hidden in the hollowed-out heels of shoes, which were below the sight of airport security x-ray machines.

Hasan's first miniature bomb was used on December 11, 1995 when it was hidden on a Philippines Airline flight. This was placed under the seat which came to be occupied by a twenty-four year old Japanese engineer, Haruki Ikegami, who was returning home to Japan from Cebu in the Philippines.

The device exploded at ten thousand feet and tore Ikegami's body in two. A hole was produced in the floor of the plane and the aileron cables controlling its flaps were severed. Only the skill of the pilot enabled the plane's successful emergency landing and prevented the death of two hundred ninety two additional passengers and crew.

This operation was planned by Hasan in the Philippines. His closest friend was acquainted with... (passage deleted by censor)...a planner of the 1995 Oklahoma City bombing. Numerous phone calls were made...(passage deleted by censor)... Reliable reports placed Hasan and...(passage deleted by censor)...at secret meetings where they discussed bomb manufacturing techniques...(passage deleted by censor)...previous attempt to produce a viable explosive failed when the trial bomb fizzled rather than exploded.

Hasan's breadth of expertise is revealed by his planning of the following barely aborted plots.

The demolition of a Radiological Dispersal Device (RDD), which combines a conventional explosive with radioactive material, in a trash receptacle in front of New York City's St. Patrick's Cathedral.

The dissemination of incendiary devices on the floors and stairwells of department stores in major American cities.

The introduction of incendiary letter bombs into the United States Postal Service.

The placement of bombs on gasoline and propane delivery trucks.

Domestic Military Activity Under The Posse Comitatus Act

Reports from reliable sources insist that Hasan is now in the United States on a mission of significance. Prior efforts to identify and arrest him, by foreign police and intelligence services, have failed. He was described in an Interpol report as being "everywhere unexpected and never where sought." An advisory opinion has been requested as to whether it would be legal to use specialized military units domestically toward this goal.

Our conclusion and reasoning on the constraints of the Posse Comitatus Act follow.

"Posse comitatus" means "the power of the county." It refers to the original power of the Western sheriff to enroll local citizens to help maintain public order. The Army was used to crush rebellious sentiment in the Southern states after the Civil War. It was placed at voting centers and became involved in civilian law enforcement. To forestall further erosion from the Army's basic mission of national defense and its possible politicization, the Posse Comitatus Act was enacted.

While considered sweeping, the Posse Comitatus Act does not apply to all domestic military activity. For example, it does not apply to the Coast Guard or to the National Guard when they are operating in their usual non-federalized status. Only then do they become subject to the limitations of the Act. Moreover, a specific purpose of the National Guard is to maintain law enforcement when regular police units are unable to do so.

Though federal courts have prohibited the use of the military in "active" law enforcement activities (arresting criminal suspects or gathering evidence), "passive" support (providing intelligence, training, or equipment) is permitted.

The Posse Comitatus Act is statutory and not constitutional and so can be easily changed, as has occurred. Because civilian authorities have been unsuccessful in reducing the smuggling of drugs across state borders, the Navy and Air Force were used to further this goal for several decades beginning with the Reagan Administration (10 U.S.C., sections 371-381). The use of military personnel has also been approved for civilian peace keeping when a state requests assistance during civil disorder (10 U.S.C., sections 331-334); or in the event of a natural disaster for up to ten days (Stafford Act, 42 U.S.C., section 5121). The further erosion of the Posse Comitatus Act followed the use of the military for indubitably civilian events, as to protect the 1996 Atlanta Olympics against terrorist attack. Had this occurred, these forces would have been involved in essentially civilian law enforcement.

When the Act was passed, the danger to America consisted of foreign armies and navies. Today, a small quantity of biological weaponry can cause millions of casualties. The President can use the military against domestic terrorism under 10 U.S.C., 331-334; or when relying on their constitutional mandate to oppose armed insurrection. While the Posse Comitatus Act does retain its meaning and enables the punishment of officers who misuse their powers in civil activity, *it does not represent a barrier against using military forces to forestall domestic terrorism.*

Thus, with the prior authorization of the President, there is no legal barrier to using military assets against the terrorist termed "Hasan," or another, who presents an imminent danger to the safety and security of the United

States which civilian authorities are unable to deter. But the use of these military forces should be part of a coordinated inter-agency effort.

Furthermore, foreign nationals who engage in domestic terrorism and perfidy* are violating international law and not protected by provisions of the Geneva Convention which govern the conduct of war. Thus they may, following their apprehension and without judicial oversight, be immediately deported from the United States for whatever further actions are deemed necessary.

A. R. Kwathwaitte (signature)
A.R. Kwathwaitte
Acting Assistant Attorney General
Office of Legal Counsel

*Perfidy is defined as deceiving the enemy by pretending to be a non-combatant and thus causing civilians to be placed in danger (for example, pretending to be a taxi driver but carrying a bomb).

Author's Postscript
May your blessings be as vast as the sky.
—Chinese saying

A friend once asked me why I wrote the novels that I did.

"What do you mean?"

"They have spiritual themes," she replied.

"That's what the public wants," I answered flippantly, without thinking.

"No," she insisted. "More readers would be attracted by sex or violence but you write of religion. Why is that?"

When I realized she was correct and that I didn't know why, I behaved like Alan in this book. I lay down and free-associated. Within minutes the real motive popped into my mind, one so obvious yet unexpected that, just as did Alan, I burst out laughing. I wrote my novels because of "C's" lifelong influence over me.

"C" was a neighbor I met during my teenage years. After college, he graduated from an Ivy League divinity school and served as a Protestant Navy chaplain throughout World War II. Then, changed by this experience, he left the clergy for other duties.

It was from him that I first learned of Paul Tillich and Reinhold Niebuhr, and read their books with profit.

I often think of "C" and, just before the September 11th terrorist attacks on the World Trade Centers, I was walking in a large American city and passed a building which had been named for his father.

"C" was the most humane person I ever met. I try to make the religious figures in my novels his equal.

"C" died several years ago and is buried in the South West which he loved. I like to think that Holly is growing up nearby.

Stanley Goldstein
Hudson Valley, New York
January, 2011
www.drstanleygoldstein.com